The Other Duke

(THE NOTORIOUS FLYNNS BOOK I)

By

Jess Michaels

THE OTHER DUKE
The Notorious Flynns Book 1

Copyright © Jesse Petersen, 2015

ISBN-13: 978-1502862075
ISBN-10: 1502862077

For more information, contact Jess Michaels
www.AuthorJessMichaels.com
PO Box 814, Cortaro, AZ 85652-0814

To contact the author:
Email: Jess@AuthorJessMichaels.com
Twitter www.twitter.com/JessMichaelsbks
Facebook: www.facebook.com/JessMichaelsBks

Jess Michaels raffles a FREE Kindle or Amazon gift certificate EVERY month to members of her newsletter, so sign up on her website:
http://www.authorjessmichaels.com/join-the-jess-michaels-newsletter/

AUTHORS NOTE

After many years and many kinds of publishing, I have decided to go full indie. This is an exciting, thrilling and terrifying time for me. Someone once said you jump off the cliff and build your wings on the way down. Well, here it goes. It's funny, though, when you go "indie" you don't do it alone. So there are a lot of people to thank for making this book, this choice and this life possible.

First, I want to thank you readers for giving me a strong enough platform to even begin to make this choice. I hope you will love all the upcoming books and come along with me as you have on all the other journeys.

Secondly, to all those who helped in the process of the book. To Mackenzie Walton, my fearless, kind and awesome editor. Thank you for all the things. To Millie Bullock, not just the best copyeditor, but the best Mommy ever. I love you! To my friends who encouraged me in this change, Grace Callaway, Delilah Marvelle, Heather Boyd, Vicki Lewis Thompson and Lila DiPasqua. Your generous sharing of information and occasional handholding made a huge difference. To Beth Neuman for raucous games of Cards Against Humanity and amazing talks that make me remember I am human as well as a writer. Weird Girls Forever!

And finally and most of all to Michael Petersen. You have taken the leap with me in every way imaginable. You are my sounding board, my best friend, my assistant and the love of my life. I could hardly breathe without you, let alone be brave enough to try this.

CHAPTER ONE

Summer 1813

Serafina McPhee flinched as the seamstress tugged a few fingers of fabric tighter around her midsection and shoved a pin through the layers to hold them in place.

"If you continue to lose weight as you have, Miss McPhee, I cannot guarantee that you will look beautiful on your wedding day," the woman snapped. "And it shall not be my fault, I assure you."

"I'm sorry, Miss Windle," Serafina said softly as the dressmaker huffed off to scribble figures into a little notebook on the table a few feet away.

"What a horrid woman she is," Serafina's best friend Emma said as she sidled up next to her and squeezed her hand. "You could never be anything but beautiful. Here, look."

Her friend turned Serafina gently until they faced the full-length mirror behind her. Serafina stared at her reflection, and her heart sank. There was a part of her that wished the nasty dressmaker was right. That she would look at herself and see that her beauty had vanished, faded, altered to something less appealing.

But she looked the same as ever. And the dress, the beautiful dress that a dozen girls would have given their pinkies to wear, only heightened what the Lord had been cruel enough to gift to her.

Her father had spared no expense, and it showed. The pale cream silk had been spun with silver and gold so that the brocading along the bodice almost sparkled in the light. The fabric was perfectly cut to fall over her body in the most flattering way possible, enhancing her bosom before it cascaded over the rest of her form, just kissing her curves.

At present, her blonde hair was bound in a simple chignon, but on her wedding day the elaborate veil on the table behind her would be perfectly set within her curls, framing her face, likely making her the envy of friends and acquaintances, all of whom had been invited to the wedding of the decade.

And all Serafina wanted to do was run.

"Oh no, don't cry," Emma whispered, retrieving a handkerchief from her gown pocket

Serafina took the offering and swiped at the unwanted tears that now threatened to fall from her eyes. She shot a look at Miss Windle, hoping the woman hadn't seen. The dressmaker would tell the world and Serafina's life was complicated enough without speculation dogging her.

"I'm sorry," she whispered back. "It's only...it's only I know *he* will only be worse once we're wed."

Emma sucked in a breath, her cheeks growing pink as she slowly nodded in understanding. But before she could speak, the door to Serafina's chamber flew open and her father stepped inside.

"Mr. McPhee," Miss Windle said with a smile, suddenly all sweetness and kindness when faced with the man who paid her hefty bills. "I didn't expect you today. Does your daughter not look lovely?"

Serafina tensed as her father cast a quick look in her direction. She expected critique, but his expression was distant and troubled as he turned back to the seamstress.

"Miss Windle, will you excuse us for a moment?"

The seamstress cast a quick glance at Serafina and then nodded. "Wh-why of course, sir."

She gathered her notebook and shot Serafina a glare, as if she had caused this request, before she stepped into the hallway. Once she was gone, Serafina's father gave Emma a hard look.

"You too, Emma. I need to speak to Serafina alone a moment."

Emma swallowed hard, squeezed Serafina's hand and then slipped from the room, shutting the door behind herself.

Serafina moved down from the elevated platform where Miss Windle had forced her to stand for the past hour. As she stretched her back, she looked at her father more closely. He looked...almost *sick*.

"What is it, Father?" she asked.

He cleared his throat a few times. "Yes, well, there is no way to say it that will ease the news, I suppose."

Serafina's heart began to pound. The last time her father had stammered and sputtered in this way had been when she was a girl and he announced that her mother had finally died after a long illness.

"What has happened?" she asked, her voice seeming to ring in the room around her.

"Serafina, Cyril is...he's..."

Serafina's errant mind swiftly began to fill in adjectives to describe her fiancé. *Cruel. Horrible. Disgusting. Hateful.*

"...dead," her father finished.

She stared at him, incapable of doing anything else. Blood roared like a raging river in her veins and her ears rang as that simple word ricocheted through her like a well-placed bullet.

"Dead?" she repeated slowly when she was able to find her voice. "What do you mean?"

Her father let out a put-upon sigh. "He was killed in a carriage accident early this morning. Messy business."

He continued to talk, but Serafina no longer heard him. Three words echoed in her mind, blocking out her father's droning.

Cyril is dead. Cyril is dead.

3

She turned away from her father and paced to the window, covering her mouth as the truth sank in. In its wake followed a reaction she could not control, one she was absolutely horrified by.

Joy. Utter joy thrilled through her entire being. Cyril was *dead*. That meant no more horrible afternoons in his company, no more false reasons to get her alone so he could…*court* her.

No more wedding.

She looked down at the gown she had despised not ten minutes before and suddenly loved it more than anything she had ever worn. She would not marry. She was free!

"But it hardly matters now," her father said with a shake of his head.

Serafina forced the giddy smile from her face and turned on him, determined not to be the worst person ever to walk the earth.

"How can you say that, Father?" she asked, measuring her tone carefully. "Cyril is dead. No matter what he was or did in life, there are certainly those who will mourn him. His mother will be devastated."

She frowned at the thought. The duchess doted on her son with a fervent desperation. This might just kill the nasty woman. Or simply drive her off the edge of sanity.

Her father wrinkled his brow as if he didn't understand Serafina.

"What are you going on about, girl? I'm not talking about Cyril's mourners, I'm talking about *your* position."

She shook her head. "My position?"

"I didn't come to tell you of this development sooner because I spent the morning going over the marriage contract with the solicitor. We are very lucky, Serafina."

The joy Serafina had begun to feel started to bleed away with the broad smile that broke across her father's face.

"How can this be lucky when my marrying a duke was of such importance to you?" she whispered, not wanting to hear the answer, but knowing she had to.

"The contract was written such so that it says you will marry the Duke of Hartholm," her father said, eyebrows lifting.

"But he is dead," she said.

"No, dukes never die," her father chuckled. "Men do. There is already a new Duke of Hartholm, you see. Or there will be once the formalities are conducted as early as the end of the day. The solicitor believes that man won't be able to break our contract. You will marry as planned, my dear."

Serafina stepped backward, staggering over the train of her gown, hearing the delicate fabric rip beneath her slippers just as she felt her heart being torn in two. It felt as if there was a rock in her stomach, weighing her down.

"But…but Cyril had no brothers," she managed past her dry throat. "So *who* is the new duke?"

Raphael Flynn paced across the parlor floor, his anger and upset rolling through his veins, rising in his chest where it choked him until he could hardly see or think or speak.

He turned on his heel and faced his family. His sister Annabelle sat at the escritoire, poring over documents without looking up or acknowledging him.

At the fireplace stood his younger brother Crispin. Despite the early hour, he clutched a glass of scotch tightly. Rafe's brother's face was lined with intense emotions, just as Rafe knew his own was.

And on the settee, their mother watched it all, her lips pursed and cheeks pale with worry.

It had been like this for two days, since news had reached them that Rafe's cousin, the rarely seen and even less liked Duke of Hartholm, had been killed in a sudden and rather scandalous accident. Two days since Rafe's life had entirely changed.

"I never even *liked* Cyril," Rafe managed to bark out,

directing his comments toward Crispin, who was his closest friend as well as his brother. "Why should I be forced to inherit his life?"

He turned to pace away again, but his mother got to her feet and stepped forward, stopping him from his relentless movement as she lifted her hands to gently straighten his cravat.

"Hush," she said, but her voice was soft and held nothing but kindness. "Have a bit of respect for the dead, Raphael."

"How can I?" he asked, even as he covered her hands with his and stared down into her face, searching for an answer she could not give him. "I do not *want* to be a duke."

Annabelle glanced up from her papers and slowly removed her spectacles. She let out a sigh that stabbed Rafe to his very soul.

"What you want, I fear, no longer matters," she said with a frown. "The articles of inheritance are very clear. As the eldest male cousin, *you* are the next in line for the title."

Rafe's temples began to throb and he reached up to cover his eyes. "And what of the *other* issue?"

His sister searched through the papers and held up a few of them. "You mean the betrothal contract?"

The nausea that had been coming and going in waves for two days hit him again and he swallowed past the bile that gathered in his throat. He struggled for air before he whispered, "Yes."

Annabelle set the papers down and slowly got to her feet. She crossed the room to him, her eyes filled with pity. Her expression told him the answer even before she lifted to her tiptoes and pressed a kiss to his cheek.

"I'm so sorry, darling. It seems the contract was written very well indeed. The solicitor was correct in his initial assessment. You have inherited Cyril's fiancée along with his title, lands and what little remains in the entailment."

Rafe pulled away from her and walked to the window. He leaned his head against the cool glass. He wished he could melt through the barrier and run away. Far away.

"God damn it," he barked before he slammed his palm against the glass, making it vibrate.

"Rafe," his mother said, her voice very tight. "Don't blaspheme."

He turned to look at her. He had not inherited much of her looks. He and his brother had always favored their father, but in that moment her expression was a perfect mirror of his own feelings. She looked sick with worry, her face pale and drawn and tired.

"I'm sorry, Mama," he said as he shook his head. "But God *damn* it."

His mother smiled slightly and crossed to him to take his hand. She squeezed gently, clearly looking to offer comfort that simply didn't exist for him. Not now. Not for a long time to come.

"I know, dearest," she said. "And I would not wish for you to have these burdens press down on your shoulders. Nor for you to wed some stranger. But we must maintain calm. After all, everything has been unstable these past few days, and who knows what will come next, for better or for worse. All we can do now is go to the funeral as planned. You will meet this young lady and her family and we will work it all out. Somehow."

Rafe smiled at her, but the expression was only meant to offer his mother the reassurance he couldn't grant to himself. After all, her words might be perfectly correct, but they gave him no solace. Because in the end, he could not believe that things would work out. They had a good many times in his rather charmed life.

But not this time.

Rafe shifted, wishing he could rip off his jacket and the

black armband tied like a tourniquet around his bicep, untie the cravat choking him and race out of the parlor. Everyone in the room seemed to take their turn staring at him. More than half had not even attended the short service at the church and the burial afterward. They had merely descended upon Cyril's home to eat his food and drink the wine that now flowed around them.

"Good God, this is a nightmare," Crispin said as he sidled up to Rafe and handed him a glass of wine. "Is this what life as a duke will be?"

Rafe downed the drink in one swig. "It seems so. Did you know four people have come up to *congratulate* me? At Cyril's funeral. As if I won a hand of cards against him or some such nonsense. I didn't care for the man, but he's dead. It's entirely unseemly."

"You have influence that comes with the blasted title," Crispin said with a shrug. "And everyone knows you've brought money to the equation too. They will be kowtowing to you for years."

Rafe shuddered. "I hate the thought."

"What will you do, abandon your post?" Crispin said with a half-smile for his brother. "That would only add to the reputation we currently hold."

Rafe tried to smile back at the teasing, but couldn't quite manage it. "It is one thing to gamble until dawn at the Donville Masquerade or drink and streak naked through St. James Park or even bed a dozen willing ladies. But to walk away from the title? It would go too far. I wouldn't do that to Mama or Annabelle. They suffer enough for our notorious reputations."

Crispin cocked his head as if he didn't understand the words coming from Rafe's mouth. "They don't complain."

Rafe shook his head. "I believe Mama's occasional sighs and Annabelle's pointed glares should be registered as complaints."

"And what of your bride? Will *she* complain?" Crispin asked.

Rafe scanned the room. "I have not yet seen her."

"Why wasn't she at the funeral and burial?" his brother asked.

"Someone was going on about women's delicate constitutions," Rafe said with a roll of his eyes. "I also heard whispers that Aunt Hesper was too hysterical to attend her only child's services and insisted that Miss McPhee not go either due to some jealousy. There are many who are anxious to tell me that Hesper does not care for her son's once-future bride."

Crispin lifted his brows. "That may count as a mark in the girl's favor, if I recall Aunt Hesper. That part of the family cut us off when I was still young, but I do remember her as not the kindest woman. Still, she is not our interest. What else do they say about Miss McPhee?"

"Only that she—"

He was cut off when a side door to the parlor opened and a young woman entered on the arm of an older man. She had honey blonde hair that was pulled back in a severe chignon, but the tight, plain hairstyle only served to highlight her face. It was heart-shaped, with lustrous, fair skin. She had full, pink lips and pale blue eyes that reminded him of icy vistas. She was wearing full black, and he realized with a start that *this* was Miss McPhee.

"What do they say about her?" his brother said, shaking his head.

Rafe swallowed. "That she is the most beautiful woman in London," he said, staring at her because he couldn't tear his gaze away.

Crispin followed his gaze and his eyes widened. "Is that the lady in question?"

Rafe managed a nod. "I think it must be."

Crispin let out a low whistle. "Then I would say the gossip is not an overstatement."

Rafe shook his head. "No. It is not."

He had seen many beautiful women before, of course. He had been with them in virtually every way imaginable.

9

Normally, he was not attracted to cool propriety or even women of rank at all. They came with too many entanglements unless they were widowed and as anxious to remain free as he himself was.

But looking at this woman, he was seized by a sudden, powerful jolt of desire that seemed to work its way through his entire body and settle most uncomfortably between his legs.

He couldn't explain the reaction. He could only assume it was because of the shock of the past few days and the knowledge that he could not escape a future with Miss McPhee unless something entirely unexpected happened, that encouraged his body to behave in such a fashion.

"When you meet with her, will you drool all over her like you are now?" his brother asked.

Rafe forced himself to stop looking at his cousin's fiancée and glared at his brother. "Shut up."

"I'm just wondering if that will be the main part of your plan today," Crispin continued, his lip tilting up in amusement at Rafe's expense.

"I do not wish to discuss this," Rafe said through clenched teeth.

His brother shrugged. "Well, you'll surely be talking about it sooner rather than later, even if it is not with me."

Rafe looked back across the room and found that Miss McPhee's father had seemed to notice him. The man said something to his daughter and then began to stride across the room toward Rafe and Crispin. Rafe straightened his shoulders and prepared for the worst.

"It seems you are correct, Crispin. Which I know you love to hear. Why don't you step away, as it seems I cannot avoid what is about to happen."

CHAPTER TWO

Serafina had always particularly hated the parlor where the mourners now gathered to eat and drink and mull over Cyril's life, as well as gossip behind her back about his death. Just two days after the accident and the details of that morning's events had already begun to spread, even reaching her ears. She blushed as she tried not to think about them too closely.

All she knew was that she felt sorrier for the whore who had been riding in the phaeton with Cyril and met the same fate he had than she did for her fiancé. That fact left a sour taste in her mouth.

Across the room, she caught a glimpse of her once-future mother-in-law. Hesper was standing with a woman Serafina did not know. The two talked together for a moment, with the dowager duchess's face angry and brittle. Then the dowager motioned toward her dismissively. Serafina turned away with a blush. From the whispers of the other mourners and the glares from Hesper, it seemed Her Grace almost blamed Serafina for Cyril's death. Which was preposterous to the core.

Before she could find a way to excuse herself for a moment and get some air on the terrace, she felt a hand on her elbow and turned to find her father at her side.

"Come," he said, gripping her arm a bit roughly. Their eyes met and she saw his determination, as if he thought she might resist. In truth, the thought had crossed her mind.

"Where?" she asked even though she had guessed what was about to happen and had little choice but to stagger in the direction that he pulled her.

"To meet the new Duke of Hartholm," he said, his voice and face heavy with grim resolve.

Serafina found herself yanking against him as sudden terror shot through her.

"No," she whispered. "I don't want to. Please don't make me."

Her father glared down at her. "There is no more escaping this now than there was before, child. Come along or I shall drag you from this room kicking and screaming, no matter how it looks."

Serafina stiffened. The world, or at least her world, was taking enough pleasure with the matter of the death of her fiancé. A fit at his funeral would make her even more a topic of gossip.

And since it would do no good to refuse, she set her shoulders and followed her father from the room of her own volition. As they walked through Cyril's twisting halls, she drew a few long breaths. Even if she was screaming inside, she had to look calm. Cyril had taught her that bitter lesson very well, and she intended to use it against his cousin just as she had against him once upon a time.

"He is awaiting us here," her father said, pushing open the door to Cyril's office. Serafina forced herself not to flinch as she entered the room with its richly paneled walls and tall bookcases filled with tomes Cyril had never touched in his life.

Come to think of it, Serafina hated this chamber as much as the parlor.

A man stood at the fire and, as her father shut the door, he turned. Serafina caught her breath.

She had never met Raphael Flynn, the new Duke of Hartholm and the cousin of her late fiancé. He wasn't titled and moved on the outside fringes of the Upper Ten Thousand. What had been said about him were murmurings of a reputation that seemed to both irritate and intrigue those in her circles. He was rich but no stranger to scandal and repeated behavior that thwarted Society's many rules.

Even Cyril had hardly spoken of his cousin in the past except to malign him, which softened her to the man considerably.

And then there were the rumors of his intensely handsome good looks. Now that she stared at him, leaning on the mantel with a haphazard nonchalance that didn't reflect the importance of the moment, she couldn't deny that he *was* utterly beautiful. An Adonis. There was no other way to describe him.

He had tousled blond hair that was a bit too long for current fashion. His face was a work of art, with a hard, angled jaw, full lips and bright blue eyes that seemed to be fashioned after the Mediterranean Sea in some of her favorite paintings. He was an angel, just like the one he had been named after, only it seemed this man would be more like a fallen angel.

But a fallen angel could still be very powerful and dangerous. She wiped thoughts of his pleasing countenance from her mind, refusing to be moved by such foolishness.

Her father stepped forward, holding out a hand to him. "Your Grace, thank you again for meeting with us. This must be a difficult time for you and your family. Such a loss, such a terrible loss."

Serafina barely held back a snort of derision, both for her father's sentiment and for his utterly ridiculous glad-handing of the new duke.

To her surprise, the handsome man ignored her father. He pushed past him, coming toward her instead. She froze in her spot, held there by surprise and distraction caused, yet again, by his good looks.

"Miss McPhee, I presume," the duke said as he stopped in front of her, looking down with an unreadable expression.

She swallowed, trying hard to remember how to form coherent words, and somehow managed a nod. "Y-Yes."

He smiled at her stammering admission, the kind of smile

that had likely seduced many with its dazzling display. He reached out and took her hand, sending warmth through her dark gloves and up her arms like he was lightning in a summer storm.

"I am Rafe Flynn, Miss McPhee. And you and I seem to have a problem. One I'm certain we can solve if we put our minds to it."

Rafe knew when he was being charming. It was a skill he had honed and mastered over the years, turning the power of charisma to his advantage. It had certainly never failed to help navigate a difficulty or seduce a lady. Or seduce a lady who was difficult.

But to his surprise, Miss McPhee withdrew her hand from his with a cool frown.

"I'm afraid you are no longer Rafe Flynn, Your Grace," she said, her tone as chilly as her expression. "At least not in the eyes of the world. As for our 'problem,' as you put it, even if you reputation tells you that you may have it all, in this case you cannot avoid the inevitable. We must wed, despite my own desires."

Rafe arched a brow. Her reluctance he had expected, but not to this depth. But then, perhaps she had loved Cyril.

He looked her up and down a second time, from a closer proximity than had been achievable in the ballroom. Her beauty was only enhanced by their closeness. He thought of Cyril and his slick hair and fat gut held in by a corset. Could a lovely creature such as this one truly have feelings for a man like *him*?

Before he could think more on the subject, Mr. McPhee rushed forward and all but shoved his daughter out of the way.

"Serafina!" he said, his tone sharp as a blade. "Watch your tongue with the duke."

Rafe looked her over another time. Serafina. Her given name had not been present in any of the marital contract documents, and now it rolled in his head. It was a very unique name, but beautiful.

It fit her perfectly.

"Step aside, girl, and let me discuss this with the duke," Mr. McPhee continued.

Rafe pursed his lips at McPhee's tone. His arrogance and dismissal of his daughter irritated Rafe beyond measure.

"Why should Serafina step aside? This topic surely affects her more than it does you."

Her father's mouth dropped open and he let out a few incoherent, flustered sounds. To Rafe's utter pleasure, Serafina turned her head, smothering a smile at her father's reaction to being set down. She was even prettier when she smiled, it seemed.

"The documents are quite clear, Your Grace," Mr. McPhee blustered when he had regained some level of composure.

Any pleasure Rafe had experienced when making Serafina smile vanished. Every time someone called him "Your Grace" it brought his now-nightmarish future into clearer view and made his stomach turn anew.

"I suppose they must be," he responded with a sigh.

"You *will* wed," Mr. McPhee insisted, his voice rising.

Rafe stared at the man. He had learned a little about McPhee since hearing of Cyril's death and the shocking fact that he might have to marry Serafina. Rumor had it the man was rich and accustomed to getting his way, but he also was grasping, desperate to be linked to an important title like the one Rafe now reluctantly held.

McPhee wanted to get what he desired, even at the obvious exclusion of his daughter's happiness. Despite knowing his fate was likely sealed, as Serafina had said it was, Rafe didn't like the idea of giving in so easily.

"We'll see," he said, enjoying the flush of frustration that came to McPhee's cheeks. "This is certainly not the place to discuss the matter, at any rate. I will call on you tomorrow and we will talk it over in detail then."

"Your Gr—" McPhee began, but Rafe held up a hand to silence him as he turned toward Serafina. She was staring at him in what seemed to be wonder, as if no one went head to head with her father and it had made him more interesting to her.

Noting that fact, Rafe smiled.

"Until tomorrow, Serafina," he said softly. "And my condolences on your loss."

The serene look on her face faltered a bit. In fact, Rafe could have sworn he saw her flinch ever so slightly at his words. But then she gave a cool nod of dismissal.

He exited the room without giving in to a strange desire to look back at her, but as he strode down the hall to gather his family and say their farewells to his Aunt Hesper, he couldn't help thinking of Serafina over and over. She was a hard one to read and that interested him even more than her intense beauty did.

Serafina kicked off her slippers and tucked her feet beneath her on the settee. As Emma handed her a cup of tea, she smiled up at her friend, then watched her take a seat in a chair across from her. Once they were both settled, Emma leaned forward.

"Now that we are finally alone, why don't you tell me about it?"

Serafina shifted. "About what?" she asked, though she knew exactly to what Emma referred.

Raphael Flynn.

Her friend arched a brow. "The weather," she said, her tone dry as a desert.

Serafina smiled despite herself. "It is quite warm this

summer and thankfully there has been little rain," she offered. "But I think perhaps you would rather hear about the funeral gathering and my meeting with the mysterious new Duke of Hartholm."

Emma shrugged. "If you insist upon changing the subject, I won't stop you, this is your home, after all."

Serafina laughed for the first time in what felt like weeks.

"This is why I adore you. Even in my worst moments, you make me laugh. And today was certainly a worst moment."

"Which part?"

"All of it." Serafina stopped, thinking of her meeting with Rafe Flynn, as he had introduced himself, despite his new title. "Well, almost all. It started out poorly enough. Cyril's mother glared at me the entire afternoon. When I approached her to give my regards, she cut me down quite viciously in front of several people."

"She's always been a bitter one," Emma said with a wrinkle of her nose, as if she had smelled something vile. "Nastiest woman in Society."

"I happen to agree. It's almost as if she thinks Cyril's death is somehow my fault. Or at least that I'm gaining from it somehow. As if I ever wanted *anything* Cyril or his title had to offer in life or in death."

"Certainly not!" Emma said, folding her arms in solidarity. "That is your father, not you."

"Speaking of my father, you should see him. He is desperate now," Serafina said.

"Why?" Emma asked, her eyes wide. They both knew what happened when Serafina's father was desperate. Bad things.

"The new duke does not bend so easily," Serafina explained with the slightest smile as she remembered how Rafe had spoken to her father.

"Yes, let us get to that subject. I am dying to know what this new duke was like," her friend said. "You have been very vague."

Serafina pondered the question for a moment. "If I have been vague, I suppose it's because I have little answers about the man. He is…well, he's terribly handsome."

"That is an improvement," Emma said with a smile.

"Yes, but I think he knows it too well." Serafina sighed. "And he has likely never had a woman in his life turn him down. Not that I shall have that option soon enough."

Emma pursed her lips. "Does he seem delighted to have the title, ready to use it and wield the power it brings?"

"No." Serafina thought of the man again and his words and actions during their brief moment. "Quite the opposite, in fact. Some might very well be crowing and strutting and enjoying every moment of their new position. Rafe seems as troubled by this turn of events as I am. And he does not seem fully accepting that we will marry, either."

Emma's eyes went wider. "Do you think you will escape the altar yet?"

Serafina barked out a laugh. "No. No matter what the new duke thinks, there will be nothing for it in the end. My father will, as always, have his way." Serafina shook her head slowly. "And this Raphael Flynn and I will both suffer for it."

Emma was silent for a moment and Serafina sank back on the settee. Now that she had stated this truth out loud, it seemed to pile itself onto her shoulders and drag her deeper into the cushions. How she wished she could sink all the way inside and hide forever.

But if she had learned anything from her very long engagement to Cyril, it was that hiding was not possible. This was her fate, one way or another.

"What if you did not have to suffer?"

Emma's unexpected question pulled Serafina from her maudlin reverie. She sat up and shook her head at her friend. "I already know my father won't bend. You know him—he's like a bulldog with a bone when it comes to earning a relationship to a title through me."

"I don't mean change your situation with you father," her

friend clarified. "I mean that if you and this new duke are both being forced into this situation, if he is as unhappy about it as you are, doesn't that leave you with some opportunity to…to…"

Her friend seemed to struggle for an explanation and Serafina leaned forward. "What?"

"Negotiate, I suppose is the best word for it."

"Negotiate what, exactly?"

Emma tilted her head. "Your future. With Raphael Flynn."

Serafina opened her mouth to protest, but then she thought of what her friend had said. She'd been so focused on what her father would have done, she had never considered that *she* might have some control—not over the wedding, but the marriage. That was what Emma meant, after all.

She thought again of Rafe and how he had approached her before her father, of how he had included her in their discussion and even put her father down when he sorely needed it. Based on what she'd heard through gossip, but also on what she'd already seen of the man, Rafael Flynn believed he could have it all.

"I suppose he *might* be amenable to such a conversation," she said slowly. "*If* he is not like his cousin."

Emma bent her head. "I certainly hope he is not."

"As do I," she whispered.

Emma reached across and caught her hand, and they sat quietly together for a moment before Serafina shook her head and gathered herself.

"He is coming here tomorrow," Serafina said as she shoved to her feet and paced the room. "So I will somehow manage to get him alone and discuss the future with him."

"At the very least, you'll learn more about his true character through the exercise," Emma said.

Serafina nodded. "And even if he isn't open, I will be in no worse position than I am now."

She looked out the window into the darkness outside and found herself smiling. Because for the first time in years, she had begun to believe that she might actually be in a *better* position than she had ever been before.

CHAPTER THREE

Rafe stood in the parlor of Serafina McPhee's home the next afternoon, pacing the floor as he awaited his host and his intended. Although he had only been left alone but a few moments, he found himself irritated and out of sorts.

Since his cousin's death, Rafe had been somewhat numb to the consequences of inheriting the dukedom. Yes, it had been the only subject of discussion within his family for days, but despite every conversation and analysis, the endeavor had not fully hit home with him until he met Serafina.

So his evening after their encounter had consisted of a great deal of alcohol and a sleepless night in his bed. A bed he would soon abandon for the ducal home, he was told by a thin-nosed solicitor who seemed to relish giving Rafe the news. The other man simply couldn't understand why someone would loathe the idea of inheriting a title. No one could.

Behind him, the parlor door opened and he turned to watch Jonathon McPhee enter with Serafina trailing behind him. Her eyes were downcast as she stepped into the room, but she lifted them for a moment and her gaze caught his and lit up with…well, he wasn't certain what emotion it was that flitted across her face, but it was not an unpleasant one.

Suddenly his upset faded a fraction.

It returned almost immediately as McPhee slammed the door behind his daughter and strode up to Rafe without the barest of preamble.

"Your solicitors have reviewed the contracts, I'm certain, Your Grace," he said, his face reddening as he hurtled himself onto the settee and folded his arms.

Rafe arched a brow at the blustering older man and promptly turned his attention to Serafina. "Good afternoon, Miss McPhee."

She nodded. "Your Grace."

"I hope you are well after a difficult day yesterday," he continued, loving how McPhee had begun to clench and unclench his fists.

Serafina seemed to take pleasure in that fact, as well. "Thank you for your kind concern. May I get you something to eat?"

"That would be quite nice, thank you," Rafe said, retaking his chair and watching as she walked to the sideboard across the room and gathered up plates. She chose two biscuits and then turned to him with eyebrows lifted in question.

"Chocolate, thank you," he said in answer to the unspoken question about which biscuit he would prefer.

"Your Grace, I must insist upon—" McPhee began again.

Before he could finish, Serafina turned toward them again. "I'm sorry, Your Grace, might I trouble you for some assistance?"

Rafe glanced over to find her motioning toward one of the plates. With McPhee still sputtering on the couch, Rafe got up and joined her across the room. As Serafina handed him his plate, she leaned in.

"Ask me to go driving," she whispered, her gaze darting to her father surreptitiously.

Rafe stared at her. "I beg your pardon?"

She pursed her lips in apparent frustration. "I saw your fancy phaeton in the drive. Tell my father you wish to go driving in the park with me, *now*."

Rafe blinked a few times, uncertain how to respond to her wild-eyed insistence. His hesitation seemed to spurn her forward. She stepped toward him until they almost touched and he got a faint whiff of the honey essence of her skin. The fragrance seeped through him, warming him, making him want her just as he had in those few shocking moments when he'd first seen her from across the room at his cousin's funeral gathering.

"Do you understand?" she snapped, still whispering, even though she seemed to be utterly exasperated with him.

"Yes, you are very clear," he said with a laugh he could not smother. He turned to move across the room and set his plate down next to a chair.

"Mr. McPhee, I would like to take a drive around the park with your daughter. I have an open rig for two, and the park is so close by. I hope you will allow it."

McPhee, not surprisingly, stared at him in disbelief. "Right *now*? When you have only just arrived and we haven't even had a moment to discuss the very important matters at hand?"

Serafina stepped forward to pass her father his own biscuit, which he took in what seemed to be stunned silence.

"Papa," she said, her voice suddenly all sweetness and light. "Perhaps if His Grace and I get to know each other, you will not have to bellow your points at him so."

McPhee shot Serafina a glare so dark that for a moment Rafe wanted to place himself between father and daughter. But when he looked at her, she didn't seem to be bothered in the slightest by her father's angry expression. Which made Rafe wonder how much worse she endured in this house with this grasping little man who would use her to obtain his own desires.

"Do you promise you will not try anything untoward?" her father asked.

Rafe turned back to him in surprise. "Untoward?"

"Your outrageous reputation with women precedes you, young man," McPhee said. Rafe almost smiled, for it seemed McPhee cared a little for his daughter yet. But the smile fell when McPhee added, "Until your obligations have been laid out and agreed to, I cannot risk you spoiling her."

Serafina blushed as she turned away from the men. "I promise you, Papa, there will be no spoiling today," she said softly.

Rafe nodded in agreement and McPhee waved them toward the door. "Go then. But this conversation is not over."

"No, it is not," Rafe agreed as he walked to Serafina and offered her an arm.

She hesitated a beat before she took it and there was no mistaking the tightness around her mouth and eyes as she marched them into the foyer. There she spoke a moment to a servant and then said, "They'll bring the carriage right away. Come to the drive and we'll wait."

He nodded, saying nothing about the subject he so desperately wished to broach. In fact, he said nothing as his gig arrived, nothing as he helped her into her place, nothing as he urged his horses into the street.

He was about to speak when the horses suddenly jolted and the mare on the driver's side leapt, slamming the carriage forward and nearly sending them both flying.

"Whoa!" he called, yanking back on the reins with all his might. His heart pounded as the horse stilled.

"What is wrong with them?" Serafina asked, her voice shaking as she gripped the edge of her seat.

"I don't know," he said, handing over the reins to her. "Hold them if you can."

She didn't hesitate, but gripped the reins without argument. She watched as he climbed down and approached the skittish mare on his side of the carriage with gentle words.

"Steady, steady, Moonfire. What spooked you?" he asked, running his hands up her side.

The animal stiffened and sidestepped slightly as his hand approached her bridle. Carefully, he slid his fingers beneath the woven bridle and drew his hand back in surprise. There was a broken piece of metal there. He extracted it from its place digging into Moonfire's flesh and drew it out to stare at it in disbelief.

"The poor animal!" Serafina gasped as he held it up to the light. "Is she injured?"

He felt beneath the bridle again, but this time the horse didn't skirt away. When he withdrew his fingers, he saw no blood and shook his head.

"She doesn't appear to be hurt," he said and moved around to examine the other horse, Sunbeam. But there was nothing to find beneath her bridle and she only kept a worried eye on the other horse rather than react to his touch.

He put the shard in his pocket and shook his head as he returned to his driver's seat.

"I'll have to show this to my stable master," he said. "And have my equipment inspected."

Serafina surrendered the reins to him and drooped against the seat momentarily. "That was certainly an unexpected beginning to our ride."

Rafe nickered at the animals and the horses began to move, this time with no dramatics. "This entire outing is unexpected," he said with a laugh.

He maneuvered the vehicle onto the street and toward the park just a short ride away. It wasn't until he turned through the huge gate marking the park that he spoke again.

"All right, Serafina McPhee, tell me—what are you up to?"

Serafina shifted slightly at both the direct question Rafe asked her and the pointed stare with which he snagged her. She had made this plan the night before with great relish, but now it was...more difficult.

"I—" she began, then stopped herself to draw in a deep, calming breath. "Since we very nearly died a similar death as your cousin together, I feel I must be honest with you. I do not wish to marry you."

His eyebrows lifted and he shook his head. "You wound me."

The flat affectation of his tone and the dancing expression in his eyes told Serafina that he was teasing her. It was odd how that easy interaction made her stomach flutter and her cheeks heat. Rafe Flynn was certainly an exasperating man.

"Please don't play, I'm being very serious," she said, folding her arms and looking away from him. It was easier to think and breathe when she did so.

"I realize that," he said.

"And I don't believe you wish to marry me either." She glanced at him again and could see he was struggling with a gentlemanly way to affirm her assertion. "You don't have to say it. It doesn't really matter anyway."

"No?" he asked. "You don't think it could all be changed?"

She shook her head at his repeated belief that things would work out for him. It must have been a remarkable life he led before Cyril ruined everything for him. She almost felt sorry for the man.

"We will be forced to do so. Certainly you must have read over the contracts."

He turned the phaeton down a little-used lane and parked it so that they looked out over the lake. Once he had secured them, he turned to face her.

"I did. As did my solicitor and, perhaps most importantly, my sister Annabelle. Your father is quite thorough."

Serafina tilted her head, taken aback by his comment about his sister reading over the contracts. She had never heard of a man with such wealth and power giving anything over to a female relative, but apparently he trusted this Annabelle a great deal.

She shook her head to clear those thoughts. "With Cyril, there was something he wanted—money—and something my father wanted, a closer connection to the power of the title

Hartholm. But with you it's different."

"How so?" he asked, lazing back against the vehicle like he was lounging at his club.

For a moment, his expression distracted her, for it made her realize what a position they were in. Although there were a few others in the park, they were actually very secluded where they were.

And she knew very well how men could take advantage. In fact, Rafe's reputation said he would very likely attempt just that. But somehow the old fear, the tension that always accompanied being alone with Cyril, did not dog her now.

"Serafina," he said softly.

She jolted at the sound of him saying her name. "I'm sorry. You must know why it's different—you have more money than King Midas."

Rafe tilted his head aback and let out a great bark of laughter that froze Serafina in her tracks. God, but he was attractive. His teeth were white and straight and there was a dimple in his right cheek that gave his grin a lopsided element. She didn't think she had ever seen such a well-favored man before.

Which made her hope even more that he might just agree to her terms.

"Not quite," he said when his laughter had faded.

She shrugged. "You don't need more."

"Some would say a man could never have enough, but I tend to agree with you," he said.

She swallowed hard. He was teasing her again, not cruelly, but as if they were *friends*. It was all very confusing.

"It seems to me that we should negotiate for what we will each receive if this travesty of a marriage must continue," she said in a quick burst of words.

His smile fell and he stared at her, clearly surprised by her statement.

"Negotiate?" he repeated.

She nodded slowly.

He examined her closely for a long moment before he leaned forward. Although the gig was open, it didn't leave much room between them so suddenly he seemed to loom up everywhere, surrounding her. She could smell the sweet hint of sandalwood and lavender, and she felt the heat of his body.

To her surprise, her body reacted very differently than it ever had to such a circumstance. Her breath came short, not out of fear, but something she couldn't name. Her heart began to stutter in her chest. She felt hot and achy. It was nothing like she had ever experienced.

"And just what do you intend to offer me, Serafina?" he asked, his deep voice as smooth and attractive as the rest of him.

But his words broke the spell. Her mind conjured quick images of Cyril's rough hands and cruelty. With a gasp, she turned her head.

"Freedom," she said, her voice cracking. "I will give you a marriage in name alone, with no expectations or connections. I will give you *utter freedom*."

Rafe leaned away from Serafina, taken aback not just by what she said, but by how adamant she was in saying it. Her pretty face was taut with strain and her knuckles were white from gripping her fists in her lap.

He had been teasing and playful with her, hoping to relax her, but now he could see he might need to take a different tactic.

"I understand your reticence," he said softly. "You were to marry my cousin up until just a few days ago and your betrothal was one that spanned many Seasons. His sudden death must be a blow. That you could not transfer any kind of affection to another man is obvious."

He watched her as she digested what he'd said. Her face

was again unreadable and he found himself wondering if she had somehow heard about the full details of Cyril's demise. His cousin had died driving his rig too fast while a whore fellated him. But those were details discussed by men, not with women. She *couldn't* know, nor should she ever, so that her illusions of her fiancé wouldn't be shattered.

"Yes, of course," she finally said, her tone oddly flat and even more tense than her expression. "What you say is right. Transferring my affections would be difficult. So what do you think of my offer? Do not trouble me and I shall also leave you be."

Rafe wrinkled his brow. That she was upset was clear, but the fact that he couldn't exactly place the reason troubled him. She agreed about transferring her affections, but he had not seen her weep over Cyril nor show overly warm emotions when she spoke about him.

So perhaps there was something else at play here. Either way, Rafe had no choice but to move forward and address her new "terms" to their marriage.

"I would not trouble you, as you put it," he said, shifting with discomfort as he tried to find a way to continue. She was a lady, after all, and might not understand. "But…we must…there are certain things we must do… things to—to consummate—"

She blushed hot, but her jaw set with grim determination. "I know what you are trying to say. So we will have a wedding night, together."

He nodded. She didn't seem shocked by the subject, so he had to assume she had spoken to a female relative or friend in preparation for her wedding night with Cyril. With their original wedding date now just a few days away, he supposed that made sense.

"But not just a wedding night," he continued. "We will also need to provide at least an heir and a spare to the title."

"Why?" she burst out, suddenly blinking far too much as she edged away from him as far as the narrow phaeton seat would allow. "*Why?*"

He frowned. She had been calm in the face of dangerously bucking horses, but the idea of bearing his children made her balk. It was very strange.

"I'm surprised a lady in your position must ask that. Because I am a duke now. Is that not the expectation?"

"But you don't want to be a duke," she argued. "Why live up to the expectations? Your reputation shows you delight in doing so, why should this be different?"

She was asking him things he already asked himself. Things he had answers to, unfortunately.

"Because I would not pass this burden to my brother in the event of my untimely death," he said softly. "Crispin would be even more ill-suited to the duty than I am. It would destroy him."

She stared at him, her panic fading, if only for a moment. "You care for him so much?" she asked softly.

"Of course," Rafe admitted with no hesitation. "He is my best friend as well as my brother."

Her expression softened at that admission, though she seemed to struggle with his request for a moment. Finally she nodded. "It would be unfair of me not to fulfill my duty. I can agree to providing you with sons."

She had said the word *duty* and it hung between them. It was funny, but looking at her, brilliant sunlight dancing off her honey hair, golden on her beautiful face, what they were discussing, sex, didn't feel much like a duty. Serafina was distant and cold now, but even if she had lingering feelings for his cousin, could Rafe teach her pleasure? After all, passion didn't have to be linked to the heart.

"Why are you looking at me that way?" she asked, her voice soft and raspy.

He shook away thoughts of laying her naked body across his bed and said, "I was only thinking that we have negotiated, as you put it, my desires, but I don't know what you want, aside from being left alone except for the purposes of procreation."

She tugged her lip between her teeth and nibbled gently. The action sent a slash of heat to his cock, and he shifted so she wouldn't see his sudden and powerful reaction.

"I would like a reasonable income so that I don't have to beg for everything I need," she said. "And a home of my own."

He shook his head. "You may stay in the ducal home, Serafina."

"No!" she said, her tone again sharp and panicky. She drew a breath that seemed to calm her, for when she spoke again her tone was much more controlled, "No, thank you. I would prefer something less...less grand."

Rafe held back a bark of humorless laughter. "As would I."

She smiled slightly and he examined her face yet again. There was most definitely something deeper about Miss Serafina McPhee. Beneath those calm waters on the surface, he had a feeling storms raged. He only wondered if she would ever trust him enough to let him see.

"Is there anything else?" he asked.

She shook her head. "No."

"Then I suppose it is a bargain," he said. She held out her hand as if to shake and he ignored it. "In this case, I believe a kiss is the proper way to seal the terms."

Her lips parted and he could see protest on her face. He held up a hand. "I promised your father nothing untoward would happen, Serafina, and I meant it. I ask for a simple kiss. I promise not to ravish you."

"Why should I believe you when you have delighted in ravishing so many women before me?" she whispered.

"I'm surprised someone would speak to you about such things," he said, searching her face.

She arched a brow. "Everyone knows it about you and your family. You are seducers and gamblers and rabble-rousers. And *many* have delighted in telling me so since Cyril's death."

"Rabble-rousers," Rafe said with a slight smile, despite her hesitation. "I have always liked that word."

"Lived it, you mean?" she asked softly.

He grinned. "From time to time, yes. But I swear to you, on all of whatever honor I possess, that I shall not force you to do anything you do not desire. Just a kiss, Serafina. The rest will happen soon enough."

She winced at that sentence, but then lifted her chin slightly. "Do as you will," she whispered.

Rafe hesitated. He had kissed many a woman and none had ever seemed so resigned to unpleasantness beforehand. It drove him to change her mind about the act, about *him*. Only he had to do it delicately.

He scooted closer and reached a hand out to gently cup the back of her head. Being careful not to disturb her hairstyle, he tilted her face for the best angle. She squeezed her eyes shut and her body went stiff as his lips descended.

His mouth touched hers, just brushing back and forth against her tightly squeezed lips. He went slowly as her body relaxed a fraction beneath him and her lips became more accessible.

She was so soft beneath him, he wanted to delve deeper, to taste her, but he forced himself to hold back and pull away before he went too far. When he did so, he found her eyes wide open, watching him with an expression of shock.

"That—that was all?" she whispered.

He arched a brow. Now he *knew* she had a female confidante who had explained some of what happened between a man and a woman. Though the fact that she had apparently never been kissed before was a bit shocking. What was wrong with Cyril?

"For now," he said softly.

She turned away from him. "Will you take me back, please?"

He opened his mouth to say more, to question her, to try to figure out why her shoulders were suddenly so stiff, her hands so tightly folded. But then he shook his head. It didn't really matter, did it? If Serafina was afraid of him, interrogating her wouldn't help.

And if she was just a beautiful prude, it would take time to work on that as well.

So he said nothing and simply urged his horses to turn back up the lane. This little outing of theirs had revealed a great deal indeed, and he had a feeling there was even more to come.

CHAPTER FOUR

Rafe helped Serafina down from the phaeton and saw her gaze dart to the side yet again. Their short ride from the park had been very quiet. Whatever headway he'd felt he was making with her seemed to be gone, though he couldn't place why.

"Did I offend you?" he asked as he held out an arm for her.

She ignored the offer and they began to walk up the stairs side by side.

"No, Your Grace, you didn't." Her voice was soft and her tone hard to read.

He explored her face as they entered the house. No, she didn't seem offended. Something else had brought their small connection to a halt. It was utterly frustrating. Only days or perhaps a week separated him from his marriage to this woman, if her single-minded father got his way. Yet Rafe had no idea of anything she thought, felt or otherwise, beyond her strange negotiation terms.

He wanted to press her further for the truth, but before he could, Serafina's father appeared in the parlor door. McPhee's face was red and sweaty and he had obviously been working himself into a froth.

"Where have you been?" he barked.

Rafe sighed. So much for his time alone with Serafina.

Now he had to deal with McPhee. He nudged passed his future father-in-law into the parlor.

"I'm sorry, did you forget our plans to ride in the park already?"

"You were gone half an hour!" her father all but shrieked.

Rafe blinked at the man's sudden outburst. "That is hardly enough time to ride there and back, let alone have any kind of meaningful conversation. Dear God, man, you do test me."

"We need to discuss—"

Rafe waved him off. "There is nothing to discuss," he interrupted. "As you have stated so many times that it makes me want to scream, the contract is clear. I might argue it, but it would take months, waste money and further ruin the reputations of all involved. Not only that, but Miss McPhee and I have come to terms."

McPhee spun on his daughter. "Terms, Serafina?"

She straightened her shoulders and gave her father a look that could have withered flowers on the vine. "Don't worry yourself, Papa. My terms have nothing to do with what you are *due*."

He glared at her before he turned to Rafe. "You will marry on Saturday."

"In three days?" Rafe said as he lifted his brows. The man must be desperate to press for such a swift resolution of the matter.

"That is when the original wedding was to take place and I have every confidence that you will be able to obtain a special license before then if you exert your new influence," McPhee said, a cruel tilt to his lips.

Rafe looked past the man to Serafina. "Will that be difficult for you, to marry me on the same day you were meant to marry Cyril?"

Serafina's expression softened, just as it had in the park when Rafe mentioned his attachment to his brother. But alongside that softer emotion, he also felt her surprise that he would ask her leave. Was it possible no one had ever obtained her consent, even in regards to the most important moments of her life? He could not imagine treating his sister or mother in such a fashion.

"I am agreeable," she said softly.

"Then so it will be," Rafe said, but found himself not ready to say goodbye quite yet to his future bride. Instead, he said, "Good day, McPhee. Serafina, please escort me out."

She tilted her head in surprise, but didn't argue. She motioned to the door. "Lead the way, Your Grace."

Serafina tried not to fidget as she and Rafe stood in the foyer together. It would not do to reveal her nervousness. Yes, she could admit it, if only to herself: Rafe Flynn made her nervous. But it wasn't in the awful way Cyril had before he died. This was something…*different*. Something she couldn't name or place, but it wasn't entirely disagreeable.

"Serafina?" Rafe's voice was soft and pulled her from her reverie as they waited for his phaeton to be returned to the drive.

"Yes?" she asked.

He stepped closer and suddenly his hand reached out, cupping her chin and tilting her face up to look him in the eyes. As it had in the carriage, her heart began to pound, her knees began to shake and not entirely unpleasant quivers started low in her belly.

"It will be better," he said softly. "Better than this."

Serafina bit her lip. What a promise to make. How she wished she could believe him. A part of her wanted to do just that, but she knew better. Until she was alone with Rafe, truly alone, she knew she wouldn't see his real character. Despite their negotiations, despite his apparent good nature, he could be utterly cruel when the chamber door closed. And he could easily renege on any bargain they made if only because it pleased him. That was the way of the world.

When she said nothing, his lips pursed. "Come to supper at my mother's home here in London tomorrow, alone," he said. "You can meet my family and see we are not ogres, despite the reputation you continue to bring up."

"My father will never agree to that," she said with a shake of her head. "He'll involve himself in it."

Rafe smiled a half-smile and Serafina felt a strange desire to lean in closer. She resisted it with great effort.

"I'll make certain your father will allow it," Rafe said. "I may not have all the power that I desire in this situation, thanks to the contracts my cousin signed. But I assure you, I still have a great deal more than your father does. Will you come?"

She hesitated. The thought of going to meet Rafe's family made her stomach hurt. How much more would they hate her than even Cyril's mother had? After all, they *had* to believe she had trapped their son into marriage, that she was as grasping as her father was.

But this was yet another thing she could not avoid.

She nodded slowly. "If you can arrange it, I will be there. Goodbye, Your Grace."

Now it was he who leaned in, his face coming dangerously close to hers. She could feel the whisper of his breath against her cheek.

"Rafe," he corrected.

She blinked. She always thought of him by his Christian name, but to say it…

"Rafe," she repeated, her voice breaking.

His smile broadened. To her surprise, he leaned down and claimed her mouth for the second time. Where the first kiss had been feather-light and gentle, this time his lips were harder against hers, filled with a promise that both frightened and intrigued her.

But he didn't force his affections for long. He drew back after just a few seconds of contact.

"It seems I have a wedding to plan for. Until tomorrow."

He released her and turned on his heel to stroll down the walkway to his phaeton. She stared after him, tracking his every move.

She was so focused on him, in fact, that she didn't hear her father's approach at her elbow until he spoke.

"Well done, Serafina," he said, and she jumped before she turned to face him. He looked mightily pleased. "He seems smitten."

She shook her head as they watched Rafe nudge the horses into movement and ride off down the drive. "I assure you, Papa, it isn't that way."

He shrugged. "It doesn't matter what way it is, as long as he weds you."

He turned and left her standing in the doorway, staring at the spot where Rafe had last been, despite the fact that he was long gone now.

Her mind turned endlessly now that she was alone to consider their encounter. She had been desperate not to marry Cyril. The very idea of it had left her on the edge of desperate acts. But though Rafe was at this point far less cruel, in a way she feared marrying him even more.

But as had been the motif of her life, she had no choice in the matter.

CHAPTER FIVE

"You can't be telling me you actually *want* to marry this woman," Crispin sputtered as he slammed his glass of whiskey down on the sideboard and sent amber liquid sloshing across the wood.

Rafe shook his head. "Of course not."

"And yet you do not fight!" his brother blustered as he paced across the parlor, running a hand through his thick, dark blond hair.

"What would be the point in fighting?" Rafe asked. "You heard what the solicitor said."

"Damn the solicitor," Crispin growled. "He's an idiot."

Rafe pursed his lips. "But Annabelle is not and she said the same thing. Nothing can be done in the end, Crispin. I would either end up in a duel or wasting a good portion of a fortune battling only to end up in the same position as I am now."

"Damn it, Rafe," Crispin said, spinning to spear him again with one of those disapproving looks. It was disconcerting to see them on his brother's face, for normally they went the other direction.

"We have a bad enough reputation as it is," Rafe reasoned.

"As if any of us have cared about that," Crispin said with a harsh laugh. "If anything, we've always reveled in it."

"It is all well and good being the Notorious Flynns—"

"We were called that *once* in a gossip page," Crispin argued. "How is it our fault that the *ton* doesn't appreciate dancing and drinking and that we win their fortunes at cards and occasionally steal their mistresses?"

"All of which has been done in public," Rafe said, his tone cool.

Crispin shrugged.

"But if I dodge this marriage, we will become worse than notorious. We will be *infamous*. And Mama and Annabelle do care what is said about us. Push too far and we might ruin our sister's chances to marry happily, or at least well." Rafe scrubbed a hand over his face. "I'm not willing to sacrifice her on the altar of my own pleasure. Are you?"

Crispin glared at him, but much of the heat had left his tone when he said, "Of course not."

"Besides, there is also Serafina to consider."

Rafe's mind turned to her, as it had been for twenty-four hours. Her beauty and her intriguing personality were both a draw to him. He couldn't deny that.

"She would be socially devastated by the breaking of the engagement," he said softly. "Especially since her father has been quite indiscreet about the fact that I will be carrying it on. The young woman is an innocent, I couldn't put her in such a position."

"Oh, an *innocent*," Crispin spat, as if the label were the darkest curse. "That sounds unbearably drab."

Rafe flashed briefly to the softness of Serafina's lips, the unexpected boldness of her negotiations when it came to their marriage, her unreadable countenance that he had begun to sense hid something far more interesting than what Crispin assumed and accused.

"You may be surprised," Rafe said, sipping his drink slowly. "You will see when she arrives tonight. Serafina is more unpredictable than you might think."

"How so?" his brother challenged, folding his arms.

Rafe hesitated. The two had always shared stories of their

conquests. Hell, they had on occasion shared a conquest or two. But with Serafina it felt different.

But his brother remained staring at him in utter disbelief, and Rafe's drive to defend the woman who would be his bride became stronger than his strange and sudden impulse toward discretion.

"She forced me to take her for a ride yesterday when I called and then demanded we negotiate the terms of our marriage," he admitted.

Crispin blinked and his smug satisfaction in the fact of Serafina's boredom faded a fraction.

"You don't say," he said slowly.

"I do," Rafe laughed. "The young woman seems to be as intelligent as she is beautiful."

Crispin groaned. "We know from the experience of living with Annabelle how dangerous *that* combination can be. Will she ever grant you peace?"

Rafe pursed his lips. If Serafina had her way, they would never speak again once the vicar had declared them lawfully wedded man and wife. He had believed that her reticence had to do with her feelings for Cyril, but now he wondered.

What secrets was Serafina McPhee hiding?

"Rafe?" Crispin pressed.

"I don't think peace will be an issue," he said, but it felt like a lie. "And certainly a little attention couldn't be so terrible from such a lovely lady."

His brother rolled his eyes. "Dear God, whatever you do, don't become enamored with the woman."

Rafe laughed the order off with ease. "No, of course not. My duty, as she puts it, will be pleasant enough, I'm certain. But I guarantee you, brother, it will change nothing."

Serafina was finding it nearly impossible to draw breath as

she exited her carriage with her maid trailing silently behind her. She took a moment to gather herself by stopping to stare up at Alexandra Flynn's townhouse. Her new future mother-in-law had used her husband's money well, for the place rivaled the celebrated homes of those with the highest title.

"Which Rafe now holds," she murmured to herself.

"I'm sorry, Miss?" the maid peeped from behind her.

"Nothing, Berta," Serafina said with a frown.

The door to the townhouse opened before them and Serafina drew back. It wasn't some finely liveried servant who greeted them, but Rafe himself. With the light from inside framing him, she was put to mind again of the angel he took his name from.

"Good evening, Serafina," he said as he held the door open to allow them inside. A servant waited in the foyer and immediately motioned for Berta to join her. The lady's maid looked annoyed, but did as she had been directed.

Serafina let out a sigh of relief once Berta was gone.

"Good evening, Your Grace. I am surprised to find you waiting for me."

He smiled. "I can well imagine you would feel overwhelmed by this gathering. I wanted you to see a familiar face before any strangers met you. I can also call your maid back. Annabelle is quite close to her own, so we are not shocked by the occasional servant at the supper table."

Serafina shook her head. "To be perfectly honest, Berta is a wretch who reports my every move back to my father. I am glad to have her gone."

"Ah," Rafe said with a sudden frown. "Then we should make sure she does not accompany you to our new home when we are married."

Serafina's eyes went wide. "Are you in jest?"

"No, I see no reason why you should staff your household with those you do not like. Annabelle's maid can make suggestions of those who might be a better companion to you and you will interview them once the excitement of the nuptials fades. I'll see to it."

Serafina blinked in surprise. "You do take care of things, don't you?"

He grinned. "What is the point of having power or money unless you can?"

She found herself wanting to smile even though his words struck a little fear in her. They reminded her of how easily he could control *anything* she did or didn't do, despite his earlier promises.

"You even managed my father," she forced herself to continue without allowing him to see her nervousness. "I admit I didn't believe you would be able to convince him to allow me to come here with only his spy as chaperone."

"I am quite persuasive, my dear, as you will no doubt learn."

She stepped back out of habit as her stomach flopped. Images of Cyril "persuading" her filled her mind and she fought to keep them at bay. Fought to remember that Cyril was dead and that this man had not yet proven himself to be anything like his cousin.

"You are pale," Rafe said, moving toward her to take her hand. A shock of heat and electric awareness jolted through her at the touch. "Are you well?"

She nodded, but the movement was jerky and she doubted it did anything to mask her concerns. "Of course. Simply...simply..."

She struggled for a word to explain herself to his man, one that would be truthful, for he was looking at her so closely that she feared he would read a lie on her face. But one that would also cover up some of her heart, some of her fears. Rafe had no right to those things.

He drew her closer as he tucked her hand into the crook of his arm. "Come, you will feel better once you meet everyone and see that we are not out of control monsters who are slaves to our worst impulses."

He led her forward toward a parlor. The door was shut, but

she could hear the murmur of voices within. Her hands began to shake, her knees tremble, and she couldn't help but cast her glance backward through the foyer toward the front door and the escape it falsely promised her.

Rafe opened the door and led her inside. She fought the urge to squeeze her eyes shut and instead looked at what awaited her.

An older woman with a pretty, open face stood by the fire talking to a younger woman who looked remarkably like her. And a man who was a slightly less handsome version of Rafe sipped a drink as he surveyed the dark garden behind the house. Rafe's mother, his sister, his brother.

When Rafe stepped into the room, all of them stopped what they were doing at once and stared. Serafina shifted, readying herself for judgments or recriminations. But instead, the older woman moved toward the door with a welcoming smile.

"Hello, you must be Serafina!" she said as she reached her son. "I'm Alexandra Flynn. How happy we are to meet you at last."

She took both of Serafina's hands and squeezed gently before she turned toward the others. "This is my daughter, Annabelle, and my younger son, Crispin."

The others came toward her, but they did not offer any less kindness than their mother had.

Annabelle Flynn smiled, and though there was some hesitation to the expression, there was also friendliness.

"Miss McPhee," Annabelle said. "I've heard so much about you both from friends and from my brother. I'm so glad to meet you. And I tell you that it will be nice to have a sister to finally balance out the men in this family."

Serafina blinked. A sister. She had never thought of it that way, that she would gain a family. Cyril had no siblings and his mother had never made things pleasant or welcoming in any way.

"Preserve us from Annabelle having a cohort," Crispin

44

laughed as he reached their small group. He held out a hand toward Serafina with a grin that put her strongly to mind of Rafe, though it didn't make her stomach wobble as her fiancé did. "Miss McPhee. Welcome to our family."

She shook Crispin's hand. Just as she had sensed in his sister, she saw the hesitation in the younger brother's eyes, the way his stare slid to Rafe briefly. For that she could not blame him.

"Thank you all for this warm welcome," Serafina said as Rafe's mother motioned them all to sit on the settees before the fire. To her surprise, Rafe took a spot next to her, his presence filling up all the space around her without even trying.

"You deserve nothing less after what you have endured," Mrs. Flynn said with another smile for her. "These are trying circumstances for all involved. I am so very sorry for your loss."

Serafina fought to maintain the proper expression when faced with such sentiments. She didn't want to offend Mrs. Flynn or the others by allowing them to see the ugly truth in her heart.

"Thank you. Cyril's death was a shock," she said, sticking to the truth so a lie wouldn't be revealed too easily.

Annabelle nodded with sympathy. "This entire situation has been such a whirlwind for us, I cannot imagine what it's like for you."

Serafina shot Rafe a look. He gave her an encouraging nod, as if giving her permission to be honest or friendly or whatever she desired to be. She wasn't certain how to respond to that, in truth.

"Yes, well, I hope you know that I understand if you cannot look at me kindly." Serafina dropped her gaze. "I realize that Rafe...that His Grace...is dear to you. My existence likely brings him harm in your eyes."

Mrs. Flynn drew back in what seemed to be true surprise. "My dear, is that your fear? I assure you, I recognize that you are as affected by these events as my son. To be forced by

Jess Michaels

contract to marry another when you had planned a different life…it seems positively medieval! I recognize your father's desire to remain connected to the house of Hartholm, but…" She trailed off. "I don't think it is fair to you anymore than it is to Raphael."

"But since circumstances are what they are," Annabelle added. "We welcome you to our family."

Rafe cast a quick glance to his brother and even Crispin managed a tight smile. "Indeed."

Serafina blinked at the tears that suddenly stung her eyes. She had been so afraid of this moment, of meeting these people, and yet they treated her with respect and care that went far beyond even her wildest dreams.

"I see Kitterage floating about by the doorway, casting glances in at us," Annabelle said. "So it must be time for supper."

They all stood in unison and to Serafina's surprise, it was her future sister-in-law who clasped her arm and drew her toward the door.

"Come," she said with a laugh over her shoulder that was directed toward Rafe. "Let me tell you all my brother's most embarrassing secrets so that you might use them against him at will."

Serafina couldn't help but laugh as well, even as she tried very hard not to look at Rafe herself. Right now she didn't trust herself not to reveal too much if she dared to meet his blue eyes.

A few hours later, her belly full and mind put at ease by the supper she had shared with Rafe's family, Serafina followed Rafe through the French doors out onto a broad stone terrace that overlooked the gardens below. The summer air hit her and she breathed in its cool freshness before she cast a side-look at her fiancé.

"Your family is… They're *wonderful*," she said.

He took her hand unexpectedly and drew her forward across the terrace, taking her toward the wall and away from the windows that granted them both light and some kind of hint of a chaperone from the people inside.

Immediately, Serafina's heart began to pound.

"Thank you," he said at last. "I happen to agree."

"Your mother has the sweetest disposition and she truly seemed to want to know about me," Serafina continued. "Your sister has a brilliant mind indeed—I can see why you had her act as solicitor by reviewing the betrothal documents."

"Annabelle is often too smart for her own good," Rafe said with a laugh.

Before, that kind of comment might have tweaked Serafina and made her question her fiancé's character, but she had watched Rafe with his sister through the night. It was clear the pair adored each other, even with all their playful teasing.

"And what do you think of Crispin?" Rafe asked.

Serafina pursed her lips. "I think he is the most standoffish of the group," she admitted. "And I don't think he has quite made up his mind about me. Despite that, he was utterly polite and I saw the charm that gossip has labeled both of you to have."

"As I told you before, Crispin is my best friend as well as my brother," Rafe said. "So I hope you don't hold any hesitation you might feel against him. I don't think it is personal."

"No, I don't either." She shrugged. "He wants to protect you, that is as clear as the nose on his face. It must frustrate him that he cannot save you from this situation."

Rafe drew back, as if surprised she had come to that conclusion about his brother. Then he smiled. "In time, you will know each other better and he will become more comfortable."

Serafina turned toward him fully. "*Will* we know each

other?" she asked. "Since you and I do not intend to have a marriage that is real, will he truly have any more relationship with me than we have now?"

Rafe blinked. "Serafina, we will ultimately have children—it was part of our bargain. I have no intention of abandoning them. We will *all* have a relationship, even if we are not a doting husband and wife. I hope we can become...friends."

Serafina swallowed. Friends. The man standing before her, looming before her, all masculine beauty and heat and charm, didn't seem like the kind who made *friends* with women. Gossip labeled him a seducer, though not a cad.

She turned away so she wouldn't have to address that issue. "All I meant to say was that they are different than I expected. Welcoming and kind, and I appreciate that a great deal."

"I assume that means my Aunt Hesper was not equally welcoming," Rafe said softly.

Serafina tensed. She had not meant to reveal that detail to him. But he had gleaned it nonetheless.

"She never liked me much. The contract was written between Cyril's father and mine, and I was never under the impression she had any say in it. She certainly always made it clear that I did not pass muster as a mate for her only child."

Rafe shook his head. "If it helps, none of my family ever passed muster either. Even at Cyril's funeral, she accused me of sweeping like a vulture to collect the spoils of her dearly beloved son's untimely death. Nasty woman."

Serafina looked up at him. Here was yet another thing she had in common with the man. It seemed there were quite a few.

He shifted as she stared and suddenly he inched closer. "Sera...may I call you Sera?"

She blinked. No one had ever given her a nickname before. Certainly no utterly distracting men. It felt very *intimate*.

"I don't know," she whispered.

He laughed. "Why don't we try it and see if we like it," he suggested. "Sera, I have been thinking about yesterday afternoon since we parted in your father's foyer."

She swallowed. "About...about our discussions?"

He shook his head slowly. "No. About kissing you."

She took a step back, but the terrace wall didn't allow much escape from either Rafe's hard body or her own mind. In truth, she had been thinking of his kiss both in the phaeton and in the foyer as well. They were shameful, heated thoughts that she had been trying desperately to squelch.

"I would like to kiss you now," he revealed, reaching up to slide the back of his hand down the curve of her bare arm. Even though the night was warm, she shivered and he smiled slightly at the reaction. "Will you let me?"

Her mind's first reaction was to say no, but to her surprise, she found herself nodding, as if her body was disconnected from her intellect. Because her body very much wanted to kiss him again.

He eased even closer and wrapped one strong arm around her waist. The embrace was gentle, not trapping, and she relaxed into it as he cupped her chin and tilted her face upward to grant him access to her lips.

Her breath was hard to find as his mouth descended, descended, and finally his lips brushed over hers in another feather-light caress. She stood still beneath his ministrations for a moment, but then she began to kiss him back. It felt like they stood together for a very long time, but it couldn't have been so very long. The only thing to disturb the perfect moment was when he parted his mouth over hers and gently probed her with his tongue.

She stiffened at the insistent pressure, anxiety rising in her chest. But he wasn't demanding, he wasn't hard or harsh, and she found herself opening to him slowly.

He let out a small, achy groan before his tongue moved inside her, gently tasting and teasing and turning her legs to jelly and her mind to mush. She lifted up to her tiptoes to get closer, tilted her head for better access and lost herself in this touch, this need she had never felt before.

He was panting when he broke the kiss, his bright eyes flashing in the moonlight.

"I *do* like kissing you, Sera," he whispered, his breath warming her already hot cheeks.

She swallowed, forcing herself not to follow when he took a long step away. Now that she was not in his arms, she realized what a precarious position she was in. In the dark edge of the terrace, he could have done anything to her.

And yet he hadn't.

"I—" She turned away from him, hands shaking. "I should go home."

"I suppose it is time," he said, coming around so she had to look at him. He explored her face and she saw his concern, his hesitation. His questions that she didn't want to answer.

The responses she would give would be far too humiliating.

"Sera—" he began.

She almost shut her eyes at that name coming from his lips. It seemed so very intimate to have this little private thing they shared. And not as unpleasant as it should have been. Kind of like his kiss.

"I'd like to say goodbye to your family," she interrupted, moving toward the parlor where the others were still gathered.

If he wanted to argue or to question her further, he didn't do so. He only took her inside and allowed her what she asked.

She could only hope that his solicitous actions would continue after they were wed in just two short days.

CHAPTER SIX

Rafe was married.

Until recently, that was not a sentence he thought he would be saying that sunny Saturday. It wasn't that he'd never thought he would marry, but he'd pictured it as something in the distant future with a faceless bride he hadn't yet met.

But as he stared across the room at Serafina, standing beside her best friend Emma and his sister Annabelle, he realized for what must have been the tenth time in the last three hours that he was staring at his bride.

She was a beautiful bride as well. Her expensive gown fit her to perfection, the creamy color accentuating her porcelain skin, the veil perched upon the soft curls of her blonde hair. Her blue eyes flitted toward him, daring to pause on his face for only a moment before they darted back to her companions.

So he still made her nervous. It was something he had to remedy over time, despite how bewitching she was when high pink color flooded her cheeks. He wanted to make that color spread all over her lush body.

"We're down to the last stragglers," Crispin said as he brought over a glass of champagne.

Rafe took it and nodded as he looked at the riffraff left behind. Family still mingled, yes, but also a few half-drunk lords and ladies. Ones he didn't know from a horse on the cart, of course. Friends had left long ago out of respect for the new couple and their odd circumstances.

"The stragglers who don't want to leave a sandwich uneaten or a drink unimbibed." He sighed. "Can you help me to move them along? I think it is high time I was alone with my new wife." Crispin nodded, but made no move to do as he had agreed. Rafe tilted his head in question. "What is it?"

His brother faced him, shifting with what was obvious discomfort. "I wanted to tell you how sorry I am, Rafe. That you have to inherit these burdens is unfair. And I would be a help to you if I can be."

Rafe smiled, a swell of love for Crispin rising up in him. "I have your sword, then?" he asked, teasing to diffuse the seriousness a touch.

Crispin returned the grin. "Always. And I will use it now to clear the room as you have demanded."

He clapped a hand on Rafe's shoulder and moved toward the remaining guests, speaking softly to them as he maneuvered them toward the exits.

It seemed to take Serafina a few moments to realize what was being done. When she did, she started and her gaze moved to Rafe again before she embraced her friend Emma and said goodbye to Emma's husband. Rafe smiled as Annabelle hugged his new bride too. In a few short days, the women had seemed to bond and it made him happy to think his wife and his sister would be on good terms.

Annabelle took their mother's arm and the two women moved toward him. Their mother sniffled, as she had all day.

"It was a beautiful ceremony, rushed though it may have been," she said as she clasped his hand in hers.

He squeezed her fingers in response. "It was, Mama. Thank you for all you've done these past few days, both to counsel me and to make Serafina feel welcome in our family."

She looked over her shoulder at her first daughter-in-law. "I like her, Rafe," she said with a soft, reflective smile. "I hope you two will be happy."

He barely contained a flinch. His poor mother had endured

a great deal over the years between two wild sons who indulged too much and a husband who had been only marginally better before his untimely death. If she knew that he and Serafina had bargained for a false marriage driven only by the creation of heirs...

Well, she would roll her eyes and say his name in that tone that spoke of her disappointment.

"Thank you, Mama," he said, briefly kissing first her cheek and then his sister's. "Good night."

They both repeated the farewell and headed for the foyer with his brother close behind. Rafe straightened his shoulders and moved to his bride across the suddenly empty room.

"Hello, Wife," he said with a smile he hoped would reassure her.

Instead, she seemed to go stiff as a board. "Your Grace."

"*Your* Grace," he corrected with a laugh. "Duchess Hartholm—how does it sound after all these years?"

She didn't smile, and her gaze went faraway. "Like someone else's dream realized."

Rafe shook his head. "Speaking of which, where is your father?"

She pursed her lips. "Off to crow and brag at the club, I suppose. He left an hour ago, foxed as can be. Did he not say something to you?"

"No," Rafe admitted.

Her cheeks turned crimson. "Badly played, Father," she muttered beneath her breath.

Rafe leaned in. "I'm not offended," he reassured her. "And it's just as well he is gone." Rafe offered her an arm. "I think we're both ready to have the rabble out of the house."

Her eyes went a little wide, though she didn't resist as he led her from the room. He took her upstairs to the chamber he had only taken over just a day before. It still contained the remnants of Cyril's life, down to the clothing in the closet, but the bed was big and comfortable and suddenly that was all that mattered to Rafe.

He released Serafina and shut the door behind them. She moved to the middle of the room and stared at the bed, cheeks pale and hands clenched behind her.

He gritted his teeth. He would have to be slow and gentle with her, for she was an innocent. That wasn't his normal indulgence. But he wanted Serafina to like what they would do together, not see it as the awful duty she had described just a few days before.

He moved to stand in front of her and saw that she her entire body vibrated like a leaf in a strong wind. He frowned and reached out to take one of her cold hands.

"I promise you, you have nothing to fear."

She turned her pale face, her frown telling him she didn't believe him. "This is your right, Rafe." Her voice was soft, but strong. "I have no intention of stopping you."

He shook his head. She remained so reluctant, as if she had been told by someone that sex was an act to fear. It made him want to double his efforts to make this a night she would not soon forget.

He reached out and ran a hand along her uncovered collarbone. Her skin was like satin, and he nearly moaned with the feel of her. He wanted to taste that skin, to feel it pressed beneath him, writhing atop him, arching to his caresses.

And soon she would be.

"I'm going to unfasten your dress," he warned, meeting her gaze as he found the line of pearl buttons that closed her wedding gown along the front.

She stood stone still, her line of sight darting away, her cheeks pinkening as he unhooked the buttons one by one. The dress drooped open, revealing the elaborate undergarments that had been designed for her special day.

Normally the reason he liked the day's fashions was because they allowed such easy access. But as he pushed the gown down around her hips, he caught his breath at the sight of Serafina standing in only a lace corset and a short shift. Her stockings were fastened to the corset.

He wanted to tear the clothes away. He wanted to pin her hands to the wall above her head and rut with her like an out of control animal. He wanted to claim her until she writhed in ecstasy and forgot everything but him.

Instead, he bent his head and gently brushed his lips against her shoulder. He nuzzled up the side of her exposed neck, not tasting, just teasing.

She tensed even further beneath him, her breath coming hard and fast as he wrapped his arms around her waist and drew her against him. Her body molded to his, her curves fitting him like they were made to do so, and he let out a deep, guttural moan of pleasure that he couldn't control.

"By God, you are something," he whispered against her ear as one hand glided from her hip to her stomach, then up and up until he brushed his fingers in the valley between her breasts. She made a tiny whimper at the touch, and he smiled and let his hand return to her stomach, her hip, her thigh. There he unhooked first one stocking, then the other.

He dropped to his knees before her and began to roll the silk away from her smooth legs, over her knee, over her calf, and lifted her foot to remove it and her slipper at once. He repeated the action on her other leg and then leaned in to kiss her bare knee.

He looked up her body to find her wide-eyed and pale, watching his every movement. Her expression was hard to read, but her breath came fast and hard, echoing in the quiet of the chamber.

"Sera," he whispered as he got to his feet. "Sweet, sweet Sera."

She nodded.

"I want to make you feel so good," he promised, dropping his lips to hers for another deep kiss.

She relaxed now, finally letting her arms come around his neck, clinging to him as she opened herself to his touch. He smiled against her lips.

When she was almost limp with the kiss, he went to work

on her corset, unlacing the back, loosening the silken ties until it drooped between them.

He broke the kiss and stepped back to tug the apparatus away. Serafina gasped, as if surprised he had undressed her without her knowledge. Good, that meant she had been momentarily lost in the pleasure. He wanted to keep her that way.

He tossed the corset aside and stared at her. Her silken, rosy chemise was the only thing left to cover her now. A flimsy bit of fabric with thin straps that barely skimmed her slender thighs.

With a possessive growl, he put his arms around her again, but this time he let his hands glide along her spine, push the fabric up, cup her bare backside as he kissed her yet again.

She let out a gasp of surprise when he lifted her. He carried her to the bed and laid her out against the pillows. She blinked up at him as he lay down beside her and rested one hand lightly on her tightly clenched thighs.

"Your skin puts the finest silk to shame," he said, massaging the taut muscles of her legs with one hand.

She turned her face away, but her red cheeks spoke volumes of her embarrassment. That was a feeling he wanted to wipe away entirely.

"Your body," he said, leaning in closer, pressing a kiss to her collarbone, "is meant to be worshipped, Sera." He kissed lower, just above where her chemise covered her breasts. "To be adored. And I'm going to do that tonight."

Now he dipped his fingers below the chemise edge and gently stroked her already-hard nipple. She gasped and arched up beneath his touch. He grinned in satisfaction. He had begun to replace fear with sensation, desire. And there was so much more to come.

"I'm going to make you quake," he continued, and pressed his mouth to the hard ridge of her nipple, outlined beneath the silky cloth. He sucked until the fabric went nearly transparent and she gave a strangled cry.

"I'm going to make you come," he growled, pushing the chemise up so that he could finally see her naked breasts.

They were small but perfect, with dusky rose tips that were dark and hard with her mounting desire. He cupped them both, loving the feel of them in his palms. He lowered his mouth and began to lick between them, pinching the nipples until she made a garbled sound of pleasure and lifted her hands to tangle them in his hair and draw him closer.

He chuckled against her flesh, but followed her silent order. He chose the right breast and began to suckle, gently at first, with teasing licks, then harder and with greater purpose. Just when she began crying out in pleasure, he switched to the opposite breast and repeated the action.

Her hips lifted beneath his shoulders, asking for what she did not know enough to request with her lips. And he so wanted to give her what she desired. But not until she was ready.

He continued to suck her nipple, gently massing her breast with one hand and with the other, he traced the length of her body, stopping only when he covered her sex with his fingers.

She bucked beneath him and stared at him with wild, wide eyes.

"Shhh," he soothed, thrumming over her nipple with his opposite thumb.

She didn't respond, but watched him cup her, stroking the outside of her sex, feeling the wetness that was beginning to grow within her, threatening to overflow.

She was almost ready.

He licked her nipple as he gently spread the outer lips of her sex. He licked her again while he let his thick thumb traced her entrance. She was so hot, so wet. He pressed against her clitoris and she cried out above him, her hands clenching handfuls of coverlet.

He pulled away with a groan and swiftly stripped off his shirt and trousers. She stared up at him when he was naked and her blue eyes went even wider.

"Don't worry," he soothed as he settled over her. He smoothed her hair back from her face even as he gently settled himself between her legs. The head of his cock found her entrance as if they were meant to fit together and he struggled to not just slide inside, claim her hard and fast.

"I'm going to fit myself inside of you," he explained softly as he positioned himself. "It will hurt for a moment, but I will make it feel good for you, I promise."

She sucked in air as he pressed forward slowly.

"Rafe—" she began, her tone suddenly sharp.

But she was silenced when he pushed forward.

He slid home in one smooth thrust and stared down at her. Her eyes had filled with tears, but they weren't tears of pain. He had not felt the barrier of her hymen, nor did she exhibit the signs that she had surrendered her virginity to him.

Because she hadn't. It was evident from the welcoming stretch of her body and the expression of guilt on her face.

She had not been untouched when he married her.

"Sera," he whispered as he reluctantly pulled from her sheath and moved away from her.

"I'm sorry," she said, rolling away to her side where she balled herself up. "I'm so sorry."

He reached out to touch her hip, stroking his fingers over her skin. Yes, he was disappointed. He hadn't fully realized until that moment how much he wanted to be the one to introduce her to the pleasures of the flesh.

"You shouldn't apologize," he soothed softly. "I'm not angry."

She moved to her back and stared up at him. "How could you not be? I am not the bride you thought you were getting."

"Of course you are," he said, wrinkling his brow. "Your innocence was a fleeting claim, Serafina. I was not promising to marry you only so I could collect it."

She blinked at him in disbelief. "So you don't hate me?"

He shook his head. "Of course not. I certainly cannot judge you. When two people care for each other, things are bound—"

She barked out an ugly burst of laughter and sat up abruptly. "*Care*? About Cyril, you mean?"

He nodded. "Or course. After so long an engagement, it isn't entirely surprising that you would go so far."

"Oh, but I didn't care. And he *certainly* didn't, Rafe."

He stared at her, watching her pained expression shatter even more. "I—what do you mean?"

She swallowed hard past the pulse that fluttered in her neck. "Rafe... I... Cyril...he...he *forced* me. He forced me more than once."

CHAPTER SEVEN

Rafe recoiled at her confession and Serafina felt the tears she had struggled to keep from falling begin to slide down her cheeks. She hadn't meant to tell him the truth about Cyril's actions.

Of course, she *had* intended to reveal that she wasn't untouched before he claimed her, but then he had kissed her, stroked her, teased her so gently. It had been so confusing. Her body revolted at being touched, it awakened a deep and powerful fear in her.

And yet, when Rafe was the one doing the touching, there had been moments when her anxiety was replaced by something far better. Pleasure. It was remarkable and her feelings, her unexpected reactions to him, had overwhelmed her reason and suddenly it had been too late.

And now she had told him the truth one person in the world other than herself knew. Even Emma had only heard the kindest version of the ugly facts.

"Rafe?" she whispered in the face of his continued silence.

He stared at her, but she couldn't read his thoughts.

"Tell me everything that happened," he finally demanded, his voice flat and hard like she had never heard before.

She swallowed hard. *Everything*. That was a difficult order. But Rafe wasn't like Cyril—the fact that he had withdrawn from her the moment he realized she was not an innocent, that he hadn't attacked her for her lie of omission, proved it.

He had once said they could be friends and she hadn't believed him. Now she felt a strange desire to do exactly as he required. To give him her story and hope he would understand and protect it in the end.

She cleared her throat. "My father and Cyril's father were old friends and the two of them made their marital arrangement for us when I was just six. You've seen the documents by now, you know how title poor Cyril's family was. In their minds, everyone would win with our match. Cyril's family would have my generous dowry money, my father would be linked to what was once one of the most prestigious titles in all the Empire."

Rafe nodded. "And?"

"I didn't meet Cyril until I was ten and he was fifteen."

Rafe recoiled yet again. "Dear God, he didn't—" he began.

She shook her head swiftly. "No! No, he didn't touch me then." She shuddered. "But I was less than impressed by him. He was pimple-faced and snide. I also thought he was uncommonly stupid when he made fun of me for reading. He told me I would stop that when I was his wife."

Rafe's lips pursed. "He was always a charming one."

"And he only grew more charming with time. Every year after that, our fathers would force the two of us to meet so that we would know each other a little when the time came to wed. I suppose it was meant to be a kindness, but as I grew older, Cyril's attitude got worse and worse. He had a long list of things I would and wouldn't do as his wife." She took a long breath, trying to maintain control as she continued, "In time, he began to ogle, then g-grope me, when we were alone."

Rafe's jaw set. "You must have told your father."

She turned her face. "I told *no one*. My father made it clear that this marriage would happen regardless of my feelings. The one time I danced around the subject that perhaps Cyril was not kind to me, my father slapped me so hard, my ears rung. So I *never* addressed the issue again."

Rafe pushed off the mattress and began to pace the room, utterly naked and not seeming to care.

Serafina blushed despite the delicate subject she was now addressing and slowly slid the sheets up to cover herself. What she was going to say next left her exposed enough in spirit that she did not want to have her body revealed at the same time.

"I was eighteen the first time Cyril—" She cut herself off, as she flashed back to images from the night she was about to describe. Rough hands, rougher lips, tearing fabric, pain.

"Shhh," Rafe said, crossing back to her. He leaned over edge of the bed and took both her hands. "It's all right."

She blinked at the concern on his face, then looked down to realize she was trembling.

"Can you go on?" he asked, his voice nothing but gentle.

She stared at him, this unexpected man who had been forced into this situation even more than she had been and yet was nothing but decent when it came to his interactions with her. And she nodded even though she didn't want to voice the truth. Rafe deserved to know it all.

"The night I came out in Society, my father insisted that we attend the ball with Cyril and his family. We met at their estate to ride over together and he took me out on the terrace. He was going on and on about how pretty I was and then he was just...on me. Pressing me to the wall, holding me too tightly. His mouth was everywhere, his hands were everywhere and then he..."

She gasped for breath, trying not to relive it all, trying not to be swept away by the memories she had so carefully kept at bay in her everyday life.

"He raped you," Rafe said softly.

She nodded, relieved he could say what she could not. "Yes. And then he took me inside, blamed my torn dress on a blackberry bramble on the edge of the terrace, and we went to my coming out ball together as if nothing had happened."

"My God," Rafe growled beneath his breath.

"Cyril danced with me, smirking the whole time, and before we parted that night he told me that I was truly his now and that there would never be an escape because he had claimed me." She swiped at the tears that accompanied her unwanted memories. "No other man would want me even if I could convince my father to undo the betrothal."

"How did you survive the night after what he had done?" Rafe breathed.

She shrugged. "I scarcely recall. It is all a blur. I went through the motions of my life, I suppose, without feeling or seeing what was around me." She shook her head. "I think that became my mode of survival. It had to be because Cyril didn't stop."

Rafe flinched. "Yes, you said he did this more than once."

"After that he went back to his usual intimidate and grope routine," she said. "But every once in a while, he would go further. I dreaded seeing him because I never knew if this would be one of the times he would 'exercise his husbandly rights,' as he would put it. I only ever told my friend Emma— you met her today."

Rafe nodded. "Yes, a lovely woman, though a bit standoffish with me. I can see why now."

"She's protective," Serafina explained with a shake of her head. "She only knew the barest details. Once she encouraged me to tell my father."

"And?" Rafe pressed.

"Of course, I couldn't. I already told you why."

"Bastard!" Rafe snapped.

"My father or Cyril?" she asked softly.

He spun on her. "Both," he growled, his blue eyes flashing with indignation, rage. All for her. It was a strange thing. She had never had a champion before.

She found she rather liked it.

"It went on that way for two years," she said with a shrug that didn't at all reflect the tangle of pain in her heart. "We were to marry after I turned twenty, but then Cyril's father died and his mother all but collapsed, so it got put off. I felt like the prison door had been cracked a bit, but it was a false freedom. It only delayed inevitable. And now, two years later, I was to marry him today. Until he quite obligingly died."

"Only you still weren't free," Rafe said softly.

She looked at him. He remained naked and somehow that comforted her. She was emotionally exposed and he physically. It was as if that put them on more equal ground.

"But you are a very different warden, Rafe," she said. "And so far, you haven't proven yourself to be cruel."

"I hope I never shall," He turned and paced the room once more. "I was such an idiot. Here I read all your hesitation as residual feelings for Cyril, despite how mad it was to me that someone like you could care for a toad like my cousin. And all along it was this ugly truth that affected all your actions."

She nodded. "Yes. It is why I wanted to negotiate for my future after our marriage. It is why I am happy to give you your freedom. It is why I hate this room."

Rafe froze and looked around himself. "Great God, this is Cyril's old chamber. He…he…?"

She nodded. "Once he took over as duke, he sometimes forced me to come up here for his fun."

Rafe stared at her, eyes narrowed, expression dark and dangerous. Then he motioned for her to rise. "Come, we're leaving."

She wrinkled her brow in confusion. "I—what?

"We certainly aren't staying in this horrible room or this awful house one more bloody moment now that I know what you endured. Get up, I shall help you dress myself and we will depart immediately."

He grabbed for his trousers and pulled them up over his hips in one smooth motion, then looked around for his shirt. All the while, Serafina watched him, uncertain as to what her new husband was talking about.

"You want to flee this house in the middle of the night?" she asked.

"Absolutely," Rafe said, hooking buttons with rapid and impressive speed.

"Where will we go?" she asked.

He paused in his dressing and looked at her, his face soft with compassion. "To my home, Sera. We'll go to my home, just two miles away. Now get up. I'll ring for the carriage and help you dress."

Serafina stared as he moved to ring the bell by the door. She didn't move, even as a servant knocked and her new husband opened the barrier just enough to say a few soft words to the unseen person. When he turned back, he smiled at her and strode back to the bed, only pausing to gather up her now-wrinkled wedding gown.

He held it up and she slowly departed the bed as if in a dream. She pulled her chemise over her head before she stepped into the gown and watched him fasten it. She had no idea what Rafe had planned or why he was spiriting her away in the middle of the night.

But she realized that for the first time in years, she wasn't utterly afraid.

Serafina fought the urge to slip behind Rafe, to hide, as the door to his fine townhouse opened and revealed a finely liveried butler waiting for them.

"Good evening, Lathem," Rafe said with a good-natured clap on the shoulder for the man. "Thanks much for rousing yourself so late and preparing for us."

The butler's stern face twitched into a brief smile. "Of course. It was my pleasure, Your Grace."

Rafe flinched. "Damn, I suppose you do have to call me that, don't you?"

The butler inclined his head. "I'm afraid so, Your Grace."

"At least to my face, at any rate," Rafe chuckled, and to

Serafina's surprise, the butler gave a warm laugh as well. Rafe turned toward her. "May I present my bride? Serafina, the Duchess of Hartholm."

Serafina tensed. She had spent nearly two hellish decades preparing to be Duchess Hartholm, but hearing herself called that by Rafe solidified that the moment had finally come. And it was as far different from her imaginings as it could have possibly been.

"Your Grace," the butler said with a stiff bow. "Welcome."

"We have found we don't care for the ducal home, Lathem, so we intend to take a few weeks here. We will need to make arrangements for the clothing that was brought to the other home for Her Grace to be moved here, as well as anything my valet took there for me. Her Grace will need a new maid as well, if you have any suggestions either from within the staff or from outside the home." Rafe fired off these rapid statements before he turned on her. "Are you hungry, Sera?"

She jolted at the unforeseen question and found both men watching her expectantly. "N-no," she stammered. "Just tired."

Rafe touched her arm briefly. "Of course you are. Lathem, we will retire."

The butler nodded. "Yes, sir. I will take care of all these things before you rise tomorrow, and I shall make sure Mrs. Lathem prepares your favorites in the morning."

Rafe made a rumbling groan of what sounded to be pleasure. "That sounds divine. Good night."

He took Serafina's arm and she followed him up the stairs and through the winding halls until they reached an open chamber door. When he urged her through, she came to a stop.

"Your room?" she asked, looking at him over her shoulder.

"Yes, and I'm afraid it is the only one currently ready for use. We were closing up the house, you see, since I assumed I would be staying at the ducal home for a while."

She faced him. "But will there be another room for me

until we settle on where I will take up permanent residence?"

She tensed as she prayed he would remember their bargain, that he would live up to his promise to provide her a place to live outside of the ducal home, away from her memories…away from *him*.

His expression softened, but it wasn't pity in his eyes. She appreciated that a great deal.

"If you would like a separate room, I'll have the lady's chamber prepared tomorrow. It connects to this room through the sitting area, but it has a lock and will be private. As for your own home…"

She clenched her hands behind her back.

"It will take at least a few weeks to arrange it, but I made you a promise, Serafina, and you will find I don't go back on my word, despite whatever my reputation says about me being a scoundrel."

She swallowed. It was strange. A scoundrel was exactly what she had expected to find in Raphael Flynn, but this man continued to surprise her at every turn.

Her gaze darted to the bed, almost against her will. It looked far more comfortable than Cyril's.

"You must be exhausted," he said, stepping toward her.

She took a big step back out of habit and he froze in place. "I only want to help you with your gown," he explained. "You can sleep in your chemise. By morning your clothing will have arrived. I'll sleep in my trousers."

She looked again at the bed. "Together?"

"Unless you wish to relegate me to the most beautiful but uncomfortable settee in the nation," he said, motioning to a velvet couch on the opposite side of the room.

She shifted. "I…"

He moved closer yet again, and this time she forced herself to stay in place. "We will only sleep, I promise you," he said softly.

She looked at him for a long moment, examining his handsome face, seeing a strangely earnest expression in his eyes.

"Very well," she whispered. She blushed, turning her face as he began to undress her for the second time that night.

He performed the act slowly, without any attempt at a seduction. Yet, knowing he was just a step in front of her, feeling his hands occasionally brush over her chest or stomach as he did his work, sent strange shivers through her.

When the dress was open, he stepped away, leaving her to remove it on her own. She turned her back to him as she did so, suddenly embarrassed for him to see her in such a state, even though they had been totally naked together an hour before.

When she finally found the courage to face him, he had stripped off his shirt and sat down to remove his boots. She watched him from the corner of her eye, admiring, despite herself, how his muscles rippled as he tugged at his footwear.

Finally he had freed himself and got up to point to the bed. "My lady."

She took a spot in the bed and slipped beneath the cool, clean sheets with a sigh she couldn't suppress. He joined her and settled in against the pillows.

Once again, she couldn't help but steal a glance at him. In the firelight he looked...*tan* against the stark white of the cotton sheets. As if he spent time outside shirtless.

An odd, unwanted thrill worked through her that she tried desperately to ignore.

"Goodnight," she whispered, turning her back to him.

She heard him blow out the lamp before he said, "Goodnight."

But even as they lay there in the quiet together, her exhaustion clouding her already wild mind, she knew she wouldn't sleep for a very long time.

CHAPTER EIGHT

Rafe had been awake since the first hints of sunlight began to peek around the curtains. Now the light brightened the chamber, allowing him to finally see Serafina fully. She was lying on her back, her face beautiful and relaxed in sleep. In the days he'd known her, he had never seen her so at peace.

And now he knew the reason why. He also knew why she stiffened at his kiss, why his hands on her made her breath hitch in fear.

And yet, last night, before she confessed the awful truth of her mistreatment at the hands of his evil cousin, he'd felt her responsiveness to him as well. Even with all she had endured, her body still craved pleasure.

She made a soft sigh and her lashes began to flutter against her cheeks as she woke. Her arms had been beneath the sheets and she tugged them free, reaching a hand up above her head.

Rafe swallowed hard. When she did that, she revealed the soft curve of the side of her breast. One he wanted to explore with his hands, his mouth. Since he had withdrawn from her wet body, his cock had been throbbing, sending him constant reminders that pleasure had been prevented for both of them.

Her eyes fully opened and she sucked in a gasp of surprised breath as she remembered he was in the bed beside her.

"Good morning," he said, smiling at her in the hopes he

would reassure her. "Or what is left of it."

She sat up partially and looked around his chamber. "What time is it?"

"After eleven," he explained.

She flopped back on the pillow with a sigh. "I have not slept that well in…it must be years."

Rafe pursed his lips in displeasure that fear had kept her from her rest for so long.

"If Cyril weren't already dead, I would kill him myself," he said softly.

Her eyes widened a fraction and she pondered his statement for a moment. "If Cyril wasn't dead, you and I wouldn't be here. You wouldn't know anything about me except that I was your new cousin by marriage. And since you had no real relationship with the man, we likely would have never met."

Rafe thought of those very good points for a moment. What she had left out was that if Cyril wasn't dead, he also wouldn't be forced to be a duke, forced to be a husband. He would be free as a bird, free as he'd always been.

And yet going back in time, changing it so that Cyril would live, didn't seem all that appealing at the moment. Certainly not so appealing as the lady currently in his bed.

He rolled to his side, moving closer to her. She tensed and inched away slightly. He froze in his spot, allowing her to flee and gain whatever distance left her comfortable. When she blushed and stared down at her clenched hands in her lap, he drew a long breath.

"I would like to renegotiate the terms of our arrangement, Sera."

Her lips parted and he saw the panic light up on her face. She began to scoot away further, but now he caught her wrist gently.

"Wait, wait," he soothed. "Hear me out."

She stared at his hand around her arm and he released her immediately.

"Please," he added.

Her eyes darted to the door across the room, as if she were considering running, despite being clad in only her chemise. Then she looked back toward him and sighed.

"Very well."

"When we opened our discussion into what our life as husband and wife would entail, I didn't know all the facts of your past," he began.

She stiffened. "I told you, I meant to confess the truth to you before—"

"Sera," he cut her off. "I am *not* maligning you. I cannot imagine the deep pain of your position. If you never intended to tell me, but only hoped I wouldn't guess the truth, I couldn't blame you even then."

"You thought you were marrying an innocent," she whispered.

He reached out, unable to stop himself from dragging a finger down her cheek. "And I did."

She shook her head. "You know that isn't true."

"I think it is. The description of an innocent doesn't just involve a body that has never been breached. An innocent has never been introduced to pleasure and I think we both know that description still stands."

She hesitated, her cheeks turning dark pink. "You are correct. I found no pleasure any time *he* put his hands on me."

He nodded once, trying to keep his boiling anger at bay. It would do nothing to help this situation.

"Then that is the focus of my renegotiation, Sera. You see, I don't want to take away anything we have agreed that I'll give you, a home of your own, an income that I cannot dictate, peace once we have created my heir and spare... I actually would like to *add* something to what I give."

She shook her head. "What?"

"Pleasure," he said softly, leaning in once more, invading her space carefully.

She drew back and her frown deepened. "I don't think that

is possible, Rafe."

"I can see how you would believe that, but I don't think it is true. After all, you like kissing me, don't you? I felt you stiffen, pull away the first time we kissed, but eventually that act became something you enjoyed, didn't it?"

She nodded. "Yes. I...I do like kissing you."

He smiled at the soft admission, the way her cheeks flamed again when she made it. "Then please trust that I can and will make the rest of the physical acts we could share just as good."

She sank her teeth into her lip and looked at him with uncertainty. He leaned closer, sliding his fingers into her bed-tousled hair, drawing her near.

"For the moment, let's continue just with kissing," he reassured her.

She let out a brief sigh before his mouth covered hers. Almost immediately, she relaxed into him, her arms coming around his neck, her lips opening to him in welcome.

He took what she offered with a hunger that surprised even him. He delved into her mouth with his tongue, tasting, testing, teasing. After a hesitation, she became bolder returning his kiss, exploring his mouth and lighting an intense fire inside of him that threatened to explode out of control.

It was only his focus on what she had already endured that kept him from simply sliding her chemise up around her stomach and taking her then and there, consummating their union and claiming her as his own.

He pulled away from her kiss after a very long time had passed. His breath was broken as he said, "I'm going to touch you, Serafina."

She immediately went stiff beneath him and he shook his head. "Not take you. I promise you I won't, no matter how much I burn to do so."

Her breath was fast and hard and there was no pleasure on her face as she stared up at him.

"I'll stop any time you'd like," he promised.

She watched him for a long time, a wary rabbit faced with a hungry fox. But finally she jerked out a shaky nod. "All right. I trust you."

Those three words, which he knew were difficult for her, set him back and he stared down at her for a long moment. Her eyes were wide, dilated with both fear and the remnants of pleasure from their kiss. He wanted to erase the first and intensify the last. He wanted to make her crave him, not have anxiety turn his touch to poison.

He returned his mouth to hers, gentling his kiss as he cupped her breast. She gasped into his mouth and once again the fire in his loins was stoked to uncomfortable heights.

He began to circle his thumb around her nipple slowly, slowly, loving how the nub tightened at his touch, rising to meet him. Serafina turned her face, breaking the kiss. Her breath remained rough and ragged.

"Y-you did that last night," she panted, not looking at his face, but at his ever-working hand on her body.

He nodded. "I did. Did you enjoy it?"

She shivered. "I don't know. There were so many sensations, thoughts, fears."

He laughed at her candor. "Well, today you don't have to fear. I know your secret. I vow to keep it well. I also vow to help you make new memories of a man's touch on your skin. Just like I did with a kiss."

She seemed to ponder that statement for a moment, and then she let out a long sigh. "What should I do?"

"Today all you have to do is allow the sensations to take you away. To tell me what feels good, as well as what you don't like."

She arched a brow, and now she did look at him. "You will admit there are things I won't like?"

He nodded. "Every person is different in what acts arouse them, what acts are not comfortable. For instance..." He plucked her nipple a bit harder now. "Do you like that?"

She gasped. "Yes," she said on a garbled moan.

He smiled before he tugged the thin fabric of her chemise past her breast and darted his tongue out to swirl it around the turgid peak.

"And that?" he asked.

"Yes," she repeated.

Her thighs were beginning to clench in a rhythm she likely didn't understand but he read perfectly. Still suckling her breast lightly, stroked his hand down her body, over her flat stomach, her hip, until he settled his fingers between her legs.

She jolted at the intimate touch and turned her face toward him. "Rafe," she murmured, halfway between a curse and a plea.

"Trust me," he repeated as he had earlier. "I'll stop anything you don't like."

She made a little sound in her throat and nodded.

He teased just the entrance of her sex first, smoothing his fingers over the pouting lips, stroking a thumb over her clitoris occasionally. She gasped at the contact, her face bright red as she stared up at the ceiling above.

"Is this wrong or right?" he asked. "Look at me, Sera."

She swallowed a few times, then looked at him. "Strange," she choked out. "But…but not painful or unpleasant."

"Hmmm, we'll have to do better than not unpleasant," he purred, and spread her outer lips gently.

Now that her sex was exposed, Serafina clenched her fists against the coverlet, her eyes fluttering shut.

"Stop me if you wish," he reminded her, even as he focused his attention on her clitoris.

The little bud swelled beneath his fingers, juices from her sex flowing to ease the friction of his touch. He watched her face as he touched her, seeing her relax as the pleasure built within her. She let out a deep, guttural moan.

"Good or bad?" he questioned, though he could see the answer on her face. Still, he wanted her to feel her control, to know that she could stop this if she wished.

"Good," she gasped. "Good. I feel like…I

haven't…it's…"

She stopped talking as he increased the pressure of his fingers against her clitoris. She arched and then let out a wail of pleasure. Her sex clenched at nothingness as her hips jerked up against his questing fingers. He continued to touch her, dragging out her release until she went utterly limp on the bed, her gasps of breath filling the air.

He lay back down beside her, watching her expression of wonder and loving that he had put it on her face.

"I-I—" she stammered, finally looking at him with wide eyes. "That never happened before."

He smiled. "It is called orgasm. The French also like to say *le petit mort*, the little death."

She scrunched up her face. "Why? It didn't feel like death to me. More like flying."

"Good. That is how it should be. Your body reaches a height of excitement and pleasure takes over, steals your control, makes you forget everything else for a moment." He smoothed his fingers over her bare arm. "And that is only the beginning. It can be even better, Sera."

"I can hardly believe that," she said with a shake of her head.

"You compliment excessively." He laughed. "But if you give me your trust, if you know that I would never do anything to force you, to hurt you, to make you feel shame, I could make what you just experienced happen again and again. If you want me to, if my cousin didn't spoil these intimacies for you."

He held his breath as he awaited her response. She looked at him closely as she thought about what he'd said. He couldn't tell how she felt.

"I promise you, there was nothing intimate about your cousin's touch," she said softly. "And when you touch me, it doesn't put me to mind of him, that is certain."

He breathed a sigh of relief before he asked, "Then will you allow me to give you pleasure for these first weeks of our marriage? At least until your new home is purchased and ready, until the intense focus on our union goes away? Will you trust me to educate you, to satisfy you like I just did?"

She nodded slowly. "You have shown me nothing but kindness, Rafe, nothing but care and gentleness. And I trust you to continue to behave in such a way for a few weeks. I admit, I look forward to creating happy memories about being touched by a man." She shifted and sat up, locking eyes with him in a way he hadn't expected. "But the rest of our agreement must stand. I *don't* want a marriage beyond one in name alone."

"Of course. I will take nothing away from our original bargain. When your home is ready, we will part ways except for the occasional reunion for the sake of creating children."

He said the words, he meant them, but somehow they felt rather unsatisfying as he stared at her, her face still flushed from pleasure, her body barely covered by her chemise.

He shook those thoughts away and reached out to cup her cheek. She leaned into his palm, still staring at him like she was trying to read his intentions, trying to read their future. He couldn't help but wonder what conclusions she ultimately came to.

"Come, my servants should have done their duty since last night. I would wager your gowns await you in the dressing area of the adjoining room. Pick one and I will help you dress."

She pulled away in surprise. "Dress? Why? I thought—?"

She glanced at the bed they sat on, and he realized with a start that she had believed they would stay here all day, with him beginning those oh-so-powerful lessons in desire.

His cock ached, but he managed to maintain the strength of his voice as he said, "There will be plenty of time for that, my dear. Right now I think we both need sustenance. Let's go down and see what the best cook in London has prepared for us to share on this first full day of being man and wife."

CHAPTER NINE

Serafina watched with a laugh as Rafe returned to the sideboard in the dining room and loaded his plate with a second helping of everything available to him. As he returned to his place at the head of the table beside her, he had a wide grin on his face that only made him more handsome than ever. And despite herself, her heart gave a terrifying little flutter.

She frowned. She didn't want to have flutters about her husband. They had a marriage by contract, nothing more. She couldn't forget that, even if his kindness, his acceptance, his pleasure-inducing touch muddled the issue.

Her body was just confused. It was the only explanation. Although she continued to stiffen, to flash to images of Cyril above her when Rafe touched her, those thoughts had already begun to fade at his gentle caress. She still tingled from his earlier intimate explorations and that made everything between them seem sharper, more focused, more intense. Once they had shared more of the pleasures he promised, certainly the wonder of the act would wear off.

"You look very serious at present," he said between bites of food.

Her smile returned at his ravenous enjoyment of his breakfast. "And *you* look like a cat who got into the birdcage. Do you always eat so vigorously?"

"No," he admitted with a broad grin. "I have been without

the delightful Mrs. Lathem's fantastic food since I moved into the ducal home two days ago. And before that, I haven't exactly had much of an appetite. Now I cannot get enough."

The good humor Serafina had felt faded at his statement about a lack of appetite. She had been so focused on her own troubles since Cyril's death, she hadn't put much thought into how Rafe must be feeling. After all, he had been dragged into a title *and* a marriage he didn't want and had not expected.

"Is the food not to your liking?" he asked as he motioned to her half-full plate.

"Oh no, it's all delicious. I was simply lost in thought." She picked up her fork and speared a sausage slice.

As she popped it into her mouth, Rafe nodded. "Yes, I see you do that quite a bit. Lose yourself in thought."

She shrugged. "I suppose I do from time to time. There have been heavy thoughts to have as of late, for both of us."

"True. But I've never been much for stewing and worrying. That's more my brother's tactic than my own."

She tilted her head at that statement. "You are lucky, then. Most people don't have a choice in their worries."

He wrinkled his brow. "Of course they do. Whatever will happen will come to pass whether I lose sleep about it or not. I do my best to prepare myself and behave in a way that will limit the troubles I encounter-"

She laughed despite the seriousness of the conversation. "That isn't what I've heard."

He grinned. "All right, I will admit that I often do not look before I leap, so perhaps I exaggerate. But what is the fun in life unless you hurtle off the cliff and see if you can fly? So often you will find you can do just that."

"And when you cannot?" she asked.

He waved his arms. "What's done is done. It is out of my purview."

"But you must be burdened by your thoughts about *some* things," she pressed, leaning closer to search his face. "You cannot *truly* be so separated from the pain reality can bring."

His smile broadened. "Well, you know I have been utterly sheltered by my wealth, my handsome visage and my notorious reputation. Isn't that what they say?"

She shook her head at his playful tone and leaned back in her chair. "A few of them, yes."

His smile faded. "You think I'm being flippant."

She hesitated. If she challenged him, would his acceptance and gentleness with her fade? She didn't think so, but there was always a chance.

Still, she found herself saying, "Perhaps a tiny bit. Although I will admit that I envy how you can be so detached. It is not a trait we share."

He shifted, and for a moment he seemed to be considering what he could say next. "Of course I worry from time to time," he admitted slowly. "About my mother, my sister, even Crispin, though God knows the man can take care of himself."

"You guard those you care for," she said, still examining him. "It is a fine trait."

"And now that guarding extends to you," he said, taking a long drink of coffee.

"Of course it won't. You protect those you care for and we already know that will not be me. It is part of our agreement that you will not entangle your feelings with me and I will certainly not tangle mine with you."

He met her gaze firmly. "You do take delight in putting me in my place. You know there are women who would have done almost anything to marry me and then would have mooned all over me to get me to declare even my barest feeling for them."

She arched her brow, sensing his teasing. The lightness of his mood was a happy change. She had been surrounded by darkness for so long that it almost felt like a lifeline to be with him.

"You would have bored of those kinds of women in a moment," she teased back. "You need a challenge."

"Probably true," he acquiesced. "But regardless of that

fact, you say I will not care for you, but that *isn't* what I agreed to."

Her heart stubbornly skipped again and she straightened up immediately. "What?"

"I would hope that over the years we will become…" He hesitated, as if searching for the right term. "That we will become very good friends."

She stared. It was the second time he'd said that to her. That they would be friends. It was as odd a thought now as it had been before they wed. And especially strange considering that just over a week ago she had been pondering the virtues of fleeing into the brothels in order to escape a marriage to Cyril.

"I would like to be your friend," she admitted softly. "I think, from what little I know you, you would be a good one to have."

He shrugged. "I would try."

"But, as your friend, I must ask you—are you not concerned in any way with performing your duties as duke?"

He seemed genuinely confused by the question. "What do you mean?"

She shook her head. "Men are trained at their father's knee for decades to take on a role that you have been thrust into almost overnight. You will have Parliament to sit on, estates to manage properly, expectations about support for your tenants and others under your care. People will come to you with questions and assume you have the answers."

His brow furrowed, and for a moment she saw a flash of anxiety in his eyes. Then he shoveled another bite of food into his mouth and grunted, "I'll learn."

She didn't have a chance to respond before Lathem entered the room with a quiet clearing of his throat. Rafe nodded. "Yes, Lathem, what is it?"

The butler held out a tray with several envelopes stacked high. "These have come for you."

Rafe stared. "What are they?"

"Invitations, of course," Serafina said with a shake of her

head. "Surely even a Society-avoiding scoundrel must recognize them."

He laughed. "A Society-avoiding scoundrel. I think I shall have that engraved on my headstone. But yes, minx, I have received an invitation or two in my time. Just not...what are there, Lathem? Five?"

The butler didn't even look down. "Eight, Your Grace."

He winced. "Eight at once. Great God. Well, respond en masse with a resounding no, Lathem."

Serafina's eyes went wide at his immediate and very firm dismissal of the very duty they had just been discussing. "You cannot mean that."

"But I do. I don't want to go to some stuffy party where I'll be *Your Graced* until my head aches. Lathem is Your Gracing me enough."

She tossed the butler a look. "Will you bring me the invitations, Lathem?"

"Of course, Your Grace." The butler stepped inside and set the tray beside her, out of Rafe's reach. "Is there anything else, my lady?"

Rafe glanced toward the sideboard with a forlorn expression. "Has your wife made any of her famous hash this morning?"

Lathem hesitated, and for a moment he went pale. "Well—"

Rafe must have sensed the same trouble that Serafina did, for he leaned closer. "What is it?"

"I would have mentioned it to you later, sir, but you see...there was an incident in the kitchen just before we brought the breakfast items out for serving."

"An incident?" Serafina asked, watching the butler wring his hands.

"A—a fire," Lathem clarified.

Rafe jumped to his feet. "A fire!"

"Yes." Lathem took a step closer. "It was small, but it started in a kitchen storage area that is rarely used and we were very fortunate that a footman, Feddington, noticed it before it got out of hand."

Serafina raised a hand to her chest to cover her pounding heart. "Lucky indeed."

"Was anyone injured?" Rafe asked.

Serafina looked at him with a smile. Of course he would be concerned for those in his employ. He was truly nothing like his cousin.

"Thankfully, no," the butler said. "And the breezes through the kitchen windows seemed to draw most of the smoke outside, which is why the smell didn't reach the rest of the house. But obviously this interrupted the preparations. Mrs. Lathem said to tell you that the hash will be on the menu tomorrow."

Rafe waved a hand to dismiss that statement. "Great God, tell her that is the least of my worries. And please let her know that I will come down later today to assess the damage and clear funds for any clean-up or repair."

Lathem nodded. "Very good. Is there anything else I can do for either of you?"

"No," Rafe said with a reassuring smile.

After the servant had gone, Serafina shuddered. "How terrifying."

"Yes," he said, sinking back into his chair with a grim expression. "A fire could have roared out of control swiftly and endangered many. We are truly lucky."

Serafina glanced toward the dining room door that Lathem had departed from. "Lathem seems a good sort."

Rafe grinned. "He is. Although I was so distracted by his news of the fire that I only just realized he followed *your* order about the invitations rather than my own. Cheeky bastard."

"I think that proves what a discerning fellow he is. He knows when a person is being unreasonable."

Rafe shook his head. "How am I being unreasonable?"

"Refusing eight invitations would be unreasonable," she said with a sigh.

"Oh, Sera," he groaned.

She reached out to cover his hand with hers. "A moment ago you said you would learn how to be a duke, yes? Well, allow me to teach you."

"You?" he repeated, staring at her hand over his, then back up to her face.

She slid away, heat rushing to her cheeks, and nodded. "Yes. I was taught the intricacies of being a duchess for years while I awaited my marriage to your cousin. Who better to teach you than I?"

He pondered that for a moment. "I suppose that is true. But you are not obligated—"

"It is not an obligation. I would simply like to help," she said softly. "You could have made these past few days a trial, but you didn't. Besides, if you have altered our bargain to include a tutelage in pleasure, why should I not alter it equally?"

"Tit for tat?" he said, his voice suddenly tense.

She shook her head. It seemed she wasn't explaining herself well enough. "No. Please, may I help you?"

Slowly, he nodded. "Very well. And your first lesson is that I cannot refuse invitations."

She laughed. "No, my first lesson is that there are *certain people* you cannot turn down."

He let out a heavy sigh. "Could I not be eccentric?"

"Not if you want to survive, Rafe."

He pursed his lips and waved toward the pile of invitations. "I will accept two."

"Three at least," she corrected. "That will be enough to make it clear you are not shunning the Upper Ten Thousand, but not so many as to appear desperate to be accepted."

He rested his head on the edge of the table. "I'm going to hate this," he said, tone muffled.

"Quite possibly," she said, using a reassuring tone, even though she could offer little reassurance. She flipped through the invitations. "Lord and Lady Aldridge are a good example.

He is an important earl."

"But I'm a duke—do I not trump him?" he asked. "Or have I been desperately misinformed all these years?"

She couldn't help but laugh at his relentless teasing. "In rank, yes, of course you are above him. But your dukedom, if you recall, was until recently in financial ruin. It was why my father was able to convince Cyril's father to arrange our match. That fact was common knowledge, and until you show them that you no longer leave the title in shambles, they will judge you for it."

"And what sort of fellow is Aldridge?" he asked.

She tilted her head. "He is a bit older than you are, but not by much. I have met him and his wife a few times and they seem like solid people. Intelligent enough, without the foppery of some of the worst of the titled."

Rafe shrugged. "Fine, respond in the positive to Aldridge. And pick two more of these invitations to respond positively to. You can teach me all about the invitees on our way to the events."

Serafina glanced down at her stack of invitations and back up to him. "You do not want control?"

"Great God, no. I trust you to make the right decisions in the matter and I promise you I shall not complain. Much."

She stared at him. In all the years she had been bound to Cyril, he had made it clear that there would be no decision made, not small nor large, in his household that would not be strictly overseen by him. To have control of any part her life with Rafe was rather…

Thrilling.

"I will do my best to pick hosts who you will like," she said.

"Very good." He pushed to his feet. "Now, all this planning has made me bored. Would you like to take a tour of my home?"

She blinked not just at his rapid change of subject, but at the way he leaned down, offering his hand to her. He smiled, and she found herself unable to do anything but take that hand and rise to her feet.

"Certainly," she managed to squeak out as they stood, face to face, him looking down into her eyes. He wanted to kiss her, that much was plain. Shockingly, she wanted him to do just that, standing in the dining room where anyone could see.

It was odd that he could touch her in his bed, awaken her to pleasure, and yet having a conversation at his breakfast table, holding his hand in his dining room...those things felt more intimate. And if there was one thing she knew, she did not *want* an intimate or emotional connection with his man.

She wanted her freedom, so she had to be careful.

"What do you think?" Rafe asked an hour later, after they had toured the entire house save the damaged kitchen. He had saved his library for last, and now she stood amongst the books, looking around with eyes wide with wonder.

"It is magnificent," she breathed.

He laughed. "The house or the library?"

"Both." She smiled in return.

Those smiles were becoming more common now and more real. Serafina was without a doubt one of the most beautiful women he had ever encountered. But when she smiled and her face lit up? Well, there was no "one of." She was simply the most exquisite creature who had ever walked the earth. And she was his.

At least in name.

He found his own smile falling. "Of course, any area of the household is yours to explore or utilize. The servants have all been told that you are the lady of the house and shall be treated accordingly.

"Likely why Lathem listened to *me* this morning," she said with a wicked glint to her eyes.

Rafe feigned a scowl. "Yes. Apparently he is of a mind that the lady of the house rules the roost."

He saw a shadow cross her face at that comment and frowned. Cyril's abuse and her father's belief that she was worthwhile only as a bargaining point had obviously scarred her.

He heard Lathem clearing his throat at the door and glanced over. The butler gave him a slight nod, and Rafe smiled and returned the motion. Lathem, as always, understood and slipped away.

"I have someone I would like you to meet," Rafe said, turning back to find Serafina had edged over to the bookcase and was staring intently at titles, occasionally let her fingertip crest over the well-worn spines of his favorites.

"Meet?" she asked, abandoning the books to look at him in question.

"It turns out Annabelle's maid has a sister in service. She trained to be a lady's companion, but could not find work and has been in another household. I've had her brought here for a trial with you, just to fulfill the role as maid since you don't have one. If you like her, wonderful. If not, then we will tell her it won't work out."

Serafina frowned. "But if she has left her current position, wouldn't this trial period result in her being out of a job? I wouldn't feel right putting her on the street."

Rafe smiled at her attention to the situation of others. In his life, he had seen plenty of women of rank and privilege who didn't think twice about those in their service. Certainly Serafina had not been taught to care for others by her father. It seemed to be simply in her nature.

"I will recommend her to a friend looking for a maid and she will be none the worse for the experience, I promise you," he reassured her gently.

She nodded. "Then let us meet the young lady."

He motioned to the door, and she followed him into the hallway and back through the house to the foyer. A young woman waited there with Lathem, a small suitcase at her feet.

"Your Graces, may I present Bridget King?" Lathem said with a nod to the maid.

Serafina stepped forward. As the two women began to talk, Rafe watched his bride rather than listened. The kind and open expression on her face obviously put the nervous maid at ease.

It was a funny thing. Less than ten days ago, he had not planned to wed, but here he was with a bride and he *liked* her. Not to mention that he wanted her. His body had been on edge for hours and now he wanted to proceed to his next lesson in pleasure and sin.

He moved forward when there was a lull in the conversation between the women. "Have you two come to any decisions?"

Serafina glanced up at him. "Woolgathering, were we?" she teased.

He laughed. "Most terribly."

"Then allow me to enlighten you about what you missed," she said. "Bridget will settle herself and then she will unpack my things in the lady's chamber."

"Excellent," Rafe said, taking his wife's arm with a slight nod to the new maid. "Take your time with that, Bridget."

The maid smiled. "Of course, Your Grace."

As Rafe guided Serafina to the stairs, she shot him a look. "What in the world are you doing?"

"I find I would very much like to be alone with you," he said softly, close to her ear.

She did not resist, but he saw her eyes widen and heard the hitch in her breath that was as much fearful as anticipatory.

"It is the middle of the day, Rafe," she said as her one and only protest.

He opened their chamber door and they entered together before he said, "Yes. And there is nothing better than a languid bit of pleasure with sun streaming through the curtains and casting the prettiest glow on a lady's skin."

He pushed the door closed as he spoke, slowly guiding her until her back was against the barrier. He bracketed her in with his arms and saw a flash of terror light in her eyes.

"Serafina," he said softly.

She shook her head, her bottom lip trembling slightly. When she drew in a few ragged breaths, she managed to speak.

"I'm trying not to think of him," she said, her voice broken.

He stepped back immediately, granting her the space she so obviously needed. She bent over, her hands braced on her knees as she sucked in air. He longed to touch her in that charged moment, to take her in his arms.

But he didn't. Not only because he wasn't sure that she would want that, but also because he hadn't yet earned that right. He might not ever, considering the method of their marriage.

"Take your time," he said, offering her the most comfort he could with his tone. "Breathe."

She did so, and after a few moments, she stood up, her face pink with upset and embarrassment and her eyes bright with unshed tears.

"I'm sorry," she whispered. "But when you held me there—"

She broke off and Rafe filled in the gap. "You felt trapped."

She nodded without speaking or meeting his gaze.

"And that reminded you of him. Something he did."

She gasped, the sound painful in the quiet chamber. He turned his face at the sound of it, at the fact that he had made her feel that way even without meaning to do it.

"I will *never* hold you steady like that again," he vowed, finally reaching out to touch her face.

Her gaze darted to his face, revealing her utter shock. "You won't?"

"No," he said. "That was what I meant by telling me what you don't like. I would never want to cause you more pain."

"Thank you."

"Come, we can return downstairs."

She drew back a fraction. "You don't want to continue?"

His mouth dropped open at her question. "You cannot wish me to after this."

She straightened her shoulders and looked at him evenly. "I would like to try, Rafe. I want to try."

He stared at her in utter disbelief. Serafina might have those flares of fear, fear she had bloody well earned over the years, but she battled them admirably. She had a brave soul— that was becoming clear with every moment he spent with her.

"You're certain?"

"Yes," she said, and her voice was stronger.

"Then remember my promise, Sera," he whispered as he leaned in and brushed his lips against hers until she relaxed against him. "Only pleasure, no pain."

She nodded as he took her hand and did not resist as he drew her toward the bed and the intimacies he intended to share with her there. Intimacies he hoped would help heal her, rather than inspire more painful memories.

CHAPTER TEN

Serafina could hardly breathe. At first that had been because of the memories that mobbed her, but now that those horrible thoughts had faded, her tight throat and elevated heart rate were for another reason.

Rafe. Rafe and the desire he inspired. Rafe and the safety he offered.

He slowly unbuttoned her gown. His gaze never left hers, even as his fingers worked along her spine. As her dress opened and he slid his hands beneath the fabric, she let out a soft sigh. His eyes went wide.

"Are you all right?"

She nodded, caught up, yet again, in how gentle he was with her.

"Good or bad?" he asked, though he didn't remove his hands from her flesh.

"Good," she admitted with a blush. "Your hands are warm."

He smiled, but his eyes went dark with his desire. A need she realized he had not yet fulfilled.

Would he now? Would he take her at last?

Her body tensed at the thought, not because she feared *him* and his touch, but because of the same kinds of memories that had been inspired by his pinning her to the door. And because she couldn't believe that what Rafe had offered with his fingers was something she could feel with his big body stretching hers. What if she didn't like it? Or what if she panicked?

"Stop terrifying yourself," he whispered.

She started. "Are my thoughts so clear?"

He smoothed his hands across her back, and then pushed her dress forward so that it slid off her shoulders and gathered around her waist.

"I can't read them exactly," he said, his voice so soft and rhythmic. "But I can see they bring you no happiness."

"I'm sorry," she said, her shoulders rolling forward a second time in further shame and defeat. "I try not to remember, I try not to think about before."

He pressed his hand beneath her chin and tilted her face toward his. "You don't *ever* need to apologize for the vile acts committed against you, Sera," he said, his gaze turning from desire-filled to rage-filled in an instant. "I only ask for you to try to remember that you're with me in this moment, not him."

She shivered, staring up at Rafe. Rafe with his beautifully sculptured body, Rafe with his easy smile and laughing view of the world, Rafe who was gentle and tender with her.

"There is no comparison between you, I assure you," she whispered as she reached out and pressed a palm flat against his chest.

He sucked in a sudden, broken breath and his pupils dilated with her touch. A thrill moved through her, despite her tangled thoughts. Touching him made him want her even more. *Her*, a woman he was forced to be with by these mad circumstances. Her, a woman whose past made her timid when it came to acts he likely could have performed willingly by a dozen other women.

And yet he still wanted *her*.

"Rafe," she whispered.

He pushed her dress lower and it hit the ground around her feel with a swish of delicate fabric.

"Yes?"

She swallowed. "I don't want to be a disappointment to

you," she admitted, her cheeks flaming with heat. "I know there are many other women who wouldn't hesitate. Women who would have given you such pleasure already."

His brow furrowed. "You think I have not experienced pleasure with you? Watching you soften to my touch, watching you orgasm for the first time, I promise you there was great gratification in that."

"But you haven't found your release," she said, shifting with discomfort at that topic. "Cyril told me—"

He lifted a hand to gently cover her mouth.

"Cyril was full of horseshit," he said. "Pardon my crude choice of words, but it is true. Yes, I would love to come inside of you, Sera. To have you milk my release from me with the quivering of your body. But we have all the time in the world now that we are wed. It *will* happen. And until it does, I am having a very good time exploring what makes you quake."

She shivered at those erotic promises, and he smiled at her reaction. Then his smile faltered as he hooked his fingers around both her chemise straps and lowered them at the same time, exposing her body inch by inch until the silky undergarment joined her dress at her feet. He looked up and down her now-naked body with a possessive hunger in his eyes that made her stomach flip with a desire she'd never expected to feel.

Was it wrong to want him like this? Wrong to ache to have this man touch her and hope he could wipe away her ugliest memories?

If it was, Rafe never made her feel that way. His smile returned as he wrapped his arms around her, kissed her, lifted her into his arms to carry her to his bed. He set her on the high edge and leaned back to remove her stockings and slippers.

His hands glided over her thighs, her knee, her calf, and she trembled as the touch sent electric heat to settle between her legs. She had no idea what he would do next, but she was shocked to find that she wanted it, whatever it was. She wanted *him*.

He stepped away and caught the back of one of the chairs beside the fire. Without breaking his gaze away from her, he dragged it to the edge of the bed and settled into the cushion. She stared down at him, confused by his odd positioning.

"What are you doing?" she asked.

He placed a hand on her bare knee and she sucked in her breath.

"Open your legs, Serafina," he said, his tone low and hypnotic.

She blushed. From the way they were positioned, if she did as he asked, her most private areas would be right before him. There would be no hiding.

His fingers glided up her thigh and he massaged gently.

"Serafina," he whispered. "Open your legs."

She trembled as she followed his directive, trying to remind herself that this man had proven himself trustworthy, at least when it came to her body.

He practically purred as she opened for him and scooted closer, draping one of her legs over his shoulder. She stared at him, cheeks burning while she watched him examine her.

"So pretty," he whispered. "So tempting."

He looked up her body with a wickedness that only intensified the ache between her legs. He clenched her hips with both hands and slid her forward so that her backside nearly hung off the bed. She fell back on her elbows with a cry at the unexpected movement. Before she could voice any kind of protest, he dragged one finger across her sex.

Her body twitched with memory of what he had done with those magical fingers earlier in the day.

"Rafe—" she began, her voice shaky and broken.

"Good or bad?" he asked.

"Please," she murmured, uncertain what she was asking for.

He smiled. "So good, then?"

He said nothing more, but he watched her even as he dropped his mouth lower, lower. Her eyes went wide. He couldn't mean to—

His lips touched her with just a feather-light brush. The unexpected caress made her arch slightly, bringing her sex closer. He chuckled, the vibrations moving through her sensitive flesh and eliciting a moan from her lips that she hadn't meant to express.

He nuzzled her with his mouth a second time, nibbling gently on the swollen outer lips of her body. She clenched her fists against the coverlet with a harsh groan, then looked down her body to watch what he would do next.

He was staring at her body, examining her most private areas like they were a beautiful piece of art. Or sweets, she supposed, since he was putting his mouth on her over and over. He gently spread her open, then leaned back down.

She tensed as his hot breath steamed over her tender flesh, making her ultra-aware of every fold and crevice of her sex. They were all alive at his touch, tingling and aching for something she had only just begun to understand.

"Please," she murmured a second time.

He glanced up at her, his eyes dark with wanting and filled with wickedness and curiosity.

"As you wish." Without another word, he brought his mouth firmly against her body.

This time it was an open-mouthed kiss he bestowed upon her sensitive, slick folds. His tongue darted out and he licked her entrance first gently, then with more force. She gripped the covers harder, swept away by the sudden intensity of the sensations. His fingers had been magic, but his mouth? That was something else.

It was as if her entire body had been suspended in water, making her weightless and unable to control how her body moved beneath Rafe's ministrations. She arched and twitched when his tongue moved over her, her breath coming short and becoming moans and cries that filled the room.

And yet he offered her no respite. His mouth tasted her relentlessly, and finally he slipped up to lick the little bundle of nerves at the top of her sex. That place he had touched before to shatter her with pleasure.

His mouth only intensified that feeling and she felt the orgasm—Rafe had called it that name—building within her. She arched to try to reach it, and he laughed against her skin as he pressed against her hip with one hand, holding her steady.

"Don't rush, Sera," he murmured, nuzzling her gently. "I'll take you there in due time."

She gave a garbled moan that likely left Rafe with little question about her desperation. But he didn't seem intent on torture, for he began to lick harder, faster, and she burned beneath him.

It wasn't until she thought she could take no more, when she was weak and ready to beg, to offer him anything in trade for release, that he slipped a finger into her body. She hadn't expected the breach, but didn't stiffen because it felt so good to have him inside her. He pressed his lips to her, sucking hard as he stroked in and out with his finger in a maddening rhythm.

Unlike earlier in the day, when her orgasm had hit her suddenly and without her understanding what it meant, this time release came slow and steady, building higher and higher as she cried out and thrashed beneath him. He continued on, not releasing her from the prison of pleasure until she was spent with desire and flopped weakly against the mattress.

Only then did he rise from the chair, lick her juices from his fingers and reposition her on the pillows. But he made no move to undress, to take her. Once again, he simply claimed a spot beside her in his bed and tucked her up against him. He held her close as her heart rate returned to normal and she caught her panting breath.

"Did I prove myself right?" he asked from above her.

She leaned up to look at him. "Right?"

"Did I not promise you I could give you pleasure ever more intense?"

She swatted at him lightly. "You are, by far, the most arrogant and self-satisfied man I have ever met. So proud of yourself."

He grinned. "I take that as a yes, then."

She settled her head back against his shoulder and wrapped her arms around him. "Take it as you will, Raphael Flynn. You will gain no quarter from me."

He leaned down a fraction and whispered, "That sounds like a challenge, Your Grace. And one I intend to meet."

She laughed at his quip, but her stomach fluttered as wildly at his promises as it had at his touch. It was painfully obvious to see that she could easily lose herself in him if she allowed that.

And she would not, *could not* let that happen.

CHAPTER ELEVEN

Rafe gritted his teeth as yet another titled fop crowded into his personal space and shook his hand until his teeth rattled.

"Your Grace, Your Grace," the man gushed. "It must be very good to be called that now, eh?"

Rafe extracted his stinging hand and tried very hard not to pull a face that showed just how wrong this man was.

"Under the circumstances, I can hardly celebrate," he said with a glare. "Remind me again of your name?"

The gentleman's enthusiasm waned a fraction. "Viscount Eames, Your Grace."

"Hmmm," Rafe said

He knew full well he would forget again in a moment, just as he had been with each and every person he had met all night. There was one thing he knew—he had been right to avoid this kind of Society for all these years. There was nothing here to tempt him. Except...

He let his gaze flit across the room to where Serafina stood with a small group of ladies. His wife was in the most beautiful gown, which highlighted her bright eyes and made her skin look almost porcelain. It was marred only by the fact that it was amethyst, a color meant to signal her "mourning" for Cyril's death.

She had put the gown on that evening with a great deal of dignity, never saying a word that wearing it bothered her, even though he knew full-well that she had despised her would-be fiancé.

Luckily, Society only judged him now as a cousin of hers by marriage who had died. They would both be able to shed the false pretenses of mourning within a few weeks.

She tilted her head as she listened to the story of her companion and smiled, and he was almost undone.

"Circumstances aside," his own companion continued, like a dog with a bone he couldn't leave alone. "You must be thrilled to elevate yourself so high. Especially considering your family's less than sterling reputation in the past."

Rafe looked at the annoying gentleman. The man couldn't be but three years older than he was, but a pampered life of excess had made him soft, fat and aged before his time by idleness.

"I don't know what you mean."

The viscount opened and shut his mouth a few times. "Why, the excessive gambling, Your Grace. The…" His voice dropped. "The women. And didn't you and your brother once have a race through Hyde Park that nearly unseated the Prince Regent from his horse?"

Rafe pinched his lips together. He had rather hoped everyone would forget that last bit. The Prince himself had been persuaded by a wildly expensive bottle of port to ultimately see it as good fun gone slightly wrong. But Rafe knew he and Crispin had only just avoided a duel of honor with royalty.

"At any rate," Eames said, filling the silence when Rafe did not. "You cannot tell me you aren't secretly delighted."

"Not everyone strives to be a duke," Rafe said softly.

The man's eyebrows lifted as if he could not believe it. "Are you saying *that* is why you removed yourself and your new bride from the ducal home?"

"Who said that?" Rafe asked, surprised that this news was something anyone knew about, let alone cared to repeat.

He knew a scandal when he saw one, and the actions he

had taken to protect Serafina from the past didn't rise to that level. Except that he and his new bride were all the talk in general.

He suppressed a moan.

"*Everyone* is talking about it," the viscount said with a shrug, even though his eyes were bright and focused with glee on Rafe's answer.

Rafe's eyes narrowed. He saw now what this man was about. Eames hoped to be the lead in some kind of salacious story. To have the answers to the question that would somehow make him important.

"Well, if everyone is talking about the fact," Rafe said, taking a drink from the tray of a passing servant, "then they must already know that it is in my nature to do the unexpected."

His companion was about to say more, but was interrupted by the arrival of their host, the Earl of Aldridge. Aldridge stepped up with a smile for the two.

"Good evening, my lords. Are you both enjoying yourselves?"

The viscount began to nod as if his head was on a spring, but Rafe could hardly keep himself from grimacing even as he said, "Of course. Thank you again for inviting us."

"You know, Eames, I believe the Marquess of Waterbury was looking for you," Aldridge said. "In the billiards room."

Eames's eyes lit up. "Was he? Then it would be rude to make him wait. Excuse me."

He darted off into the crowd. Once he was gone, Aldridge sighed. "That man may be the greatest idiot in Society. Which is saying quite a bit."

Rafe nearly choked on his drink at the unexpected comment. He eyed the earl carefully. Once Rafe had met him earlier in the evening, he had realized he had been at Eton with the man what seemed like a lifetime ago. He recalled having no quarrel with Aldridge, but he had no idea what the earl's personality was now, decades later.

"Then why invite him?" he asked, observing the answer carefully.

Aldridge let out a long, playfully put-upon sigh. "He is a relation to my dear wife, I'm afraid. Third cousin, or something to that effect. And he tends to come to parties even if he hasn't been invited. You'll soon find out."

Rafe wrinkled his nose. "I have no intention of hosting parties."

"As a duke, it will be expected of you."

Rafe groaned. "Great God. Being titled is tedious."

Aldridge gazed out over the crowd with a far-away look on his face. "It can be, I agree. But it can also be of great benefit to the causes and people you care for."

Rafe drew back a fraction. He'd never considered that before. Although his brother could care less about Society, his sister might be interested in coming to this world, in "marrying well" as she put it.

"I'm not certain I have any causes," he said with a grin.

Aldridge returned the expression. "I have a few. Come by the house in a few days and I can persuade you to take them up, as well. With our combined finances and influence, perhaps we could change the world a bit."

Rafe glanced at the man. Aldridge didn't seem to be in jest, so he nodded. "Certainly."

"And now I see my lovely wife is alone for what must be the first time since this party began. I must take the opportunity to dance with her." Aldridge inclined his head. "I'll see you soon, Hartholm."

Rafe muttered some kind of goodbye, even though his attention was drawn again to his own wife. Although she wasn't alone like Lady Aldridge had apparently been, Serafina drew Rafe to her like a moth to her bright and beautiful flame.

He moved toward her, his gaze never wavering from her exquisite face. When he was a few feet from her, she finally seemed to sense his approach, for she sent him a look from the corner of her eye. Her cheeks darkened in a blush that made him want to sweep her away where he could act out every fantasy she inspired.

Instead, he gave a dashing smile to the women in her small group and said, "Good evening, ladies."

He saw Serafina exchange a brief look with her best friend Emma Richards, and then she managed to give him another side-glance and joined the others in their good evenings.

"Would you all mind very much if I stole my wife away? We haven't had a dance tonight."

Despite the fact that his wife stood beside him, a few of the women looked Rafe up and down. He felt their stares and saw the way they tossed him flirtatious glances, but he never stopped looking at Serafina. No one else held even a fraction of his interest compared to her.

"I would be happy to dance with you, Your Grace," Serafina finally said. "Excuse me, ladies."

He locked her hand into the crook of his elbow and led her to the dance floor.

"They're all looking at us," she said through a clench-toothed smile.

He started and looked around to find she was correct. It seemed almost the entire room had ceased what they were doing in order to watch the couple of the moment take the dance floor.

"You *do* know how to dance, don't you?" she asked softly.

He laughed. "I said I don't know how to be a duke, my dear, not a man."

The music began in that moment. It was a waltz that the orchestra played, so he pulled her close and swept her into the steps, guiding her gently.

Her eyes widened as it became clear that he was proficient in this act.

"I should not have doubted you," she said with a laugh that cleared the worry from her face.

"No," he teased. "You should not have." He looked around and found the crowd was still enamored. "Though I've certainly never had an audience such as this."

She shook her head. "They all want to know about you, but also about *us*. It isn't all that often that a man inherits a title and a bride in one act. Especially one with as much scandal as Cyril's death."

Rafe frowned. From her very tight expression, it seemed she knew more about the truth of Cyril's accident than he had given her credit for.

"How much do you know?" he asked.

She shrugged even as they spun effortlessly. "Enough to recognize that the men are still talking about it. That I was, in male terms, a cuckold. In truth, I do not care. I wish Cyril would have stuck to his whores. Though I do feel sorry for the poor girl who died in his..." She cleared her throat and wrinkled her nose. "...service."

"You are truly remarkable," Rafe breathed.

"Oh stop," she said, ducking her head with a blush, stumbling in her steps for a brief moment.

"I mean it," he continued. "You have such dignity in the face of a painful and humiliating situation. I greatly admire you, Serafina."

She tilted her face to look at him and then nodded slightly. "Thank you," she whispered.

He examined her more closely, so beautiful, so strong, so intelligent and sensual. And more than anything in the world, he wanted to touch her.

"Will you go home with me?" he asked.

She did not answer, but he saw her gaze slip to the crowd at the edge of the dance floor.

"Surely we've put in enough of an appearance to satisfy the curious," he said as he tightened his fingers around her waist. She sucked in a breath at the action and he smiled in triumph. "I want to be alone with you."

"Yes," she said softly.

His eyes went wide, for he had guessed he would have to be more convincing than that. "Yes?" he repeated.

She nodded. "After we say goodnight to our hosts, we may go home."

The music began to slow and Rafe found himself loath to release her, but he finally did so, and she made a pretty curtsey before she took his arm and let him lead her away through the crowd and directly toward Lord and Lady Aldridge.

Because after two days of teasing, he was ready to take his passion for Serafina to the next level. And he couldn't wait even a moment more to do so.

Serafina had felt the heat of Rafe's passion before, she had sensed that he desired her. But as he dragged her into his lap in the carriage, kissing her with wild abandon, she could tell this was something different.

In the past, even the recent past, such ardor would have frightened her, made her think of things Cyril had done or forced her to do.

But Raphael was not Cyril, and she no longer took even a moment to compare the two. No, with her arms around his neck, her body nestled against him, her mouth open and tongue tangling with his, the only thing she felt when she thought of what would come next was...longing. If she was right about his increased fervor when it came to her, then tonight she would finally be claimed as his in every way physically possible.

Even if that was a fleeting gift, she wanted to own it.

Their carriage slowed and Rafe released her with a throaty groan that spoke of his desire just as much as the hard ridge of his erection that had been growing for the past fifteen minutes did.

"I am both disappointed to let you go," he murmured, "and so very excited to be home with you."

A footman appeared to open the door to and assist them

from the vehicle, but Rafe waved the man off. Instead, he got out himself, then turned back to help her. The steadying hand he placed against her hip lingered too long for propriety and she suppressed a shiver as she took his arm.

"Upstairs," he said, but she wasn't certain if it was a suggestion or an order. Either way she nodded, and he led her up to their chamber without allowing anyone to even take their wraps.

Once inside, once the door had been closed and locked, he leaned back against the barrier and simply *stared* at her.

"All night I have dreamed of being alone with you," he said softly. "And here we are, and I almost don't know where to start."

She bit her lip. She had never been bold. It wasn't exactly in her nature, and with Cyril she had lived to discourage, not take control. But here with this man in this moment, she wasn't afraid. She was just...*ready*. Ready for him. Ready for what they had begun on their wedding night and had been cut off. Ready for it all.

"Why don't we start with my wrap?" she suggested softly as she unbuttoned her heavy shrug and tossed it aside without a care for where it fell. "And your top coat."

He nodded and did the same as she had done. She began to work on her gown, which happily fastened in the front, and he caught his breath as he watched her undress for him. Her fingers faltered from time to time, partly because she so rarely undressed herself and partly because she could hardly breathe and her fingers felt thick and useless when he watched her so closely. Finally she managed it and let her dress fall away, kicking it aside.

"Are you going to take something else off or will I be the only one naked yet again?" she asked.

He smiled as he made short work of his tailored formal jacket and then nearly tore his cravat in half as he untied it.

"Had I allowed myself to be naked with you since our wedding night," he explained while he unbuttoned his shirt and tugged it over his head, "then I would not have been able to exert the control I have with you in the past few days."

"And why did you?" she asked, staring unabashedly at his shirtless form. Oh, she had seen him like this on their wedding night, of course, but she had been so anxious and afraid, she hadn't exactly enjoyed what she saw.

Now she took her time drinking him in. He was perfectly formed. Lean muscle roped his arms, his chest, his stomach, his tapered hips. And dear God, but he was tanned, proving he was very wicked when he wasn't in London and could roam about the countryside in far less than appropriate attire.

"Why did I what?" he asked, dragging her back to the moment.

She blinked. She had almost forgotten her question, but it came back soon enough. "Why—why did you exert such control?"

He tilted his head. "Because you needed it," he said. "Because you had to believe that I am not the brute my cousin was."

She stared at him a moment, then slowly approached him. She lifted her hand and stroked his cheek with the back of it. "I do not believe that, Rafe. I know it."

His face softened slightly before he bent lower and kissed her deeply. Any hesitation she might have felt, any fear, melted away with that kiss and she reached up to clutch his bare upper arms as he guided her to his bed.

He laid her across his pillows, then stepped away to shed boots and trousers. She turned her face, still uncomfortable with the sight of his engorged member. She was curious about it, yes, but looking at it remained difficult.

If he noticed her hesitation, he made no comment on it, but joined her on the bed where he returned to those passionate kisses. She wrapped her arms around him, relaxing into the pleasure he created with his mouth, his hands as he guided them to her chemise and lowered the straps. When he could go no further, he drew back and freed himself from her arms to undress her fully.

Once he had gotten the undergarment off, he balled it up without breaking eye contact and tossed it to join the other tangled remnants of their very proper night at the ball.

She thought he would move back to kiss her, but instead he looked up and down her body slowly, taking in the sight of her with dark, appreciative eyes.

"Only pleasure," he reminded her.

She smiled. "Always pleasure," she corrected him.

He cupped her breast and began to stroke his thumb over the distended nipple, rubbing a gentle, hypnotic rhythm against the sensitive peak. She let out a shuddering sigh at the attention and let her eyes slide shut so she could savor just the feel of his touch.

She didn't open them, even as he replaced his hand with his hot mouth. He sucked her nipple, swirling his tongue around and around, lapping at her like a man starved for her flesh.

She couldn't stop the moans now. She didn't try to do so, but let them loose as intensive pleasure mobbed her, building the familiar wall of the orgasm that would soon shatter within her.

His hand moved lower, brushing seductively over her stomach, edging over to cup her hip as he had earlier in the night, although this time it was bare skin on skin and oh, so seductive.

He let that hand massage across her thigh, and finally he cupped her sex just as he had the first morning they spent together, when he had promised her pleasure as part of their bargain. He had given her that in spades since, but now she wanted *more*. Her eyes came open finally and she watched as he teased her with his fingers, opening her, readying her. And all the while, he sucked from one nipple to the other, playing her like an instrument that was part of a magnificent orchestra of pleasure.

He drew away from her breasts and looked up at her with a

wicked smile. His fingers continued to play as he moved up to slide his nose against hers. But he didn't kiss her. Not even when she lifted her chin in silent demand.

"Oh no," he whispered, ducking her plea. "My eyes won't be closed when I am finally inside of you, Sera."

He urged her legs wider with those insistent hands and she was too helpless with desire now to resist. Then his hand was gone and he rolled on top of her, positioning himself between her legs, even as he remained true to his word and kept his stare firmly locked with hers.

"Are you ready?" he asked.

She tried to catch her breath, tangled between fear and longing, the past and a future she had never imagined. A future she could only take if she let him fully consummate their union.

"Yes," she said on a shaky breath.

He positioned the hard thrust of his sex against hers, and she held her breath as he slowly glided inside of her. Unlike the first time he had done so, she wasn't caught up in fear and she shivered at the feeling of being stretched by him, filled by him, taken by him in this primal way.

To her surprise, there was intense pleasure in the slide of their bodies. In the slick welcome he had created and the hard invasion he had resisted until now.

When he was fully inside of her, he stopped moving and looked down at her.

"Breathe, Sera," he said with an encouraging smile. "Don't forget to breathe."

She dragged a gulp of air into her lungs and found herself relaxing. It was in that moment that he thrust for the first time.

She had been ready for that thrust, even before they married. She was ready for discomfort. She was ready for a stomach-clenching wish that it would end.

But this was *not* that. When he slid through her, almost all the way out and then back in again, her body didn't revolt. It didn't clench. It didn't respond with pain or discomfort.

Instead, the fire he had built previously with his fingers, his mouth, his seduction, suddenly flamed higher. The pleasure she had come to expect from this man was in this act as well. In every swivel of his hips, in every heavy thrust of his body.

She arched to meet him on the next strokes, clenching around him in a rhythm that was as natural as breathing. The dam of pleasure strained with his expert claiming, with the way he watched her like she was the most fascinating creature who had ever existed.

All of it came together, and when he swiveled his hips another time, hitting the perfect spot in her body, the orgasm crested over her. And just like with his hands or his mouth, he didn't offer her hesitation as a respite. He thrust through the crisis, dragging her higher with the rapid pistoning of his hips until the quakes of her release weakened and she could barely moan his name.

"Great God, Serafina," he panted, staring at her as if he'd never seen her before.

Suddenly the movements of his body grew erratic and he let out a garbled moan before she felt the explosive burst of his seed deep inside of her. Then he collapsed over her and held her close as their heartbeats pounded in time.

CHAPTER TWELVE

Serafina sighed as Rafe rolled away, separating their bodies, then gathering her to his side. She could hardly believe how light she felt. How warm and satiated.

She had never thought lovemaking could be like that. But Rafe had given her that gift. And so much more.

"My God," he said as he smoothed her sweaty hair away from her face. "You are gorgeous. Absolutely beautiful."

She stiffened at the compliment. If she thought she hadn't made her displeasure clear, his chuckle proved her wrong.

"The look on your face," he said, stroking a thumb across her cheek. "Why do you hate it so much?"

She shook her head. "Hate what?"

He laughed again. "Don't be coy now, I think we've gone too far for that. I have seen you make a face each and every time someone has complimented your loveliness. Yes, sometimes you hide your annoyance better than others, but it is always there." He leaned closer and tapped the tip of her nose playfully. "Some ladies actually *like* being complimented for their looks. So it fascinates me that you despise it. Would you like to tell me why?"

Serafina rolled to her back, dragging the sheets up around her chest as she pondered what he had said. She had never confessed to anyone her true thoughts on her looks. She had never even considered it. But here Rafe was, asking her the truth without any kind of ulterior motive behind the question. To say what was in her heart was an almost undeniable draw.

She sighed. "What I'm going to tell you may make you think I'm arrogant. You may even like me less when I'm finished."

"Your warning intrigues me further, but I will tell you that I do not think I could dislike you," he said, the laughter gone from his voice and from his face as he watched her carefully.

"I know I am beautiful," she said, her cheeks flaming with embarrassment at the conceited admission. "Empirically it is true—I see it in the mirror each day. And I have also heard it almost every day of my life."

He leaned away a fraction. "So you are terribly bored of it," he teased gently.

"I'm being serious, Rafe. It isn't that I'm bored of hearing the world wax poetic on my physical attributes. It is that…that…"

She trailed off, stopped by the fact that she was about to reveal yet another piece of her soul to a man who already knew so much about her. A man she was supposed to be distancing herself from, not inviting further into her confidence.

"Tell me," he urged, his face serious as his hands moved to cover her clenched ones in her lap.

She let out a long breath. "When I was five, my mother told me I was beautiful. I suppose she must have told me that before, but it is the first time I recall her saying it. I was pleased, of course. I knew being pretty had value. But she followed that with more and more compliments on my physical appearance. As I grew older, she was almost obsessed with my gowns, my hair. I was her doll to dress up and display, to show off to her friends and then gossip with me afterward about how much uglier their girls were."

Rafe nodded. "I can see how her excessiveness would make you uncomfortable."

She pursed her lips at the memories that mobbed her. "And it was worse. She wasn't only obsessed with my being a pretty girl, but that I would be a pretty woman. She harped on how curvaceous I should be. Was I too thin? Was I too fat? How I should never wear yellow because it 'didn't suit me.'"

"How old were you?" he asked, his voice filled with disbelief, tinged with horror.

"It was before I was betrothed to Cyril, so…six, perhaps?"

"And what of after? Surely she must have relaxed when she believed your future secure."

"On the contrary, she grew even more determined. She was thrilled I had landed a future duke, of course, but she feared I would lose his interest if I didn't use my beauty. That became her only mantra. *Use your beauty, Serafina. Use your beauty.* I had to sneak books because she didn't want me reading or studying."

"Why?" Rafe asked.

"I didn't need to be intelligent or witty. I needed to be pretty."

"That explains why you were surprised when I said Annabelle had reviewed the betrothal contract," Rafe mused.

She nodded. "If my mother had thought I could decipher a document like that, she probably would have locked me in my chamber as punishment. I had to sneak my learning, my study, and keep my thoughts to myself."

"How terrible," he said with a shake of his head.

"She died when I was eleven. She drew me in to her bedroom at the end and asked my father that we be left alone. I looked at her, wasted away by a long, terrible illness. She was in obvious pain. And I loved her, I did, so I hoped she would say something meaningful to me. I wanted her to tell me she loved me or was proud of me. At the very least I hoped for some advice in surviving life alone with my father."

"She didn't tell you any of those things?"

She shook her head. "No. Instead, she told me once more to use my beauty. Those were her last words to me."

Rafe was silent for a moment, as if letting those facts sink in. "I have met your father, so I cannot believe he would be any better."

She bit back a bark of humorless laughter. "He didn't have as much beauty advice, but he certainly only ever spoke of my looks when he listed my attributes. When I was fifteen, he had me end a friendship with a girl because she became too fat. It was always about looks. And my looks are why Cyril was so awful."

"What do you mean?"

She tilted her head. "Surely you must know that my beauty was part of why Cyril wanted me. To have me on his arm, a trophy, was vastly important to him, nearly as much as the damned money in my dowry. Had I been a little uglier, perhaps he would not have—"

She broke off. Her memories of Cyril's abuse had begun to fade a little with Rafe's gentle touch, but when she spoke of it so plainly, her stomach still turned.

"A man like Cyril will victimize regardless," Rafe said softly.

She shrugged. "Either way, you must understand how difficult it is only to be judged by something that has nothing to do with my character, not even something truly in my control. My looks will fade with time. I have often looked forward to that day, actually. But what will I have left? No one has ever thought of or been interested in my intelligence or my kindness or my wit or anything else except how nice I look in a dress."

She looked away toward the fire, absently watching the flames dance. "I just wish someone saw more."

He placed a hand beneath her chin and turned her face toward his again.

"I see more," he whispered.

Her eyes went wide not just at his words but at the firm, certain way he said them. She stared at the earnest honesty on his handsome face.

"How can you when you hardly know me?" she asked, more to herself than to him.

He traced his thumb over her lower lip. "I'm beginning to

know you, Sera."

She swallowed hard, because she feared that claim might be all too true. It *felt* like Rafe knew her in a deeper, more meaningful way. Despite the fact they had been acquainted less than a fortnight, despite her hesitations and barriers, she couldn't deny that he truly seemed to *see* her.

But luckily she didn't have to respond to his claim, nor even think about it overly much. He didn't allow a response as he leaned in to gently kiss her.

She melted at the brush of his lips, lifting her shaking hands to drape them over his shoulders and sink into this heavenly caress. She couldn't help the shuddering moan that entered his mouth as he lowered her back on the pillows, his heavy, hard body moving over hers, pinning her to the bed, awakening the fire in her body that she had never thought would be possible.

"So soon?" she murmured as he began to kiss her neck.

He lifted his head to grin at her. "Are you protesting?"

"No, I just didn't think that people...*did* this more than once a night," she said, cheeks flaming at the subject.

He tugged the protective sheet down to reveal her bare breasts and gently sucked on a nipple until her back arched.

"As long as *people* are enjoying themselves, they can do it as often as they'd like," he said as he moved to tease her opposite breast. "Are you enjoying yourself, Serafina?"

She could hardly breath as he cupped her ribs and guided the sheet lower, lower, revealing more and more of her body. Everything tingled. Between her legs she *throbbed*.

"Sera?" he repeated.

"Yes," she said on a broken breath. "I never thought I would crave your body inside of mine. I never thought that this could be anything but a duty I endured with dignity. But you have set me on fire, Rafe. And only one thing can put that fire out."

His pupils dilated, and she could see the surprise on his face at that admission.

"What will put the fire out, Sera?" he whispered.

She pursed her lips. He wanted her to say the words?

"Tell me," he said, his tone low and even and so seductive that she felt like he was touching her intimately.

She swallowed. "You," she whispered. "You are the only one who can set me free from the very prison you create with your touch. I need you, Rafe. I need this."

She wasn't certain if he would torture her more at that admission, if he would use the power she gave to him. But he didn't. His mouth crushed down on hers, hot and hungry and more out of control than he had ever been when he touched her.

His ardor should have frightened her, for it contained a wildness she normally wouldn't trust. But she wasn't afraid at all. She was excited by his passion, by the way he tore the sheet fully away and pushed her legs wide with his knees. His member was hard and ready as he positioned himself at her entrance, and he was panting as he slid forward, gliding deep inside her waiting body with a long, loud moan.

"You think I put out your fire," he growled, his face too close, his breath too hot, his body too perfectly fitted into hers. "You stoke mine. And until I'm inside of you, I burn, Sera."

She dragged his mouth down and kissed him with everything in her. All the things she couldn't say, all the feelings she couldn't express, all the need that shattered her. He began to thrust hard into her, a rhythm unlike any other he had shared with her. Despite his roughness, her body throbbed with pleasure, arched to meet him, fluttered around his invading member with just the hint of the orgasm to come.

He broke their kiss with a grunt and slid his hands down her body, cupping first her hips and then her naked backside. He rocked her against him in a grinding, relentless rhythm, and suddenly a thousand starbursts exploded before her eyes. She screamed out his name as wave upon wave of powerful pleasure rolled over and through her.

It was as if her pleasure was his permission, and he cried

out in unison, pouring his seed deep into her quaking body. Then he pulled her even closer as he buried his head into her shoulder, his arms shaking. And he held her that way until they had both fallen asleep.

CHAPTER THIRTEEN

Rafe stepped from the door of his club and onto the drive with a sigh. He had once *liked* visiting there, but now he felt everyone *watching* him and heard his name whispered as he passed. Even old friends treated him differently.

It was yet one more reminder that his life would never again be the same.

But he would adjust, of course. Already he was doing so with Serafina. The past two days between them had been a heavenly experience of mounting passion.

He smiled as his carriage was brought to the club drive. As his driver began to step down, he raised a hand to stop him.

"My brother's home is so close by and the weather is fine. I think I'll walk."

His driver smiled. "Of course, Your Grace. I will meet you there."

The carriage took off again and Rafe sighed. A walk would do him good. At least it would give him time to reflect.

He strolled down the walkway in the direction of his brother's home. The sun was shining, the birds were singing. Two weeks ago, he wouldn't have had a care in the world to ruminate upon. But now he found himself considering his wife again and again. Her body, of course, but more than that.

It was almost a week since they wed and he grew closer to her each day. More interested in her with every moment they shared. He felt her relaxing in his presence and she was slowly revealing more of herself when they talked.

But she *still* insisted that they would part as soon as a house could be procured for her. A house, Rafe had to admit, he hadn't even begun to seek out, despite his promises.

He frowned as he approached the intersection to his brother's block of the street. He looked for approaching vehicles and riders and when the street was clear, he stepped out to make his way across.

He'd taken no more than three steps when the tremendous thundering of hooves echoed toward him. He turned toward the sound and gasped as he saw a carriage careening toward him at full speed. There were screams from other walkers as he dove forward and rolled into the gutter just as the vehicle screeched past him and veered around the corner so quickly that it nearly toppled itself over.

Rafe rolled to face the carriage, certain it would stop and the driver and occupant would have an apology or explanation for their reckless behavior, but the vehicle kept going. It weaved through the traffic on the next street, nearly colliding with other drivers as it disappeared from view.

"Sir!"

Rafe looked up to see a man reaching out for him. He took the offered hand of assistance and climbed to his feet.

"Are you injured?" his helper asked him as Rafe dusted himself off.

He tested his arms and legs and found no serious pain in any of them. "A bit bruised, perhaps, but no injury," he assured the Good Samaritan and the others who had stopped to gape at him.

"Bloody lucky—it came right for you," the man said with a shake of his head. "A fine carriage it was, too, to be driven so wildly."

Rafe looked again in the direction the carriage had escaped. "Lucky indeed that I was not struck," he murmured. "Thank you again for the assistance."

The man nodded and walked away, leaving Rafe to his own devices. He wiped a suddenly sweaty brow and shook his head. He had never been so close to death before and he found it made him think even more about his wife...and his future.

Despite the fact that those two subjects were supposed to be mutually exclusive.

"Great God, don't *you* look a fright," Crispin said as Rafe entered his parlor a few moments later.

Rafe glared at his brother and said nothing as he poured himself a hefty glass of scotch from the sideboard near the fireplace. When he'd taken a gulp, he turned toward his waiting sibling.

"I was almost killed," he said, then explained what had just happened in the street.

Crispin stepped back in stunned surprise as Rafe finished his story. "My God."

"Quite," Rafe agreed as he paused at the mirror above the fireplace to fix himself. Once he had done so, he turned back to Crispin. "But I survived, so..." he trailed off with a wave of his hand.

Crispin shook his head, his frown deep and dark. "Always so nonchalant."

Rafe smiled, but inside he felt anything but nonchalant about the day's events. "I refuse to dwell on what *might* have happened," he lied.

His brother took a drink and examined him closely. "Very well. Then perhaps you would prefer to dwell on what has."

Rafe shook his head. "What do you mean?"

"How do you find being a duke suits you?"

Rafe looked over the edge of his tumbler of whiskey and glared at Crispin, whose tone was now laced with sarcasm and whose eyes glittered with the same.

"Did you invite me to your home today to delight in my pain?" Rafe asked.

Crispin shook his head. "You know I could never do that, Raphael. I have had many a sleepless night as I pictured you on this hellish path."

Rafe wrinkled his brow. "You may be overstating it a bit, Crispin."

"Am I? You were free as a lark not a fortnight ago, without a care in the world. And now you are surrounded by foolery. Nearly being mown down in the street is almost a metaphor."

"Crispin—" Rafe began.

His brother ignored him. "I've heard via Annabelle and Mama that you've been invited to some of those ridiculous Society parties we took so much care to avoid over the years. Is the new duchess dragging you there?"

Rafe stiffened at the way Crispin referred to Serafina. "I thought you liked 'the new duchess'. If you do not, I think you should hold your tongue. That is my wife to whom you are referring."

Crispin's rigid posture collapsed a little and he sank into the closest chair with a sigh. "I like her as far as I know her, yes."

Rafe frowned. He could see the true concern all over Crispin's face and he loved his brother for it. Rafe set his drink aside and took the seat beside him.

"It isn't so bad as all that," he reassured Crispin softly. "As I settle in, I realize more and more that there is a great deal of responsibility, yes. I have an entail to rebuild thanks to the utterly foolish business decisions of Cyril's part of the family. I have tenants."

"You had tenants before, on the Sussex estate," Crispin sighed.

"Yes," Rafe acknowledged. "But not like this. There are probably twice as many, if not more, in Cyril's holdings and they haven't been treated particularly well over the years.

There are amends to be made."

"And what of the balls and the frippery?" Crispin asked, giving him an even look.

"My first inclination was to avoid such things, of course." Rafe shook his head. "But Serafina has made some very good points about cutting myself away from men who would be my peers. Men who could help me as I made my transition into the House of Lords."

His brother grumbled even more dissatisfaction and Rafe smiled again at Crispin's over protectiveness.

"I think the elder brother is supposed to watch the younger like a hawk, not the other way around," he teased.

Crispin, for once, didn't join in. "I don't want to see you forced into some other person's life, Rafe."

Rafe flinched. That was exactly what had happened since Cyril's death. And yet, there were parts of it that weren't so terrible.

A brief flickering image of Serafina arching beneath him passed through his mind and he exerted effort to make it go away.

"At any rate, Sera isn't dragging me into anything. But she has been raised and taught to be a duchess almost her entire life. She is offering me help to be the best duke I can be and I appreciate that. So should you. Trust me, without a guide, the entire endeavor would be far less tolerable."

Crispin stared at him for what felt like a very long time.

"What is it?" Rafe finally sighed.

"*Sera*?" his brother repeated, somewhat incredulously.

Rafe rolled his eyes. "It is a shortening of her name, *Cris*, nothing more. What of it?"

Crispin smothered a smile at the old nickname Rafe had called him as a child, but then his face was serious again. "Nothing at all. I just thought you and *Sera* had agreed she would be moved into her own home after the wedding."

Rafe pushed to his feet and paced away. He'd been just thinking that same thing not ten minutes before.

"These things take time, Crispin. I'm trying to find her the perfect accommodation." He stared out the window, thinking of her. "She deserves nothing less."

His brother made a sharp sound, and Rafe turned to find Crispin on his feet, staring at him. "Tell me you aren't developing feelings for Serafina."

Rafe clenched his fists at his sides, but it wasn't because Crispin was out of line. It was because he had just broached a subject Rafe had been trying very hard to avoid.

He cleared his throat. "Feelings? I suppose I am."

Crispin's face contorted with something akin to horror.

"I *like* her," Rafe explained. "I am developing respect for her. I'm constantly surprised by her. Those are all *feelings*, Crispin."

"Rafe."

"Crispin."

His brother shook his head slowly and his tone was gentle when he said, "Don't get caught up in romantic notions, Raphael. You two were thrown together by ridiculous circumstances, and she *is* beautiful. No one could deny that fact."

"She is far more than that," Rafe said softly, thinking of their conversation of two nights before when she had expressed a wish to be seen as more than her looks.

Crispin's lips pinched. "Perhaps she is, but she was never *your* choice. And you were never hers. You may swoop in like a white knight in some attempt to make her more comfortable, but don't mistake that notion for anything deeper."

Rafe stiffened. His brother was closer to the mark than he knew. Crispin didn't know what Serafina had suffered at their cousin's hands, nor did Rafe have any intention of sharing Sera's secret, even with his best friend and brother. But Crispin was still correct that Rafe *did* want to give her so much to make up for what she'd endured. She deserved that and so much more.

"You are being an idiot," he breathed, trying not to meet

his brother's seeing eyes.

Crispin shrugged. "Then I am an idiot. And you will do the best thing for everyone involved and get Serafina the house she wants for herself. You will move her out of your home. And you'll get a mistress to warm your bed."

Rafe gripped a fist at his side, but his tense posture didn't put Crispin off a bit.

"What about that widow…what was her name…Lady Braehold?" Crispin smiled. "You liked each other well enough."

Rafe scowled. "The viscountess and I had one night together, Crispin, over a month ago. And while it was certainly pleasurable, it wasn't something I am aching to repeat."

In fact, he wasn't aching to repeat anything with any woman. Except Serafina, who kept wending her way through his thoughts until he could see her perfectly when he closed his eyes.

"Then find someone else," Crispin encouraged. "I could make inquiries on your behalf."

Rafe arched a brow at the desperation that laced his brother's tone. "Why are you so set upon my finding a mistress? Why not let me have a few weeks to play husband before you hurtle me into some other woman's arms?"

Crispin ducked his head and drew a long breath before he replied, "I suppose I worry that you may get caught up in this ludicrous life that has been fitted over your own. That you will lose yourself."

Rafe stared at him, taking in his knitted brow, his tight frown, the concern in his bright eyes, so like Rafe's own. He reached out and squeezed Crispin's shoulder.

"You are worrying over nothing, I assure you. Things will be different, of course, now that this unexpected change has happened, but I have no intentions of abandoning you." Crispin's gaze snapped up and Rafe saw that he had struck upon the real issue. "Nor will I lose myself."

But as he made that promise to his brother, Rafe couldn't

help but wonder if he could keep it. After all, when he heard the words in his own voice, he recognized that they were a lie. He was already beginning to lose himself. To the title, to the future…and to the woman who had wound her way into his life and his bed.

Serafina folded her hands in her lap and tried very hard to make her right foot stop tapping anxiously beneath the hem of her gown.

"I don't want to be here," she murmured to herself as she looked at the door across the room. But escape was wishful thinking. Just as it always had been when dealing with Cyril or his family.

As if on cue, the door to the parlor opened and Cyril's mother swept in. The dowager duchess was draped in black from head to toe and her face was pale and drawn with grief.

In that moment, Serafina felt nothing but pity for Hesper and rose to offer her assistance to a seat. But as she neared her once-future mother-in-law, Cyril's mother recoiled, her glare sending a perfectly clear message of her continued hatred for Serafina.

"Good afternoon, my lady," Serafina said with a slight incline of her head.

"Good afternoon," the dowager said in an icy tone as she motioned Serafina back to her place. Once they were settled, Hesper looked Serafina up and down with a loud sniff. "Wearing color, I see."

Serafina flinched at the accusation. "My lady, once I married Rafe, your son became my late cousin. You know that the mourning rules for a cousin are different than those of a spouse. I am wearing violet, of course, out of a respect for Cyril."

Violet that she despised more than any other color she had

ever worn. She couldn't wait to pack her mourning gowns away for good and wear greens and blues and joyful reds again. They would certainly reflect her renewed spirit far better.

"*Rafe*," the dowager said, practically spitting the word out like it was a curse. "You call him Rafe."

Serafina shifted. She hadn't realized she had used Rafe's nickname so casually. It was difficult not to when she always thought of him that way. Rafe Flynn forever, regardless of what propriety dictated.

"If you feel that is flippant, I believe you know I mean my husband, His Grace, the Duke of—"

Suddenly Cyril's mother was on her feet. She swung, and her hand connected with Serafina's cheek with a hard slap that turned her head and left her face stinging. She staggered up and backed away, staring at Lady Hartholm in shock.

The dowager was panting, her eyes flashing hatred and violence and her hands shaking at her side.

"*Never* call him that," the dowager warned. "Not to me."

Serafina swallowed hard, folding her emotions carefully away, just as she had always been forced to practice with Cyril and his family.

"Why did you ask me here, my lady?" she asked, glad her voice didn't tremble too much.

Hesper's face contorted into another mask of hatred and pain. "I've heard you and my nephew have been parading around London, flaunting your ill-gotten gains at parties."

Serafina shook her head slowly. "I assure you that is not true. Yes, Rafe—"

She cut herself off. What should she call her husband if Lady Hartholm didn't like his nickname or his title?

"My husband and I," she began again, "have gone to one party and accepted invitations to two other events, one tonight and another Sunday afternoon. But we flaunt nothing, I assure you. We are currently a novelty due to the tragedy surrounding Cyril's death and the shock of his cousin inheriting both a title and a bride. I'm certain that interest will fade soon enough. My husband is only trying to maintain a dignified view of the title."

"Dignified," Lady Hartholm jeered as she paced to the window and stared out at the sunny garden. "What would *anyone* with the last name of Flynn know of dignity? That man and his family have been a blight on my husband and son for decades. That *he* would hold the title my son earned...it sickens me."

Serafina pursed her lips with displeasure. She so wanted to ask this woman how Cyril had *earned* anything in his life. By sitting around on his aristocratic backside? By abusing anyone he considered beneath him? By being a pompous know-it-all when he was quite possibly the most stupid man she had ever had the displeasure to meet?

Instead, she took a deep breath and tried to remind herself that his mother had loved him deeply. Almost to his detriment, for she had allowed him his every whim, which had never improved his personality.

But his loss had clearly destroyed this woman.

"I can imagine how difficult this must be for you," she said softly, not meeting Lady Hartholm's gaze for fear her true feelings would be clear. "But I cannot change what has already transpired. Is there anything my husband and I can do to ease this transition?"

Lady Hartholm spun around and speared Serafina with a dark and angry glare. "Ease this transition? Yes, my dear, I think there is something."

Serafina moved forward a step. "Of course—please tell me."

"*Die*," the other woman said. "You can both die like my son and let the title die with you. I would rather have it buried in the ground than belong to a Flynn like Raphael or Crispin. And you...you killed my son and you can rot with your new husband."

Serafina recoiled at the ugly, bitter words. "My lady!" she gasped. "I—I—"

But there was nothing to say in the face of such hate and

vitriol and madness. So she inclined her head slightly.

"I'm so very sorry for your loss, my lady. I will leave you."

She backed from the room, noting how Cyril's mother tracked her each and every move, her puffy eyes wide and wild. It was only in the foyer that Serafina turned her back and exhaled a breath she felt she had been holding for ages.

"My carriage, please," she managed to whisper to the dowager's butler.

She looked over her shoulder as she awaited his delivery, suddenly uneasy with the dowager being so close when her rage was a bubbling cauldron that felt ready to overflow.

"Your Grace," the butler said, pulling her from her thoughts and motioning for the front door and the carriage that had pulled up on the drive.

She nodded and moved out into the fresh air, which she gulped in like a woman starved. Her footman nodded as he opened his door.

"Tell Waters that I would like to go to Mrs. Richards'," she said with a shiver as she looked back up at the dowager house. "I need to see her."

CHAPTER FOURTEEN

"Great God, how unpleasant," Emma said, refreshing Serafina's long-cold tea with a shake of her head. "But that woman was always hateful, just like her horrible son. You are better free of them."

Serafina sighed. "But in a way, I'm not free at all. She is still the dowager, Emma. And Rafe's aunt. She can press her influence if she chooses to do so. And when she said we should die…"

"Are you worried?" Emma cocked her head. "Honestly, it sounds like the ravings of a woman crazed by grief and…well, simple nastiness."

"Perhaps," Serafina conceded, though the situation didn't feel that straightforward.

Emma shrugged. "She adored Cyril. She must feel his loss keenly."

"She does, I'm certain," Serafina agreed. "And that I'm getting something good from this arrangement chafes her even more."

Now Emma grinned. "Yes, let us get to the something good and stop talking about nasty Cyril's even nastier mother!"

Heat flooded Serafina's cheeks at the knowing look on Emma's face. "Emma!"

"Oh, come now. I have met the new duke and he is terribly handsome. But I know you are not keen on change, so the fact that you have moved yourself into his London townhouse rather than continuing to live at the ducal estate makes me think he is something *more* than you expected."

Serafina pushed to her feet and paced away from her friend to look out the parlor window. Thinking about Rafe was confusing, and nothing seemed to make it less so.

"Serafina," Emma said in an almost singsong tone. "You cannot pretend my statement away."

"I'm not trying to. I'm just thinking of a way to explain." Serafina sighed. "Rafe is different than I thought he would be when we met. When I met him, I was wary, both because he is related to Cyril and also because he *is* so terribly handsome. He knows it too. So I assumed he would be…well, perhaps just as bad as his cousin."

As she turned to face Emma, her friend leaned forward. "But?"

"But although he is a rake and a rogue and very aware of his looks and the power they grant him, he is also…"

She hesitated, because to say out loud the things she had seen in her husband seemed too intimate. And terrifying. Because once they were said out loud, she couldn't pretend she didn't feel them.

"You delight in leaving me in suspense," Emma huffed, though her eyes twinkled with teasing. "Or are you trying to find the words again?

Serafina covered her hot cheeks with icy fingers. "Rafe can be very kind. Even when he found out that I was not…*untouched*, he was never accusatory or hateful."

Emma's smile fell, and she flinched. "He realized it?"

She nodded. "He's experienced enough, of course, that he knew. I expected judgment and even that he might despise me, but it is Cyril who Rafe despises because…because I told him the truth."

"The truth?" Emma repeated. "You mean you told your husband that his cousin forced himself on you?"

Serafina nodded slowly.

Emma's mouth dropped open. "But you've never told—"

"Anyone but you." Serafina completed the sentence quietly. "I know. *That* is why we left the ducal home. Rafe didn't want me to have to endure the memories left there for me. It was an unexpected kindness he did not have to perform."

Emma's eyebrows lifted. "I see."

"I see? What does I see mean?" Serafina asked with a glare.

"I have known you for almost ten years," Emma said softly. "I know your expressions. And you have never looked so...*soft*...when you were speaking about a man."

"Soft?" Serafina barked out, panic suddenly gripping her.

Emma shook her head. "I only mean that it appears you actually like him. Is it possible that this union with Raphael Flynn is actually a good one?"

Serafina frowned. Once again, Emma had struck upon a topic that felt far too intimate to answer. Worse, it made Serafina think of things she didn't want to consider. Like how much Rafe had moved her in just a week of marriage.

"It's certainly better than any life would have been with Cyril," she finally admitted.

Emma arched a brow. "That isn't what I mean."

Serafina turned her face. She knew that. But she wasn't about to address the underlying implications of what Emma asked.

"I don't know what else you could mean," she said, pacing the room restlessly.

"Rafe is a kind man, he values your needs. And is he an— an—" Her friend blushed. "An attentive lover?"

Serafina felt hot as she thought about Rafe's touch. Attentive was not the word she would use when describing the magnificent things he did to her, woke in her.

"Yes," she whispered, unwilling to say more.

Emma smiled softly. "I'm glad. You deserve to have some pleasure after the pain you endured. But you also deserve love."

At that word, Serafina stiffened. "Don't be ridiculous," she snapped, more harshly than her friend deserved. "I may be very pleased that I have ended up with a husband I do not despise. However, I won't be so foolish as to allow for anything else to develop between us. Love is a weakness I cannot afford and do not desire."

Emma shook her head. "Oh, Serafina."

Serafina moved forward. "I adore you for wanting what you think is best for me, I truly do. But what has made you happy is not the same that will make me happy." She glanced at the clock on the mantel. "And now I must return home. The duke and I agreed to meet and discuss some of his duties after our calls this afternoon."

Emma looked as though she wanted to say more to her, but instead she simply sighed. "Very well. Let me escort you to the foyer."

Serafina nodded and when Emma had taken her feet, they walked arm and arm to the foyer. As they waited for her carriage, Serafina turned to face her best friend.

"I hope you don't think me harsh when it comes to my husband. It is only that our current arrangement is *not* permanent." She said it firmly, but in her heart she wasn't certain if the words were for Emma's sake or her own. It was a reminder she felt like she needed at present.

Emma squeezed her hands gently. "I do not think you are harsh, my dearest, sweetest friend. But I *do* think you are scarred by the past. I just hope you won't let the thickness of your skin keep you from allowing someone into your heart."

Serafina drew in a sharp breath at both Emma's words and the pity in her friend's eyes. But she was spared from responding when her carriage arrived. So she merely pressed a kiss to Emma's cheek, said goodbye and all but fled.

Rafe looked at the clock again and then pivoted to pace across the parlor. It was a quarter of an hour past the time he and Serafina had agreed upon to return to the house, and he found himself restless as he awaited her. Not just because he wanted to see her, but because of his earlier near-death experience. It made him nervous, but also made him want to be close to her.

As he moved to look at the clock yet again, he heard the rumble of horse hooves on the drive, and his heart leapt into his throat. It was the oddest of sensations, for he had never felt such anticipation when it came to being with a woman. Not just in bed with her, but *with* her.

The foyer door opened and shut, and Serafina talked briefly with Lathem.

"His Grace is in the green parlor, Your Grace. And tea is waiting there," he heard Lathem say.

Rafe was almost vibrating as Serafina opened the parlor door and stepped inside, a vision in her latest violet gown, her blonde hair framing her spectacularly beautiful face.

In that moment, he couldn't resist. He crossed the space between them in four long strides, wrapped his arms around her and kissed her.

She opened to him right away, giving a shuddering sigh as he sucked her tongue, splaying his hand across her trembling back and feeling her melt against him.

And yet, long before he was satisfied, she suddenly broke the kiss and stepped away, eyes wide and breath short.

"Good afternoon, my lord," she managed to squeak out.

He studied her expression closely. He could see the desire lit up in her eyes, burning there just as it burned within him, but as always, her hesitation also remained. No matter how much she allowed, she always held some part of her away from him. It shouldn't have mattered, and yet it did.

He drew in a long breath and didn't push her, even though he wanted to crowd into her space, wrap her against him, make her crave him until need wiped away reluctance.

"We have tea," he said, turning on his heel to motion to the set that had been placed on a table between the settee and a chair in front of the fire.

She nodded and moved forward. She took the settee and he settled into the chair to watch her pour a cup. Everything about her was graceful, from the way she lifted the pot to the way she tilted her head at him. She blinked a few times as her expression changed from one of serenity to something different, something pained.

"What is it?" he asked.

She shook her head. "We have been married for nearly a week and I don't know how you take your tea."

"We have been busy learning other things about each other."

She bit her lip. "But I should know this. After everything you've done for me, I should know this simple thing about you."

He sucked in a breath at how deeply upset she seemed to be by her lack of knowledge of such a silly thing. He covered her hand with his and whispered, "There is one way to remedy that, you know?"

She stared at him. "And what is that?"

"Ask me."

She gave him a wavering smile, and he could see she was gathering herself after her outburst. Finally, she cleared her throat and said, "How do you take your tea, Your Grace?"

He leaned back, driven to tease her a little if only to keep the conversation light. "Ah, the question at the core of every relationship in the empire."

Now she laughed, and the room lightened at the sound. "It is of vital importance, I agree."

He met her eyes, holding her stare for long enough that she shifted slightly and her pupils dilated.

"I like everything in my life to be sweet and creamy," he said softly.

Pinkness filled her cheeks at his double entendre, but to

her credit, she did not turn away. "Then it is sugar and milk for you, Your Grace?"

He nodded once. "Plenty of both. I doubt there can ever be enough."

She swallowed hard and then dropped three sugars and a generous dollop of milk into his tea. She stirred gently before she handed the cup over. He smiled when her hand trembled slightly. Then she quickly flavored her own beverage and took a gulping drink of it.

"And now you know something new about me," he said with a grin.

She nodded. "It seems I do." She turned her face and shifted with discomfort. "We have a party tonight," she rushed to add.

Her words were an obvious change of subject from the one he had been dancing around.

His pleasure faded, and he set his tea aside with a groan. "Again."

She shook her head, but she was smiling. "You know, Rafe, I have heard told from multiple sources that you actually *like* parties."

"I like parties with my friends. Parties where the alcohol is not watered down to nothing. Parties with laughter and genuine conversation."

"You are so dramatic, Your Grace."

He furrowed his brow. "Dramatic? I think not. I am stating what is an obvious difference between what I once was and what I am forced to be at present."

"I do understand the concept of being forced into a future, Rafe. Truly. And I realize you're still adjusting to everything that has happened in the past two weeks."

He watched her closely. She could so easily wipe her feelings away from her face, but did she still have them burning in her heart? Hidden where she had to confront them alone?

"I think you must still be adjusting as well, Sera," he said softly.

She turned away. "I was to marry a duke, and marry a duke, I did."

He frowned. "I would hope I am not interchangeable with my cousin."

She jolted, and her gaze slipped back to him. "No," she whispered. "You are most definitely a vast improvement." He opened his mouth to say more, but she didn't allow that and continued, "Either way, I promise you that you will find many of the things you just described at the parties we now attend."

He huffed out his breath, and she shook her head with a smile. "I challenge you to tell me you did not like Lord Aldridge."

"I'll grant you Aldridge, yes. He's a decent fellow."

"He's not the only one," Serafina insisted. "But you know that. You went to school with many of your new peers. I'm certain you didn't despise them all."

Rafe rolled his eyes. Damn, but she would use logic against him. "No, I admit I did not."

She looked him up and down. "In fact, I would wager that your charisma and charm made you a leader of many of the men who later took up titles."

"My charisma and charm, eh?" he repeated with a grin and leaned closer.

She blushed once more, and he couldn't help but think of her arching beneath him at the height of her pleasure, the same fetching color darkening her skin.

"Don't pretend you don't know your strengths," she said with a shake of her head. "And that you haven't used them in the past to get what and *who* you want."

He shrugged. "I suppose I have."

"And it isn't as if you are coming in off the streets to be duke. You have already lived your life as a man of vast wealth and reasonable power. This is only a shift in that dynamic."

"It is just so tedious, though," he groaned.

She met his gaze, and her one pointed look shamed him

with its underlying judgment. "I suppose your life as the idle rich might have been more fun. But you could do so much good if you will only try."

He watched her for a long moment. Although she maintained that serene expression that was a wall between them, he saw a flutter of desperation in her blue eyes.

"Doing good matters to you," he said. A statement, not a question.

She hesitated and he could see she struggled with trusting him to say more. "It does," she finally admitted. "I always knew it would be impossible to influence Cyril to be more than the bastard he was. If I was to do something for others, I would have to do it on my own, possibly even in secret, and with my pin money."

"That is probably correct," Rafe said with a scowl. "He was always a greedy ass."

She nodded. "Earlier you asked me not to equate you with your cousin, but you must see that I don't. I think you are so much more than him, Rafe. And I think if you dedicated yourself to this path, you could be even better."

He sighed. "It seems you have a plan."

Her eyes lit up at that small surrender. The expression was almost worth the pain that caused it.

"I do!" she admitted. "I want to give you a list of those I think might be the best to make friendships with at these gatherings. Men who are not idle, but involved in the betterment of those around them. Also, men of good nature who I think you will *like* if you get to know them."

"Very well. And then?"

"We will find a cause to support," she said with a shrug. "Also, we will need to visit your tenants. As you know, Cyril badly mismanaged and abused them. They'll need to meet you soon to assure them that we are not of the same ilk."

"We?" he said softly.

She blinked at his interruption and then she shook her head. "I mean you. *You.* Obviously I will assist you in any way

I can, but we will soon have separate lives."

He flinched at her blunt statement of that fact. Of course he knew that was her desire. He even fully understood why. And it should have made him happy to know that he could have such freedom in his future.

And yet it did not.

"You must also think of the future. Your children will thank you for setting their path in motion now."

"My children," he repeated softly. "*Our* children."

She clenched her hands in her lap. "Yes," she whispered.

He leaned in once more and lightly traced her hand with his thumb. She shivered at the contact, and he thought she might give in to him. She quaked a little, but then she jumped to her feet and paced away.

He watched her go, confusion mobbing him. This was the second time she had pulled away from him, and now he was beginning to wonder why she was so skittish.

"Where did you go today?" he asked as he settled back into his chair and watched her stop her pacing. Her back was ramrod straight and stiff before she turned to look at him.

"Why do you ask?"

He arched a brow at her reticence to speak to him. What was she hiding?

"Because you're nervous," he said, bringing the issue straight into the light. "And I want to know why. To help you, if I can."

She shifted, and again he saw her battling about whether to tell him the truth or not. She still didn't trust him. Would she ever?

Finally she sighed. "I went to see your Aunt Hesper, Rafe. And her rage was all but overpowering."

CHAPTER FIFTEEN

Serafina didn't know exactly what reaction she *thought* Rafe would have to her admission about seeing his aunt, but his casual shrug wasn't it.

"Aunt Hesper has always been a dreadful old biddy," Rafe said. "Why did you go there?"

Serafina blinked, not entirely certain she understood the question. "She asked me."

He draped his elbows over his knees with a bark of laughter that made her jump. "Now that Cyril is dead and you are duchess, you are not a marionette on her strings. Refuse her if she asks you again, especially since she is unpleasant."

Serafina stared at him. Rafe always did what he liked, when he wanted to do it. His wealth and lack of responsibilities had allowed him to do as he wished for a long time. And the idea that she could adopt some of his laissez-faire attitude brought a thrill through her entire body.

But he had not seen Cyril's mother. He had not heard the venom in her tone. Serafina still shuddered when she thought of it.

"You don't seem to be reassured," he said, exploring her face with those all-too-seeing bright blue eyes of his.

She shook her head. "I am not. What I saw today with the dowager went beyond a woman venting her grief. It was different. She was...was..."

He cocked an eyebrow. "Was?"

She swallowed. "Enraged. Violent, even."

That made him straighten up. "Are you afraid she might harm you?"

She jolted at the sudden concern to his tone. He had been dismissive until he asked that question, but now he was on high alert. For her.

"No," she said. "Well, at least not first. I'm more afraid she might harm *you*."

After all, Hesper's vitriol had been mainly focused on the destruction of *her* family's title by Rafe. Her eyes had glittered with rage and the way she said that Rafe should die…it hadn't felt like an idle threat.

He smiled, his earlier tense posture returning to his normal relaxed one, but she saw something flicker in his eyes.

"Me?" He laughed. "I cannot even imagine she would attempt such a thing, Sera."

"Then why do you look like you're secretly pondering something?" she asked.

His eyes widened. "What would there be to ponder?"

She pursed her lips. "I don't know exactly. There have been a few troubling things since we met, though."

"Such as?"

He wasn't making this easy, and she huffed out her breath.

"The horse with the shard of metal in her bridle the first day we rode together, for one. And the mysterious kitchen fire in this very house."

He arched an incredulous brow, and she shook her head at how foolish she must seem to him. "I realize there are only two occurrences and—"

She cut herself off when he turned his face slightly.

"What is it?" she asked. "Twice you have looked *guilty*."

He cleared his throat. "I will have to remember your ability to read me in the future."

She folded her arms. "*Rafe*."

He met her gaze. "I was almost hit by a carriage today."

Serafina staggered back as her heart seemed to twist into a painful knot of terror in her chest.

"Sit down. You're pale," he said, rising from his own seat.

She held up her hands to ward him off. "No. I won't sit. Rafe, why didn't you tell me this as soon as I arrived home?"

She took an unbidden step toward him, suddenly wanting to touch him and reassure herself that he was whole, but she forced herself to stay still.

"Are you hurt?" she asked.

"No," he said softly. "I'm fine. Serafina, I can see how you might think these things are related, but it is far more likely that they are merely badly timed coincidences than some deeper plot."

"Despite the fact that they have all occurred in a span of less than two weeks?" she asked, even though she desperately wanted to believe him.

He frowned. "The kitchen fire was likely because my house was being closed up. My staff didn't expect us here that morning and mistakes happen under those circumstances. As for the carriage today, it could very well have been an inexperienced driver or a foxed one who had been harangued by his employer to hurry."

What he said did help, but she couldn't fully shake her anxieties. "How do you explain the horse with the metal?"

He shook his head. "My stable master doesn't know how that could have happened, I admit, but I still think it more likely to have been an accident or an equipment failure rather than a conspiracy to hurt me launched by my *aunt*, of all people."

"You didn't see her. She was very serious in her words and actions," Serafina whispered, although she couldn't help but feel more at ease with how dismissive he was at the thought.

"I promise you, Sera, she has been railing about how our family should be stricken from the earth for at least a decade. Ever since Crispin seduced Miss Genevieve Kitterich, a once famous actress, and made a splash across the gossip rags for six months."

Serafina raised both eyebrows. "How old was Crispin then? Eighteen?"

He smiled that beautiful, mischievous, lopsided grin. "You know what they say. Notorious Flynns. Please put your mind at ease. And take my advice—you do not ever have to see her again."

He had been holding back, but now he crossed the room toward her, his gaze suddenly predatory despite the lazy quality to his movements. He was like a cat that had all day to play with the mouse.

She shivered at the thought despite herself.

"But I do appreciate your concern on my behalf," he said as he reached her.

He caught her elbow and inched her forward until she leaned against his muscular frame. She could hardly breathe now—everything around them seemed to fade and the only important thing left was him. Them. This.

His smile widened as he dipped his head to capture her lips with his. Earlier she had been able to push him away when she thought of Emma's accusation that Serafina might come to care for him, but now?

He was far too intoxicating a draw not to surrender. She did so with a muffled moan and lifted her arms around his neck to draw him even closer. He guided her toward the settee she had abandoned a few moments earlier. He lowered her back against the pillows gently and then stood to stare down at her.

"I'll lock the door," he said, his voice rough and low as it danced down her spine.

She stared up at him, unable to keep her eyes from going wide. "Here? Now?" she asked, hoping he would understand what she meant.

His widening grin told her he did. "Oh, my darling, there is still so much more to teach you, I can see."

She blushed at his gentle words and stared as he crossed

the room and turned the key to grant them the privacy he required. When he turned back, he began to shed his jacket, loosen his cravat, and she sat up to observe him divest himself of propriety and become the lover she had begun to crave.

Crave, but not quite touch.

So far, their encounters had been entirely driven by him. His tutelage had been powerful and wild and gentle, but he had never demanded she give him anything more than her surrender.

When he tugged his shirt free of his trousers and yanked it over his head to toss to the floor, she wanted to give him so much more. She found herself wanting to *touch* him the way he did her. Not just to make certain he wasn't hurt by the accident he had described, but to please him.

Despite her unhappy memories of Cyril stealing what he wanted, she still had the need to gift it to this man.

He leaned over her, his bare chest now within hand's—and mouth's—reach. She extended her fingers and pressed a palm to the bare skin, and he hissed a sound of pleasure at her touch. He tensed as if to move closer, and she pushed him back out of reflex.

He froze immediately. "Do you not want this?" he asked, his voice strained.

She forced her gaze to flicker from his bare chest to his face, and the heat that flooded her cheeks was unstoppable.

"I do want you very much. But I—"

She cut herself off, unable to say the words. Instead, she looked at his half-naked body again and curved her flat hand to stoke her fingertips against his pectoral muscle.

He cleared his throat with difficulty. "You want to explore?"

She nodded. "I do. Does it make me a wanton in your eyes?"

His face twisted in displeasure. "It makes you human. Ripe and filled with desire. That is *nothing* to be ashamed of, Serafina."

He shifted to sit down on the settee beside her instead of pinning her there with his superior weight. "I am yours to command," he said softly. "I'll submit to your desires as long as I can."

"And when you can't?" she asked, her gaze flickering to his.

He smiled. "I may lose control at some point and need to be inside of you. But I assure you I will give you more than fair warning that the moment is coming."

She shivered. Now that he had given her permission to explore, she wasn't sure what to do. She had never had carte blanche, nor had she wanted it with Cyril. He had forced and demanded the way she touched him and she had given in because the alternative was far worse.

She had never pictured herself in the situation where exploring a man's body would be...enticing.

But it was. She shoved the past aside, hid it as deep as she could manage and focused her attention back to Rafe. He was what mattered now. What she wanted in this charged moment.

She angled herself on the settee to face him, leaning in until his body heat wended its way around her, seeped into her. She saw a few bruises that she hadn't noticed when he was standing. Purple marred his left arm and side.

"Rafe—"

He shook his head. "I promise you, I'm fine. Though if you wish to verify that statement, I give you permission, Doctor Serafina."

She smiled at his teasing, but her hand shook as she reached out to press it, once again, to his bare chest. She felt his muscles tense as her fingers glided over his flesh, watched his cheeks suck in as he took a sharp breath.

"Why is your skin so tanned?" she whispered as she traced the lines of each defined ridge along his chest and stomach.

His eyes went wide at the question, but he quickly smiled. "At my estate in Sussex, I do what I like. Including ride and work outside without the confines of a shirt." His smile broadened. "And I also take the occasional naked dip in my lake. Which leads to a bit of color on a man's skin when the weather allows for sun."

Serafina's mouth dropped open in shock at that admission. "I—you—"

He laughed, revealing such straight white teeth, his eyes lighting up with life and mirth. He had never been so utterly attractive, and she actually jolted with how much she wanted to lean into him, weave into him...never let him go. It was as if he offered her escape from the confines of her past, that with him she could find a way to be something so much more than what she'd been forced to be so far.

But if she stayed, she feared she might come to care for him. That was a terrifying notion for so many reasons.

"You look as though I've told you I own an elephant," he said, dragging her from her troubling thoughts.

She shook her head. "I feel I would be less surprised by that admission now. I've just never known a person who was so utterly free as you have been."

He shrugged, but his bright eyes continued to hold hers mercilessly. "Would you like to hear about it? Hear about my past?"

She hesitated. She had shared her own secrets, in part because of necessity. But if he told her his, would that bind them further? Complicate a relationship that was already feeling more and more complicated each day?

Perhaps, but she found herself wanting the answers anyway.

"Yes," she whispered.

He leaned in until their faces were but inches apart. "I will tell you everything you want to know. But only if you keep touching me. I cannot have you distracted from what you so desired."

She worried her lip with her teeth for a moment and then nodded. "Very well."

In truth, his words might distract both of them a fraction

from what she was doing to his body. Wouldn't it make these acts less intimate?

She pressed her palms flat against him and pushed him back on the couch until he half-reclined on the pillows. He grinned once more.

"As you well know, my father was the brother of Cyril's father. The second son of a duke. But what many forget is that they had very different mothers. Cyril's father's mother died when he was just a boy, and very quickly their father remarried and had several more children with his new wife, including my father. Cyril's father always hated my grandmother. He was quite a few years older than his brother, so he was away at school. The second marriage was a love match. They went to the country, they laughed. Apparently my grandfather was quite a different man with my grandmother."

Serafina listened, but she stared at Rafe's upper body, stroking over his broad shoulders, his hard chest, his toned stomach. Occasionally his voice cracked as she touched him one way or another, but otherwise, he didn't try to interfere with what she did.

"That would explain the rift between your two parts of the family," she said softly.

He nodded. "Cyril's father despised us, and he taught his wife and his son to do the same. *My* father, on the other hand, was sad that he and his brother were estranged, but focused his life on the pleasures it contained. He gambled and drank, occasionally to excess and in inappropriate places. He rode horses and raced phaetons, always too fast. He taught my brother and sister and I that life was a feast worth partaking in."

"Those Notorious Flynns," she mused with a laugh.

"So very notorious," he admitted. "There are so many stories, Serafina, you will be shocked once you hear them all. As for my father, there was only one place he refused to stray into wildness, and that was with women. He adored my mother—it was another love match."

Serafina jerked her head up to look at him. He was staring at her, but it didn't seem to be because she was touching him intimately.

She lowered her head, determined to distract him from whatever thoughts were in his head. Gently, she dragged her tongue over his salty flesh. He stiffened beneath her and his hand came up to rest against the back of her head.

She focused now, tasting his shoulder, nipping along his collarbone, and finally she wrapped her lips around his flat nipple and sucked gently.

He grunted out a low, needy sound of pleasure, and she smiled against his flesh. There was something very powerful in what she was doing. For this moment, at least, he was at her mercy.

And she wanted to test how far he would allow her to go before he could not speak, before he would snatch control back and take her.

"Please continue," she murmured against his flesh.

His breath was heavier now and he shook his head. "I can scarcely recall what I was talking about."

"Your father teaching his children that life was a feast," she offered before returning her lips to his flesh and doing a bit of feasting of her own. He smelled so clean, so male, and he tasted just as good.

Rafe's voice was strained as he said, "We were encouraged to play as children, to laugh. We ate as a family, and although we had governesses, my parents raised us without separating us from their lives. My father taught me to gamble. He took my brother and me to races. And when we began to be associated with scandals, he only laughed. He never helped us to escape our troubles—he told us we had to learn to do that ourselves, but he never saw the harm in a good time. Even a good time gone slightly wrong."

Serafina lifted her head from his tempting flesh and stared at him. "That sounds heavenly."

He nodded. "It was."

For a moment, she was overcome with jealousy for his happy childhood. And with a deep desire to give her own children such unconditional and unconventional lives.

But she and Rafe would be different. Theirs was not a love match, after all. They would have children, but there was a vast difference in how they would be raised. After all, she could not picture Rafe taking them from her, legal right to do so or not. So while they would be exposed regularly to their father, it wouldn't be the same.

She shook her head and instead put her thoughts back to his body. He still wore his trousers, and she could see his erection pressing against those. She wanted more of him now.

Blushing, she turned her face so he wouldn't fully see her expression when she said, "Will you remove the rest of your clothing, please?"

He said nothing and didn't move for so long that she forced herself to look up at him. He was staring at her, a fire burning bright in his eyes that let her know he was on the edge of taking back control. Of taking her.

"Rafe?" she whispered.

He nodded slowly. "Of course, Your Grace. Your wish is my command."

She slid away from him to allow him to get to his feet and watched as he removed his boots, tossing them aside without breaking the intensive eye contact he had made with her. He kept it as he began to unfasten his trousers, slowly, tortuously, until she all but licked her lips in a desire to see him fully naked.

Finally he pushed the remainder of his clothing away and stood before her, naked and proud. He was aroused by her earlier touch and his hard member jutted up against his stomach. She had never thought she would crave that instrument, but oh, how she did.

She couldn't help herself. She reached out and touched him with the tips of her fingers.

He sucked his breath in with a gasp of what sounded like

pain, and she snatched her hand away with a blush.

"Did I hurt you?" she asked.

He shook his head. "God, no. When you touch me, it is anything but painful. My cock is merely sensitive."

She stared at him again. "Your cock?"

"Yes. It could be considered a vulgar term, but I prefer it to many other ways a man refers to his penis."

"What other ways?" she asked.

He gave a wicked smile. "A rod, a whore's pipe, a lady's delight, a pego, a plug tail. There are more, but you understand."

She shivered at the blunt conversation, but couldn't tear her eyes away. He stood before her, hard as steel but cloaked in velvet flesh. She knew what he could do with his *cock*. She knew what pleasure it could bring.

"Fascinating," she murmured as she reached out to touch him again. She just traced the length of him with the edge of her fingernail and this time didn't pull away when he gulped in breath.

She briefly recalled the things Cyril had forced her to do, this time not with a shudder, but with the question if Rafe might like the same attention.

There was only one way to find out. She wrapped her hand around him and gently stroked him once. He stiffened with a low moan, and she looked up at him. She didn't have to ask if he liked what she did. His expression told her he did, very much. And the fact that she had brought him pleasure made her want to give him more.

She stroked him again, paying attention to the sounds he made, the sweat that broke out above his lip, the way his body jerked toward her. She increased the rate of her hand, then decreased it in accordance to his reaction.

It was odd how her body reacted to the things she did to him. Although she was fully clothed, not at all stimulated, her sex began to tingle. Her nipples hardened beneath her gown and her breath came short. It was exciting to please him. There was power in knowing that she had some small control over his feelings and reactions.

She wanted more. Her breath caught as she considered the "more" she knew about. An act she had never liked, but now, as she stared at Rafe's swollen cock, it didn't seem so very repugnant.

Leaning in, she licked her lips, swallowed hard and then closed her mouth around the head of his member.

He let out a cry of surprise that was garbled with pleasure.

"Serafina!" he barked, his fingers tangling tighter in her hair.

She withdrew carefully, still sliding her hand over him. "Do you not want this?"

Perhaps she had been misled that it was an act men desired. Although when she thought of Rafe's mouth on her so intimately, it made her shiver in pleasure, not disgust.

"No, your mouth is amazing. But you don't have to do this," he said, his voice broken with need.

"I want to pleasure you," she whispered. "I've never felt such a drive before, but with you...I want to do this."

She saw him battling within himself. The gentleman who wanted to protect her from whatever she had suffered in her past resisted, but the man who wanted her touch drove for more.

She was determined to reach the second and force the first away for a while.

Covering him with her mouth again, she sucked on his cock. His knees buckled a fraction, and he gripped her shoulder for purchase. She stroked her mouth over him, teasing him with her tongue, sucking to make him shudder, and all the while her heartbeat increased. She realized she was rotating her hips against the couch, grinding for her own pleasure as she worked him toward his.

Suddenly he pulled away, popping free of her mouth and fist and staggered back, his face red and his eyes wide and wild.

"Rafe—" she began in protest.

He didn't let her finish. He yanked her to her feet and crushed his mouth to hers, his hands rough as they roamed over her body. He sat down on the settee he had abandoned and pulled her over him, helping her open her legs and shove her skirts up around her hips.

His fingers slipped into the slit in her drawers and he touched her sex. He smiled.

"Already wet," he murmured. "Good, so good."

She could hardly listen—she was too busy reaching between them, finding his hardness and rotating to line up their eager bodies. Slowly, she lowered herself over him, and they sighed in tandem at the joining of their bodies.

"Move over me," he grunted, gripping her hips through her bundled gown. "Oh God, move, Serafina."

She rolled her hips, clinging to his bare shoulders as she struggled to find a rhythm that made her moan. Once she found it, she arched faster and faster, stroking her sex with his, building toward orgasm that, when it came, utterly shattered her.

She couldn't help but cry out as the waves of pleasure mobbed her. Her hips moved out of control, her release pushed on by the way Rafe lifted his body into hers insistently. Finally, he let out a cry and she felt him pump into her, soothing her sensitive flesh and bringing on a final end to the spasms of release that had held her hostage since the first flutterings of her orgasm.

She collapsed forward, pressing her forehead to his, her breath heavy and her body weak with him. He gathered her close, cradling her in his arms, stroking her sweaty hair, whispering mindless words of pleasure and sweetness until they could both think again.

"Rafe?"

He opened his eyes and looked at Serafina, still bundled at his side on the narrow settee, her hair cockeyed, her cheeks pink, never more beautiful than she was in that moment.

"Yes," he purred, still reeling from their powerful sexual encounter.

"Do you miss your father?"

He stiffened at the question and allowed the painful emotions that it inspired wash over him. Sometimes it was good to feel them. It let him know he was alive, that he had loved.

"Yes," he answered after the moment had passed. "Every day, I miss him. Never more so than when Cyril died and this duty passed to me."

"Because he would have counseled you?"

He laughed. "Because he would have been the one to take it," he teased.

She smiled. "I can imagine your mother would have been heartily surprised when he was expected to marry me."

His laughter grew at her unexpectedly cheeky quip. "Yes, it would have been a very awkward breakfast table." They laughed together and he pulled her closer, smoothing her hair as he shook his head. "No, of course it is his opinion I would have valued. Although you are proving to be a far better guide about what to do as a new duke than he likely would have been."

Her cheeks darkened with a blush. "So far I'm only dragging you to balls. Not an auspicious beginning."

"And reminding me that with my new power comes unavoidable responsibility and also an opportunity to do something of value in this world. I would say that is quite promising."

She seemed to ponder what he had said for a moment. "I envy the childhood you describe, Rafe. Not for the freedom you had, though that does sound like great fun, but for the family. I was never a part of something like that. It is a lovely thought."

She turned her face, but he still saw her profile. There was sadness in her face, regret, but also strength and intelligence. He wanted to wash away the first feelings. He wanted to keep her from ever feeling alone again.

And it was in that moment that he realized he had begun to do exactly what he'd vowed never to do.

He was falling in love with his wife.

CHAPTER SIXTEEN

Rafe leaned his head against the glass of the carriage window and stared across the vehicle at her forlornly. "I do not want to do this."

She laughed at his sad puppy dog expression. "You have said that for two balls and one garden party and now this!"

"And *that* is exactly why I don't want to do this. I am exhausted by people." He folded his arms in an open challenge of her.

Her laughter grew because this playful exchange seemed to be the norm between them. As if he were the petulant student and she the stern teacher bound to drag him through his education.

"You know it is only your family we are going to see," she reminded him.

"Who is more exhausting than my mother, brother and sister?" he asked.

"My father," she offered softly, the teasing suddenly leaving her voice as she thought of the fact that her father had been invited to the gathering tonight as well.

It was a kindness of Rafe's mother to include him in this family event, but one she wished Mrs. Flynn had not bestowed. She had not seen him since her wedding, now almost two weeks ago. Sadly, she had not missed him despite the fact this was the longest time they had been parted.

"Serafina," Rafe began softly, reaching across the space between them.

She forced herself to smile to lighten the mood. "I only mean that it is *I* who should be hesitant about tonight, not you."

He held her gaze for a moment, then leaned back against the leather seat. She could see he wanted to discuss the situation with her, but he returned to teasing her instead to make her more comfortable.

"If you are having second thoughts, we could go home." His smile turned wicked. "I could think of better things to do together."

She blushed, as she always blushed when she thought of making love with him.

"But you always want to do the same thing," she said with a shake of her head. "We have done that *thing* plenty of times. Creativity is key, Rafe."

She expected him to smile, but instead the desire they had been dancing about in the conversation suddenly flared higher, and there wasn't a hint of joking in his tone when he growled, "You have no idea of the heights of my imagination when it comes to you."

She dropped her gaze into her lap because the intensity between them felt like fire, and playing with fire was something dangerous and undeniable. The fact was, she might say they had made love enough, but she didn't feel like it was true at all. To her utter shock, since she had been allowed to play with Rafe, touch him, stroke him while he did nothing but allow her power, her desire for him had only grown. She had given up sleeping in her own chamber at all, forgoing privacy for heady nights of passion with him.

But it would come to an end soon enough. They had made their joint appearances to show the *ton* that they were wed and not a subject of continued scandal. Rafe was looking for a home for her. She couldn't imagine it would be more than a week or two before he found something and had it readied for her.

And then they would only have their friendship between them and occasional times of passionate joining to create their sons and daughters. These first weeks of their marriage would become nothing but a joyful memory for her. She would go on with her life, free of confusing emotions, free to obligation to do as she was told, free as she had always wanted to be.

At least, that was what she told herself when she allowed herself to think of the future. It never made her feel better.

"You have become very serious," he said. "Has something fascinating developed in your lap or has your mind fled my company?"

She glanced up. "I'm sorry. I didn't mean to float away."

"As long as you come back," he said, and now he did take her hand, squeezing gently before he released her with a sigh. "We are turning up the drive."

She nodded. "Indeed we are."

"Would you like to present a united front to the families? It could very well be our best chance of survival."

She smiled and nodded, but inside his comment stung a fraction. A united front with Rafe was only a dream. It wouldn't last.

And that had begun to trouble her more and more, despite the fact that it was entirely her own choice.

Rafe found himself tracking Serafina's every move as she stood across the parlor with Crispin. Despite his younger brother's hesitations about Rafe's wife, it seemed she had weaved a spell over him.

Just as she had done with him. Rafe had realized he was in love with the woman across the room not a week before and had said nothing about that to anyone. Perhaps he had hoped the intense emotion would fade, that he would discover it was only the byproduct of passionate love-making.

But it wasn't. The more distance he moved from that initial discovery of his heart, the stronger the feeling became. There was no denying it now. He *was* in love with Serafina.

And she wanted nothing to do with love or even a shared future with him. The terms of their bargain had not changed for her, even though they had been altered irrevocably for him.

He frowned and forced himself to look away from his wife. Instead, he found her father standing across the room with his mother. Jonathon McPhee talked on what seemed to be an endless stream, and his mother briefly glanced across the room toward Rafe. Her expression was a combination of both apology and a desire to be saved from another moment with the man.

He doubted McPhee would be invited to more family gatherings. And yet, Rafe's rage toward Serafina's father and his willingness to trade on his daughter's future was unmitigated. At some point, he *would* have it out with the man.

"Excuse me, Your Grace, have you seen my oldest brother? Raphael is his name."

Rafe turned toward the voice that asked the question and smiled down at his sister, Annabelle. He could see the concern in her brown eyes.

"Don't tell me you think I am so changed since becoming duke," he said, almost happy to stop thinking about Sera and her father, though this new topic was no more comfortable.

"I'm not certain it is becoming duke that is changing you," his sister said softly. "I approached you and all the laughing playfulness was gone from your face. I saw a very serious man in my brother's body."

He shrugged. "Isn't it you who is always telling Crispin and me to be more staid? To stop cultivating notoriety for our family name with our recklessness?"

She frowned slightly and then nodded. "I suppose I have said that. And meant it when it was said. But I didn't intend for you to lose yourself in the process."

He let his gaze slip to Serafina once more. Crispin had

gone to refresh her after-supper drink and she stood alone in the middle of the parlor. She was utterly beautiful, completely irresistible.

"I actually think I may have found myself, Annabelle, not lost myself."

Annabelle stared at him, then followed his gaze toward his wife. Her eyes went wide and she suddenly grasped his arm and began to drag him from the room.

"Mama, I am going to show Raphael my new pianoforte," she called out in a singsong tone no one in the world could have trusted.

Their mother glanced at the two of them and her face still sought escape from her companion. "Perhaps you could—"

Annabelle cut her mother off. "We'll return in a moment."

As they exited the room, Rafe made an attempt to shake off his sister's remarkably powerful grip, but she continued to drag him away.

"Mama was trying to get rid of Serafina's awful father," he said as she all but flung him into the music room and shut the door behind them.

"I know what she was trying to do, but I cannot have a conversation with you while *that man* is in the room." Annabelle straightened her skirts. "I will make it up to her when I return and insert myself in their conversation as respite."

Rafe looked around. "And what do you need to talk to me in private about? Because I assume you know I don't give a damn about your pianoforte."

Annabelle waved her hand. "Neither do I."

Rafe frowned. His sister was vastly talented in her music but dismissed it regularly. But that was a topic for another conversation.

"What is it?"

"I could ask *you* the same thing." Annabelle folded her arms. "You were mooning over Serafina a moment ago. *Mooning* Rafe! I've never seen you do such a thing."

Rafe tensed. Was he so obvious? But he was not about to talk about this with his youngest sibling.

"Mooning? You must be daft." He rolled his eyes.

She caught his arm and shook it. "Don't lie to me Raphael Flynn. I'm not stupid. I know what I saw."

"She's a very pretty woman," he said, minimizing everything he thought or felt about Serafina. "And I do desire her. Perhaps *that* is what you see."

Annabelle made a face at his mention of desire, but she didn't seem stopped by that topic she hated. "Rafe."

He turned and walked away, passing by all the instruments his sister was so talented at playing. He stopped before the aforementioned new pianoforte and stared blankly at its shiny surface.

"Truly, you are seeing phantoms."

She said nothing for a moment, and Rafe dared to believe he had been saved from her intrusion. But then she slowly crossed the room, turned him toward her and reached up to cup his cheeks.

"You know I adore you, despite any desire I may have had about calming your wild nature for my own selfish motives." She smiled up at him. "Obviously there is something going on, and who else will you talk to? Crispin wrecks himself every night, creating scenarios about your unhappiness of being forced into your title and marriage. And Mama will meddle out of a desire for your good."

Rafe pursed his lips. Both those statements were utterly true.

"You are left with me," Annabelle said softly. "I only want to know what is in your heart now, so that I can help you."

"You can't help me," he groaned.

She frowned. "Then allow me to simply be a confidante. I will not judge, not you and not her."

Rafe pulled away from her gentle hands and sighed as he stared down at her. Annabelle wasn't like her brothers. While they went wild, she had tried to cultivate whatever she thought a lady should be. Sometimes he saw a glint in her eyes that spoke to her untamed Flynn nature, but very rarely did she express it.

And yet he knew she loved him as deeply as she had just claimed. And since she was of an age with Serafina, and trustworthy… she might be correct that she was the best person with whom to discuss this thorny problem.

He cleared his throat. "I—I am in love with my wife."

It was the first time he had said it out loud and he waited for it to ring false in the air around him. It never did. In fact, it had never felt so true.

She leaned forward. "I beg your pardon?"

"You will have me declare it again? Very well. I am in love with Serafina."

Her smile broadened. "Oh, Rafe, that is wonderful. I wish you every happiness—"

"She is not in love with me," he interrupted with a frown. "In fact, she is insistent that we are going to have separate lives as soon as I can find her a new home to flee to."

Annabelle stared at him with an unreadable expression for what felt like an eternity. Then she shocked him by tilting her head back and letting out a peel of laughter that echoed in the room just like the music that was normally played there.

Rafe glared at her.

"I'm happy my pain causes you so much pleasure," he ground out. "You are a heartless thing."

His sister reached out to touch his arm with one hand while she wiped away tears of laughter with the other.

"You misunderstand. I find no amusement in your pain." She tried to catch her breath. "It's just that…that…"

She trailed off with more laughter and Rafe huffed out his breath and turned away. She followed him, gathering her composure along the way

"I'm sorry, I'm sorry. I only find it funny because I don't think I've ever known a woman who hasn't looked at you and had little fantasies about a future as your loving wife. All my friends even had designs to tame you and love you for all time. For years, I had to listen to so many of them rant on and on. It was disgusting."

Rafe's eyes went wide. "What?"

"Oh yes, taming a rake is a very common fantasy, I assure you. And now you find someone and she has no interest in taming you at all." Another giggle bubbled from her lips. "No wonder she appeals to you—she is indeed a singular creature."

He swallowed. "She is that. But her reticence isn't the appeal, I assure you. She is…she is…"

"Beautiful," his sister suggested.

Rafe frowned. "Yes, of course, but there is so much more to her. She has a wire of strength that weaves through her in everything she does. She has endured hardship with Cyril that—"

He cut himself off as anger mobbed him, and gripped his fists at his sides.

Annabelle paled and all her laughter vanished in an instant. Her voice was a mere whisper when she asked, "Was our cousin very cruel?"

"More than you could ever imagine," Rafe managed through gritted teeth. "As was her own family in turns. And yet she has retained a light, a humor, an intelligence, a desire to better those around her that is admirable to her core."

Annabelle's face softened. "If what you say is true, and I have no doubt that it is, I think I shall like my sister-in-law a great deal."

"You will," Rafe agreed. "The two of you have so much in common, actually." He sighed. "It could be so perfect, except she doesn't want a life with me."

"Why?"

He shook his head. "That cruelty we spoke of earlier, it scarred her inside. She wants freedom from being forced into a role or a life or a marriage."

Annabelle nodded. "I can understand her desire to escape her past and the expectations it entails."

Rafe frowned at the way she said those words, as if they were something more she had in common with his bride, but she continued before he could question her further.

"So what do you wish to do?"

He sucked in a breath. "I want to win her. To woo her. To give her a reason to stay."

Annabelle blinked up at him. "And do you truly intend to love her for all time? Is this something more than a passing fancy because she is all but unattainable?"

He nodded without hesitation. "My love for her has only grown since I admitted it to myself. I think of no one but her, in a way I have never experienced with even the most talented of lov—"

Annabelle held up a hand with a shudder. "Please don't say lovers. It is too much for an innocent sister to bear. I don't want to hear of your conquests from you, news of them has circulated to me over the years more often than I would have liked."

"There will be no more of those, I assure you," he said.

"Good. You've had plenty." She frowned.

He shook his head. "Crispin would disagree."

"Crispin has had plenty too," Annabelle growled. "And you must realize he may fight you on this. You settling down seems to be a threat to him, although despite that feeling, he appears to like your wife very much."

"He wants to protect me." Rafe sighed.

"Don't allow him to protect you into heartbreak," she said.

"And that is your only advice on the matter?"

She laughed. "No. I am an endless fount of advice on all topics."

He rolled his eyes. "Of that, I am fully aware. Let us start with this one, shall we?"

"Very well. I assume based on your friendly exchanges the few times I have seen you together that Serafina does not despise you. She merely resists a future together thanks to her fears, yes?"

"You are right. We get along splendidly, actually."

"You talk, you share more than mere, uh, physical connection?" His sister blushed almost purple.

He nodded. "Yes."

"Then you are beginning to recognize what she values, both in others and what she wishes to be valued for."

He thought of her claim that no one ever saw her for more than her beauty. "Yes."

"Gift her those things. Strive to be a man she can admire. And admire *her* for her true gifts rather than whatever others see her to be. If a man does that..." She dipped her head. "Well, a woman could not help but fall in love with him."

"That's actually very good advice," Rafe said, examining his sister's face closely. "Is it from personal experience?"

Annabelle turned away. "No one has ever done those things for me. It is only a lifetime lived as a woman that gives me an insight."

He leaned in and caught her hand briefly. "You deserve no less than what you describe, you know."

She shrugged. "But this is not my story, Rafe. You focus on your future and I will focus on myself when the time is right."

He frowned. There was something in his sister's face, a vague expression of...*desperation* that made him want to press her further on the subject, but she turned away from him and walked toward the door without allowing his prying.

"Now, come with me. As you know, Mama requires saving from Serafina's God-awful father. We shouldn't keep her waiting any longer."

He trailed behind her back toward the parlor where the rest of the party was gathered, his thoughts a jumbled mess of Annabelle's advice and mounting plans of how to make his wife *his*.

CHAPTER SEVENTEEN

Crispin Flynn laughed and Serafina couldn't help but stare. There was so much about this man that put her to mind of Rafe and yet she could see the differences too. Crispin had a harder edge than his brother, a darker intensity. And while he was certainly nothing but polite to her, she was well aware he was feeling her out, determined to protect Rafe.

She couldn't hate him for it. In fact, she rather envied that her husband had so many people in his life who cared so deeply for him.

"And how do you think my brother takes to being duke?" Crispin asked.

She felt the edge to his tone and straightened up out of a protective reflex. "I think he is adjusting well enough, though he will never love his position."

"Do you aim to change that?" Crispin asked softly. "To seduce him into embracing this new future?"

She blinked at the double meaning of the question. "I doubt I have the power to seduce a man as intelligent and strong as Raphael into anything," she replied evenly. "But if I can ease the transition for him, I will certainly do anything I can to help."

"Parties seem to be the main thrust of the plan."

She knew it was a subtle putdown, but she shrugged it off. "Aren't they always? It is amazing how much business is done on the ballroom floor. Right now Rafe must show his face to the Upper Ten Thousand. He must claim what has been placed on his shoulders and behave as though it is comfortable to him."

"Until it truly is?" Crispin asked.

She tilted her head. "You behave as if the time when your brother will be more accepting of the inevitable is a bad thing."

"He was forced into a life that wasn't his own," Crispin said, his eyes darkening. "I can't help but hate that fact."

She reached out and briefly touched his arm. "You are a good brother and I cannot imagine how difficult it is for your family to stand by and watch Rafe get sucked into this unwanted change. But may I suggest that a better help to him than stewing about it may be to accept some of the invitations that have been sent your way?"

He stiffened, and she hastened to explain herself. "I've been told by several ladies that you and your mother and sister have been invited since Rafe's inheritance."

He nodded. "Over the years our family has had enough money and influence that we were asked to the parties of the titled occasionally. My father hated that rot and we never went."

Serafina smiled. "Yes, Rafe has told me a bit about your father. I wish I'd had the chance to meet him."

Crispin's gaze narrowed. "My brother confided in you about our father?"

She nodded.

He seemed to ponder that fact for a long moment with a troubled expression he finally wiped clean. "You are correct that the invitations to those kinds of things have begun again."

"I realize you don't want to do it, that perhaps it even goes against your nature, but it might help Rafe to have you there."

His eyebrows lifted. "To show our acceptance of this folly?"

She shook her head slowly. "No. I meant more as a comfort to him. He is surrounded by those he knows vaguely at best. I know he loves his family deeply and your presence at his side might simply make him more comfortable."

Crispin drew back in what seemed to be surprise at that statement. Then he gathered his composure. "I'll consider it."

"Good," she said, smiling.

He stared at her even closer. "You truly are unexpected, just as he has said."

"Unexpected?"

"It is a compliment, I assure you," Crispin said with a laugh.

She wanted to ask for elaboration, but before she could, she felt a touch on her shoulder. When she turned, it was her father standing at her side. Her heart sank. Although he hadn't interacted much with her this evening, his presence had been like a constant rap on the back of her head. Annoying and worrisome.

"Father," she said with a falsely bright tone. "Are you enjoying yourself?"

He nodded like his head was on a spring. "Oh yes, very much so. Mr. Flynn, your mother is a wonderful hostess."

Crispin forced a smile, not very believably. "Thank you. We like her."

Her father's gaze moved to Serafina again. "Will you excuse us? I would like to speak to my daughter in private for a moment."

Serafina did her best to keep her heart rate down, but those words gripped her in the way no others could. But there was no escape without causing a scene. Rafe had left the room with Annabelle a few moments earlier and no one else knew how much she dreaded her father's presence.

She smiled apologetically at Crispin. "I hope we'll talk again later."

He inclined his head slightly. "I'm sure we will."

Her father took her arm and maneuvered her away from Crispin. When he walked toward the door, she tugged back a fraction.

"What are you doing?"

His lips thinned. "I wanted to speak to you in private, Serafina. Mrs. Flynn told me we could use the parlor across the hall."

Serafina barely contained the urge to flee and allowed her father to take her to the opposite room. When they entered, he released her and crossed to the fire.

She steadied her nerves with a deep breath and then said, "What is you need to discuss that requires privacy?"

He glared at her. "You have not contacted me since your wedding. I want to know how things are going between you and the new duke."

She smoothed her skirts. "As well as can be expected," she began. "We are of a mind on more issues than I believed we would be. He is kind and intelligent and—"

Her father cut her off with a wave of his hand. "Do you think I care about any of that?"

She shook her head, fighting the swell of sadness that accompanied his dismissal of her feelings. She expected it by now, but oh, how it continued to sting. Especially when confronted with Rafe's family and their strong bond. His mother, his sister, even his brother only cared about Rafe. His happiness was paramount to all of them.

And here was her father, leaning in, his eyes glittering with his own desires.

"Then what do you want to know?" she asked softly. "If my contentment means as little now as it ever did."

Her father frowned, and there was a flash of desperation in his eyes. "When you were to marry Cyril, he was established and respected. Our bargain benefited me as much as it did him. But with Flynn, it is different. So, tell me—is he being accepted? Is he interested in the influence that comes along with his title? Or is he as frivolous as gossip says?"

She folded her arms, suddenly defensive of Rafe. "He is anything but frivolous. In fact, I would say Cyril was a far emptier vessel than Raphael."

"Answer my question."

"Rafe is charismatic and handsome as well as rich. When he walks into a room, he commands it naturally, so he garners a great deal of interest, more than he likely desires. But he knows the responsibility that has been laid upon him and I have no doubt he will thrive as duke. You needn't worry about his future influence."

Her father took a long step toward her. "Good. I would hate to think I'd lost something in this bargain."

"The bargain *you* insisted we carry out, despite our mutual protest," she said softly.

He jerked his face toward hers. "Watch your tone. And while we're speaking on these things, you need to move yourselves back into the ducal estate. London is talking endlessly about the fact that you two hole up in Flynn's bachelor home. This does nothing to negate Hartholm's notorious reputation."

Serafina shook her head. Her father was likely correct in that assessment, but she couldn't imagine Rafe would care. He was not ashamed of his past. And he always encouraged her not to be embarrassed by hers, either.

"Once you are where you belong," her father continued, "you will have a ball and invite all the best of Society. And me."

Serafina turned away from her father and strode across the room. "I do not doubt that at some point Rafe will take up residence in the ducal home. But I won't be with him."

"What?" her father snapped.

"His Grace and I have come to our own arrangements, Father. I will not be living with him. Of course, I shall provide him heirs and spares; I would do nothing to humiliate him or lower the way he or the title is seen. But this marriage was not something either of us wanted and we have already determined that we won't destroy ourselves by pretending otherwise."

She said the words, but they did not ring as true as they once had when she made that very bargain with Rafe. After all, he was so much more than she'd ever thought he could be. She *liked* him. And yet *this* was where they stood.

She looked at her father over her shoulder, surprised he had not responded to her shocking announcement. His face was red as a vibrant rose and his nostrils flared.

"You cannot be serious about that foolish statement," he finally said, his tone filled with anger and betrayal. It was as if she was doing something to *him*.

"I most certainly am," she said, wishing her voice didn't tremble in the face of his obvious anger. "And as far as a party at the ducal home is concerned, I do not see that happening any time soon. I don't wish to arrange it and I doubt Rafe feels differently."

Her father moved across the room at surprising speed and his hand closed over her upper arm like a steel trap. He shook her once, digging his fingers into her bare flesh as he hissed, "Do you think you can deny me just because you are no longer in my house? I am your father, Serafina, and I will not be deprived of the small benefit having you and raising you has provided."

She squeezed her eyes shut, trying to meter her breath, trying to think of some kind of response in the face of his anger and threats.

But she didn't have to say anything. There was suddenly the sound of a throat clearing at the door and she opened her eyes to see Rafe standing in the entryway, his glare locked on her and her father.

"McPhee, I would suggest that you take your hands off my wife," he said, his tone low but filled with undeniably dangerous warning.

It was obvious her father heard it as well, for he let her go immediately and pivoted to face Rafe. "I am owed—"

"*You* have been paid in full," Rafe said, his face never changing, but his eyes burning with an increasingly high and hot fire.

"She's *my* daughter," her father whined.

Rafe arched a brow. "She is my wife. Whatever claim you had on her left you the moment the wedding ended. Now I would suggest that you gather your things from my butler and depart this gathering early."

"And why should I do that?" Her father attempted to sneer and yet the catch in his voice told Serafina of his fear. She said nothing, but her heart swelled at that unusual sound.

Rafe took a long step into the room. "Because if you don't leave, you will truly suffer the headache I will be telling my family you are experiencing as an excuse for your departure."

"You threaten me?"

Rafe leaned forward. "I *promise* you. Do I make myself clear?"

"Crystal," her father said softly.

He tossed her one glare before he strode toward the door. He eased to the side, out of Rafe's way, as he left the room and went into the foyer, where Serafina heard him call for his horse.

She heard nothing more, for Rafe quietly shut the door behind himself and stepped closer.

"Is your arm bruised?" he asked.

She lifted it to look at it. There were a few red marks from her father's tense fingers. "Not yet."

His lips thinned. "I ought to follow him outside and beat him until he bleeds."

She moved forward and swiftly closed her hands over his. "Don't," she whispered. "Rafe, you did enough."

Suddenly she was aware of how close he was, how warm he was, how much she wanted to wrap her arms around him and show him how much his defense of her meant.

"I did nothing," he said, but his gaze darted to her lips, as if he shared her passionate thoughts.

She almost laughed. "That is the first time I have ever been defended against his demands and attacks, Rafe."

His brow furrowed and he shook his head slowly. "How did you survive him? How did you ever survive any of it at all?"

Her lips parted. "I—I—" She swallowed hard. "I always had a tiny hope that I clung to with both hands. Perhaps some part of me knew you were coming, knew that you would save me from the future they had planned for me."

He cupped her chin with one big hand and tilted her face toward his. "If you need saving, I will always be there."

His mouth covered hers and she allowed the surrender she had been craving. She lifted her arms around his neck and melted against him, sighing as he traced her lips, then gently dipped his tongue into her mouth and tasted her like she was some kind of fine wine.

After what seemed like far too short a time, he released her and stepped back, his eyes glazed with a desire she matched.

"Serafina," he said, his voice rough. "I think you should cut him out of your life."

She blinked, still under the spell of his kiss. It took her a moment to realize of what he spoke.

"My father?" she murmured.

He nodded. "If you can call him that at all. In my mind, a father is a confidante, a teacher, a guide down a tricky path, even a friend. Certainly, at the very least, he should give a damn about the happiness and well-being of his child."

She shook her head. "Not all of us are as lucky as you were in your father."

His face grew sad. "Indeed, that is true."

She slipped her hand into his. "I understand why you might want for me to cut him away, but Rafe, if I do that I will have no family. No one."

He flinched as if that statement cut him and then he squeezed her hand gently. "That isn't true. You will share my family."

Her heart lurched and she stared at him in surprise. "I—"

"I know you don't want me," he continued. "But as my wife, you cannot deny them. They'll love and accept you."

She leaned back. "Do they know our plans to live apart?"

He hesitated long enough that she knew the answer before he said, "My brother knows. And I just told my sister. But it wouldn't make a difference, Sera."

She blushed as she pulled away. "How can you say that? I can only imagine what your mother will think, what *all* of them will truly think when they realize I'm living in my own home. The scandal—"

He cut her off with a burst of laughter. "My darling, I assure you we know of scandal in my family. *This* will not rank in even the top five."

She pursed her lips. "But they still cannot possibly want me in their lives when the truth comes out."

He arched a brow, caught her hand and before she could protest, led her from the room. "Why don't we find out?"

"Rafe," Serafina whispered as she tugged against his hand.

He ignored her protests and entered the parlor where his family remained.

"I'm sorry to say that Mr. McPhee was stricken by a sudden headache and had to leave us," he said.

From the expressions on his entire family's faces, he could see none of them believed that, but for Serafina's sake no one said a word except for his mother, who stepped forward.

"I'm so sorry to hear that. I will send a note to him later. But at least we'll get a bit of time together this evening."

Serafina glanced up at him, her expression filled with pleading that he not reveal what she considered to be their "secret", but he ignored it. Until she understood true acceptance, he would have no chance to make her fall in love with him and see that a life with him had value.

"Actually, there is something else I would like to discuss. Annabelle and Crispin, you are aware of this, but I think it's best if we speak about it in the open, as a family."

His mother tilted her head. "Oh dear. What is it now?"

"Please don't," Serafina said softly, her eyes cast down at her slippers and her voice trembling.

"You all know that Sera and I were forced into this arrangement due to circumstances beyond our control." He cleared his throat. "And because Serafina is a wise woman, she approached me with a proposition that we would marry, that we would provide heirs to the title, but that there was no reason we should be forced to live a lie."

His mother blinked and her gaze moved to Serafina. His wife had not looked up, and he flinched as a tear escaped her eyes and glided down her cheek.

"What are you saying?" his mother asked softly.

"Serafina will have her own home and her own money and we won't live together as husband and wife." He squeezed Serafina's hand gently and found it to be very cold and stiff. He smiled to reassure her. "I believe she fears this will make you all despise her, that she'll have no place in this family if you know our desperate little plan. So I leave you all to address this issue."

Of course it was Crispin who stepped forward first. "I don't understand why we would like you less, Serafina," he said, smiling at her. "I cannot condone anyone living in misery if they can choose something else. I will happily claim you as my sister no matter what."

"As would I," Annabelle said with a shake of her head. "I think you've been forced into a life you didn't want long enough. If having your own home, living your own life, is what you desire, it only seems fair that you should have your way."

Serafina stared at the two of them, and he could see the depth of her disbelief. And why wouldn't she doubt this kindness? She had experienced so little of it throughout her life.

She turned her attention to his mother, who slowly moved across the room to take both her hands.

"Serafina, I married a rogue and I've watched my

sons…and even occasionally my daughter…involve themselves in tomfoolery you cannot imagine. Rafe lit fire to the Duchess of Waterburg's favorite gown once. While she was in it. And that is the *least* of our family's eccentricities."

As Serafina's eyes widened, Rafe stepped forward. "Now then, that was an accident and she escaped unscathed."

"And in her undergarments," Crispin added almost beneath his breath.

"In the lake," Annabelle said with a chuckle.

"To be fair," Rafe said, turning to Serafina. "This was *not* a recent occurrence. I was eight."

"But this isn't a childhood transgression," Serafina said softly, holding his mother's gaze. "People will talk, you may be asked to make explanations…"

"People have talked since the beginning of time, whether you give them a subject or they make one up." His mother took Serafina's hand and lifted it to her chest gently. "And my only explanation will be that this is the decision that makes my son and my daughter-in-law happiest. *Does* this make you happy?"

His mother looked at Rafe and he saw a flicker of concern in her eyes. As if she somehow read his heart without him telling her.

Serafina sighed. "It is what is best, I think, for us both."

Rafe glanced down at her. Serafina had not said that the separate lives she insisted upon would make her *happy*. Which gave him a slender thread of hope.

"Then it is what you will do and none of us will think less of you for it," his mother insisted before she pulled Serafina in for a brief embrace.

She stiffened at first, but then wrapped her arms around his mother and hugged her back. When they parted, both women were wiping away tears.

"Now, if you don't mind, I'd like to hear more about the duchess's dress," Serafina said with a laugh.

"Oh, it is the best story," Rafe's mother said, drawing her to the settee.

Crispin followed, calling out, "Don't forget that it started when he and I released the hunting dogs on Papa's orders."

"How could I forget?" his mother sighed.

Rafe moved to follow them, but Annabelle caught his arm and held him in place.

"What are you doing?" his sister asked softly, so the rest couldn't hear.

"What do you mean?"

"You told me you loved the girl," Annabelle said. "And then you make the announcement to the world that you will not live together. How is that wooing?"

He looked across the room at his wife, tucked onto the settee between his mother and brother, her mouth gaping and her eyes filled with laughter at the stories of his reckless childhood. She was lit up from within and he loved her more than he ever had.

"You told me to give her what she has always wanted. Well, she has never had the choice to live as she chooses. She's never had any kind of freedom whatsoever. I think, if I give her those things, she will be more receptive to me than if I demand she do exactly what she claims she doesn't want."

Annabelle wrinkled her brow. "That is taking a risk."

"It is. But if she truly doesn't want a life with me, I'll have no choice to let her go rather than force her into something she doesn't desire."

His sister blinked. "You do truly love her."

He nodded. "I do."

"Well, then I hope it won't come to loving her enough to let her go."

She squeezed his arm and moved to the settee to add her part to the story. Rafe sighed.

"So do I."

CHAPTER EIGHTEEN

Serafina glanced up from her book and caught her breath as Rafe walked into the sitting room. Her husband truly was the most beautiful man she had ever known. He was like a light when he entered any room, making it a better place.

And if it were just his physical appearance she was attracted to, perhaps it wouldn't have made her stomach twist. But it wasn't. The more she knew him, the more she realized that his heart and his soul matched his external appearance.

But she didn't want to care for him. She didn't *want* to care for anyone. In the end, that wouldn't lead to happiness, but to despair and disappointment and a life she would have no control over.

"You look as though you are a cat that just found a way to open the birdcage," she said, setting her book aside and praying her tone sounded even and unaffected by his appearance.

He smiled, but there was a nervousness to the expression. In fact, it was the same nervousness he had been exhibiting since their gathering with his family a few days before.

What had changed since then to make him so...*odd* around her?

"I have something for you," he said.

She swallowed hard. "Something?"

"A gift. It's in your dressing room—will you come with me?"

She stood slowly and gave him a look. "Are you attempting to seduce me, Your Grace?"

She teased, but the fact was that the physical connection between them was something she had come to truly crave. He so often found her midday or midmorning or at midnight or any time he pleased—and spirited her away for passion. She loved every minute of it. That, at least, she could admit.

He grinned. "That is a wonderful idea, Your Grace, but perhaps we can save it for *after* the gift."

He held out a hand, and she took it. The entire way up the stairs, she watched him. She'd never seen him like this before, almost vibrating with excitement he was trying hard to hide. Whatever his gift was, it meant something to him. And he thought it was going to mean something to her.

Suddenly she felt exposed, nervous, and as they reached her dressing room door, she hesitated.

"You don't have to give me gifts, you know," she whispered, catching his eye. "It isn't part of our bargain."

Some of the light in his eyes dimmed at her statement and tension tightened his jaw for a brief moment. Then he shrugged one shoulder and opened her door.

"I do it because I like to do it."

She turned toward the dressing room and caught her breath at what she saw. A dress form had been placed in the middle of the room, and on it was the most beautiful dress she had ever seen. It was a ball gown cut to flatter her slender frame and to accentuate the attributes she knew Rafe liked most.

But beyond all those things was something else that made the gown special. Or at least special to her. It was made in a beautiful buttercup yellow fabric decorated with sunnier hand-stitched flowers along the sheer overlay.

She turned toward him, mouth slightly open in shock.

"You said your mother told you not to wear yellow," he said softly. "And I think it is far past time for her voice, for your father's voice, for Cyril's voice, to leave your mind. For you to do as you'd like without any fears of recrimination."

She felt her lip begin to tremble with emotion and she spun away so she wouldn't reveal too much about how much his gift meant to her.

"It is beautiful," she managed to squeak without bursting into tears.

She felt his fingers close around her shoulder, felt his warmth at her back, beckoning her to lean into him, to trust him, to surrender more than just her body to him. And she wanted so much to do that.

But her fear palpitated, filling her ears with the rush of blood, making her hands shake at her sides. Giving herself entirely to any other person was such a terrifying thought.

Sucking in a breath, she pulled away from him and moved further into the room to examine the dress. It was more and more beautiful the closer she came. When she touched it, the silk glided through her fingers like water.

"How can I repay you?" she asked, turning toward him, braver now that there was distance between them.

He frowned. "It wasn't given in the hopes of some kind of quid pro quo," he said. "If you wear it and enjoy it, that will be enough for me."

"Rafe—" she whispered.

"Please don't say whatever is on your lips."

She stopped. "What do you mean?"

"Just listen," he continued. "You've made it clear what you want, and I would not deny you that. But I hope you won't deny *me* any attempts to change your mind."

Her eyes went wide as the shock of that sentence froze her in her spot. "Why would you want to change my mind?" she finally asked, her voice shaking.

He moved toward her slowly. "You are a very smart woman. I'm certain you will figure that out on your own."

He stopped in front of her and reached out to cup her chin. Slowly, he tilted her face toward his, searching her eyes as if he could see into her soul. She wanted to turn away, to shut him out, but the draw of him was too powerful. She found herself leaning up into him, willing his mouth to lower to hers.

He followed her silent demand, pressing a kiss to her lips that seemed to make the room hotter and the air around them thicker in an instant. She gripped his arms, fisting his jacket in her fingers. She wanted him.

But she also wanted the physical connection they shared to somehow mute his unexpected attempt to create some deeper emotional bond. Something that frightened her and made her want to run.

If he sensed her desperation, he didn't seem unhappy about it. He groaned her name against her lips and put his arms around her, cupping her backside with both hands and pressing her against the hard ridge of the erection that already pushed against his trouser front.

She moaned at the feel of his tempting cock and all it promised to give. Her fear faded, her anxiety faded, until all that was left was him, was her, and was what was about to occur between them.

"Hurry," she whispered as she stroked one hand between them to press against the needy length of his cock.

He grunted with pleasure, but his smile was wicked as he looked down at her. "Why hurry? I have all day."

She gasped, but her words were cut off as he dropped his mouth to her again and guided her back through the dressing room into his bedchamber.

Once inside the room, once he had closed and locked all the doors to keep out any intruder who might interrupt their pleasure, he stalked toward her. He held her gaze steady as he undressed her, taking his time with every button, every hook, every piece of fabric.

When she tried to help, he pushed her hands aside. When she tried to speak, he silenced her with kisses until finally she stood naked before him.

A month ago, this state would have terrified her. But now she almost preened as he raked his hot gaze over her flesh. She knew what the look of her did to him now. She *liked* how she could control a man who was otherwise uncontrollable.

More than that, she liked that they were equals in their pleasure. And she could give as good as she got.

"You have finished with me," she whispered. "Why don't you take your turn?"

"You think I'm finished?" he growled as he ignored her request and instead cupped her backside again.

This time his hot fingers pressed into her bare flesh and the corresponding ricochets of pleasure were almost too much to bear.

"Rafe!" she cried out.

He all but tossed her onto the bed, looming over her with promise glittering in his bright blue eyes.

"Oh yes, love, you will say my name. Scream my name. Sigh my name. Because I'm not going to hurry. I'm going to take my time with you as you deserve and as *I* desire."

She stared up at him, thrilling at his words, her body aching for him even before he'd truly touched her. She didn't have to wait long. He climbed onto the bed with her, his warm hands covering her naked ankles, then making a slow slide up her calves, her knees. She shivered beneath his touch, her back arching almost against her will as he stroked skin over skin.

When he reached her thighs, he gently pushed, urging her to open to him, to reveal her sex, to show him that she was already wet and ready for him.

She did so without hesitation, without even a hint of the embarrassment or fear she had once felt when his eyes burned on her or his hands stoked over her. Now she felt nothing but a desire that curled in her stomach, tingled through every inch of her flesh, awakened each and every nerve ending she possessed.

In this, at least, she belonged to him, and she loved every heated moment they shared.

He spread her wide and stared down at her with a wicked half-grin on his handsome face.

"So many things I can do to you," he murmured, as much

to himself as to her.

She shivered. "What will you do?"

He cocked an eyebrow and slowly lifted his gaze to her face. "Taste you until you quake and beg, then make love to you until we are both weak."

His statement was direct and it hit her in the gut, but it was the look in his eyes that truly froze her in her spot. He was speaking of seduction and pleasure, but there in his stare she saw something else. Something warm, something gentle, something tinged with the emotions she did not ever wish to feel.

When he dipped his head, she could no longer see the evidence, but her nervousness remained. *Could* he feel something for her?

She had no time to ponder it further because Rafe tore all rational thought from her mind when he pressed his mouth to her weeping, sensitive sex. Electric sensation immediately rippled through her body and she cried out with the instant pleasure that seemed to light her on fire.

"So responsive," he murmured, his words vibrating against her tender flesh and making her clench her sex against nothingness.

"Please," she whispered, her voice hardly carrying because her breath was gone.

He grinned up at her. "Please you? Oh, I intend to do just that."

He brushed his lips over her a second time, feather-light teasing that did little to release her from the prison of his touch. She gripped fists against the coverlet, reaching for something she couldn't receive without his help.

He smiled again, and then he darted out his tongue and traced her sex from bottom to top, stopping at the throbbing bundle of nerves that gave her so much pleasure.

"Do you know what this is called?" he asked before he stroked the flat of his tongue over her, and she yelped when a jolt of pleasure arced through her entire body.

"N-no," she murmured.

"Your clitoris," he explained, stroking it again. "If I stimulate it enough, you'll orgasm."

"Please do it," she all but wailed.

"I will," he reassured her with another chuckle and a lick that teased rather than relieved. "But first…"

He trailed off as he brushed his fingers over her. He peeled her open, revealing her fully and then, without preamble, he gently pushed two thick fingers deep within her core. She clenched around the invasion, loving how she stretched to accommodate him.

"Inside of you," he whispered, his mouth still a fraction of an inch away from her aching clitoris, "is another place where I can make you come. Right…" He maneuvered his fingers and gently curled them.

She almost levitated off the pillows as a deep pleasure seemed to bloom inside of her, not fully in release but something close to that sensation.

"Right there," he said with a smile. "So what do you think would happen if I touched you in both places at once?"

She stared at him, unable to keep the wild need from her voice as she murmured, "Show me."

His pupils dilated with her breathy request, and she saw a shift in him from teasing lover to a man driven to possess her in the most primal way possible. Power swelled in her to know that she could inspire his need even as he teased and taunted her so sweetly.

"Be careful what you wish for, Your Grace," he said, his tone tense.

He dropped his mouth back to her and sucked her clitoris between his lips. As he began to lave her with his tongue, his fingers worked deep inside of her, stroking and curling, teasing and touching until he finally found a rhythm that drove her mad. In one stroke he would curl his fingers inside of her, in the next, he licked her clitoris, back and forth until her hips arched helplessly and her sex clenched around pleasure so intense it bordered on pain.

And just when she thought she would possibly die from the tension he had created, the orgasm hit her.

She had come before, but it had never been like this. As Rafe continued to stimulate her with that relentless cadence, her body began to tremble, the trembles turned to quakes and the quakes to shuddering that seemed to move through her entire being. She lifted into him, screaming because she couldn't control her voice, clinging to the bed covers because her clawing hands were out of her control.

He stroked on, watching her come from his position between her legs, his dark eyes filled with building desire that threatened to consume them both.

It was only when the bursts of pleasure faded slightly, when the tremors became occasional twitches, that he withdrew his fingers and his tongue and pushed to stand up.

She reached for him as he went, making a wordless sound of need that made him sway a fraction.

"I'm not leaving," he reassured her. "I need to undress."

She sat up on her elbows to watch him do just that, lazy desire ratcheting up as he divested himself of everything he wore bit by bit.

His body, always a draw to her, was even more appealing at this moment. She wanted to wrap herself around him, to rake her hands and teeth over him, to feel him pulse inside of her as he lost control like she had lost control.

When he was naked, he moved to cover her, supporting his weight on his hands. She opened further for him, allow him to settle between her legs, his hard cock nudging her soaking sex.

"My God," he growled as he eased forward, taking her inch by hard inch until he was fully seated.

Her body was already ultra-sensitized by release and his invasion only intensified the sensations. Already she fluttered around him, on the edge of a second orgasm. She lifted, pushing to find that pleasure a second time, despite how spent she remained.

"You are a minx," he moaned at her aggressive movements. "But this is mine today, mine to control."

She stared up at him, uncertain what he meant. But then he slowly circled his hips and she let her eyes shut with a shuddering sigh.

"Look at me," he whispered, his voice broken as he took her with slow, steady strokes. "Look at me, Serafina."

Her eyes came open with the second, more strenuous order and watched his face. He strained with effort, the veins in his neck stretched and his cheeks red with exertion. Their eyes locked, and it was as if he had placed her in a prison, only it was a beautiful place she couldn't escape.

In that moment, with his body stroking into hers over and over, their gazes locked, she had never felt so fully connected to him. So lost in him. So one with him.

It was terrifying, but she couldn't pull away. Not just because of the pleasure building in her again, but also because this connection was so utterly magnificent.

The second orgasm mobbed her in that moment, and she whispered his name as her sex milked him. He gritted his teeth and groaned as he spilled his seed into her.

He pressed kisses along her neck as he collapsed next to her and dragged her into the crook of his body, so they were lying with his front to her back, cradled together like spoons. He said nothing, but continued to kiss her flesh, his arms around her in warmth and comfort.

After some time had passed, she felt his body relax and realized, with a start, that he had actually fallen asleep. Slowly, she turned to look at him, able to explore his face without his knowing it.

Relaxed in slumber, he seemed younger, and she couldn't help but reach out to gently trace his lips with her fingertip. He smiled but didn't stir.

She sighed as she thought of the dress he'd had made for her, waiting for her in her dressing room. He'd claimed that was the gift he had for her that day, but now she wondered.

Was the greater gift not the connection they'd shared while making love? Which was the more frightening? The gift that said that he knew her well or the connection which proved he did, despite her desperate attempts to keep him at arm's length?

Either way, she had felt the shift between them and she wasn't certain she was ready to face what that meant for her future.

CHAPTER NINETEEN

"I think he is wooing me," Serafina whispered as she looked across the crowded room toward Rafe.

He was standing with his brother. Crispin looked highly uncomfortable, but Serafina couldn't help but be pleased he had heeded her suggestion and come to offer support to Rafe. No matter what she felt at present, she wanted her husband to be happy and at peace. Even if it couldn't be with her.

Emma smiled at her side, blissfully unaware of Serafina's thoughts. "Good. No one deserves wooing as much as you."

She glared at her friend. "I don't *want* to be wooed."

"Of course you do," Emma said with a wave of her hand. "All women do."

"No, I do *not*."

Emma let out a great put-upon sigh. "And why not?"

"You know why," Serafina hissed, even as she offered a weak smile to the marchioness who said her hellos as she passed by.

Once the woman was out of earshot, Emma continued, "Because you refuse to have tender feelings for a man. Which made sense when it was awful Cyril, but Rafe is different."

"I know, which makes my reticence all the more reasonable," she said with a shake of her head.

"I'm afraid you'll have to explain that logic," Emma said with a laugh.

"Rafe is a rake who was forced into this position. He may have some…" Serafina struggled for a word that would express the changes she was so desperate to ignore. "He may have some tender feelings toward me, but do I really want his affection due to pity for my past or out of gratitude for my help in his transition to being duke?"

"Do you really think that is his only motivation for how he behaves toward you?"

Serafina could hear the disbelief in Emma's voice, but ignored it. "What else could it be? We have known each other less than a month, and while I admit that our physical connection is—"

She stopped as another lady hesitated in front of them. "Your Grace," the woman cooed. "That yellow is divine on you."

Serafina managed a nod as she glanced down at the gown Rafe had ordered for her. She did love it and had never felt so beautiful, inside *and* out, as she did when her maid helped her into it that night. Bridget's oohs and ahhs had only exacerbated her feelings about the dress.

"Oh, thank you so much, my lady," Serafina managed to squeak out.

The woman squeezed her hand and moved away.

"Who was that?" Emma asked.

"I don't even know," Serafina whispered. "*This* is how distracted I am—I cannot even recognize a peer when I was forced to memorize the name, title and often the circumstances of everyone around me for years."

"That sounds awful," Emma said with a shake of her head.

"It was," Serafina agreed.

"Then perhaps it's best that your husband distracts you so much that you cannot recall those things. He doesn't *expect* you to know them."

"He *should*. He needs me to know them more than Cyril ever did." Serafina sighed. "My focus should be on helping my husband become accepted and comfortable as duke. And it should be on moving into a new home and starting my life."

"I think you already have," Emma said softly, her gaze moving toward Rafe.

"Well, I can't do *that*, don't you understand?" Serafina shook her head. "He found out I liked Madeira, so he had the best sent from Portugal. I have a *case* of Madeira, Emma. What do I do with it?"

She laughed. "Drink it. Though not all at once, I think."

Serafina stared at her friend. How could Emma be so dismissive? Couldn't she see how desperate the situation was?

"There are flowers in my dressing room every day."

"Every woman likes flowers," Emma said.

Frustration mounting, Serafina said, "He bought me this gown I'm wearing right now."

"And you have never looked so lovely. The color suits you in every way."

Serafina huffed out her breath. "Two days ago, I was given a new book from the shop and a hairbrush decorated with what I sincerely hope are paste sapphires because they reminded him of my eyes."

Emma's face had softened. "Everything you are telling me is so romantic."

Serafina narrowed her eyes. "You are not helping."

"I don't know how I can help you," her friend said. "You don't want what he is trying to offer, though I think you are a fool not to take it."

"What, jewels and baubles?"

Now was Emma who pursed her lips to express her frustration. "*Love.*" Serafina flinched, but didn't interrupt as Emma continued, "He is watching you right now, my dear."

Serafina jerked her head to look and found that Emma was correct. Rafe tracked her every move and when he met her eyes, he smiled at her in a way that made her heart all but skip a beat.

"I will tell you that the expression I see on his face is not one of pity or gratitude, but love," her friend continued.

Serafina swayed slightly and gripped Emma's shoulder to keep from collapsing at that statement she had been trying to avoid for days.

"He can't love me," she whispered.

Emma steadied her further. "No, I'm afraid that isn't true. You may not want him to love you, but he most definitely *can*—and I think he does."

"Well, I don't love him," Serafina whispered, and hated how false the words sounded when she meant them so deeply.

"Are you certain?" Emma hesitated as a gentleman passed them by with a brief hello that they both answered in unison. With a frown, Emma caught her hand and drew Serafina away to a quieter corner of the ballroom. "Are you certain you feel nothing for the man?" she repeated softly.

"Of course! How can you ask me?" Serafina whispered on a broken breath.

"I ask because when you are with him there is a light in you that I've never seen before. Anyone within ten feet of you can feel the connection between you. And it isn't just a physical attraction, but something deeper and more important."

"That isn't true," Serafina said.

Emma arched a brow. "Very well. Then perhaps I don't believe you are immune to his considerable charm because you have wanted so much to have your own home and yet you continue to live in Rafe's house with him."

Serafina froze. "He—he is looking for a new home for me. Until he has something—"

"Is he?" Emma interrupted. "Have you spoken to him about it recently? Has he asked your opinions on anyplace he has seen or taken you to see if you would like to live there?"

She sucked in a breath. She'd been so wrapped up in…well, in *him* that she hadn't had a frank conversation with him about the standing of her house hunt. He'd mentioned it to his family nearly a week before, but Emma was utterly correct that the subject had hung, unaddressed, between them since then.

"I will speak to him about it," she said, suddenly numb as she glanced across the room to him again.

Rafe continued to chat with his brother, but he continued to occasionally glance at her from the corner of his eye. She felt every look like a stab to her soul.

Emma took her hand. "Please don't be rash, Serafina," she whispered. "I understand your fears, I truly do, but to throw away love…you *will* regret it."

Slowly, Serafina extracted her hand from her friend's and shook her head. Emma couldn't be right. She didn't want to love Rafe or have Rafe love her. She wanted her freedom, her independence. Didn't she?

The situation was confused, but she had to recall all her very good reasons to keep her life separate from his. She couldn't let his physical seduction make her believe in a silly future that could never come to be.

"No, Emma. I'll regret it if I allow myself to believe that a fairytale could be true. It is better to embrace reality now and save everyone further heartache later. Excuse me."

She turned and began to walk toward her husband. She heard Emma softly calling her name, but ignored it, focusing instead of Rafe and what she would say when she reached him. She could hardly think, hardly breathe, and there was a lump in her throat that she didn't wish to think about as she struggled for strength in the face of unexpected desire.

How could this have happened? How could they have come to this when they had planned a loveless marriage so carefully?

"Good evening, Serafina," Crispin said as she reached the men.

She tried to force a smile for her brother-in-law, but could hardly manage it as her gaze slipped to Rafe. "H-hello Crispin, I'm so glad to see you here," she stammered.

Rafe tilted his head and examined her face closely. "Are you well?"

She nodded. "Yes, of course. I only wished to speak to you

THE OTHER DUKE

alone for a moment, if we could. Perhaps we could find privacy on the terrace?"

Rafe's face lit up with pleasure, but she saw Crispin frown from the corner of her eye. It was as if her brother-in-law knew she was driven to refuse whatever advances Rafe had recently been making.

And despite all the acceptance Rafe's family had promised, she could not imagine they would continue to like or support her if…when…she hurt him.

"Of course," Rafe said as he offered her an arm. "Will you excuse us, Crispin?"

His brother murmured something appropriate, but Serafina barely heard the words. She only felt his stare on her as Rafe escorted her across the room and out the double doors onto the terrace outside. As he released her and shut the doors behind them, she sucked in a great gulp of air.

"I admit, I rather like that you desire to be alone with me, Serafina," Rafe said, moving toward her with lazy seduction in his eyes.

She stared at him. Crispin had obviously sensed her discomfort, the impending doom of her request, and yet Rafe was blissfully unaware. Which made this situation all the worse.

"Rafe," she said, backing away so that he couldn't get her in arm's length. If he touched her, she might convince herself that this conversation could wait.

And it couldn't. At least, she had felt so strongly that it couldn't up until this moment when fear and regret gripped her.

He stopped moving and a frown creased his face. "What is it?"

She cleared her throat. "I wanted to discuss where we stand with my separate home."

His brow wrinkled and his desire faded a fraction. "You brought me out to the terrace in the midst of a ball to discuss your house?"

She nodded, although when he put it that way, it did sound

189

strange. "I had a realization when talking with Emma that we had not reviewed the topic for some time. I thought it best to broach the subject immediately."

His lips pursed slightly. "I see."

There was a long silence between them that made Serafina shift with discomfort. "So what is your response?"

"I have an agent seeking out homes on my behalf," he said, waving off the topic.

"And?" Serafina urged when it seemed that would be his final word on the subject.

Rafe huffed out a sigh and walked passed her to the terrace wall. He looked out over the garden rather than at her as he said, "Thus far none of the available options have suited either the agent or myself."

"So you *have* looked at homes," she said.

He swallowed, and the way he looked at her from the corner of his eye told her the story. "No."

She gripped her fists at her sides. Panic had begun to squeeze her chest.

"Then perhaps I should be the one to search. After all, this home will be mine. It isn't fair that you should have to determine what will best suit my taste and needs."

"I have not done so badly so far, have I?" he asked, looking pointedly at her gown.

She felt heat rise to her cheeks and turned her face. "You have been kinder than I could ever have hoped for," she admitted. "But—"

He moved toward her a step. "But what? Why rush into a new home, Serafina? Are we not getting along well?"

She caught her breath. "Of course. We get along fine, Rafe. But we had an arrangement."

"Made before we knew each other," he said softly. "Before we had talked about anything important or shared a bed. Don't you think the situation has changed between us?"

Serafina squeezed her eyes shut. She couldn't look at him because she saw that he had convinced himself he cared for her. And as bewitching a concept as that was, she couldn't allow it. If she did, she would fall headlong into all the emotions she didn't want to feel. She would utterly lose herself. There would only be pain down that road. Perhaps for them both.

"I do not wish to renegotiate," she said softly.

"Serafina," he said, his voice harsh and pained.

She turned toward him, straightening her spine as she gave him the respect he had earned with his kind treatment of her over the past month.

"I will not deny that the marriage we have shared thus far is not an unpleasant union," she said, keeping her tone detached and as uninterested as she could. "And I like you Rafe, I truly do. But there is nothing more to my feelings than that. So I see no reason not to continue exactly as we initially planned. I will move into my home and you can go back to whatever..." She hesitated before she forced herself to continue. "To whatever activities you once involved yourself in."

His face seemed to harden to stone, for he had not moved a fraction since she began speaking. Now he folded his arms. "And there is nothing else to say about it?"

She managed to nod once. "I don't think there is."

"Then allow me to speak," he said. "Serafina, I am—"

She gasped and rushed to him, covering his lips with her fingers as the tears she had been trying to control filled her eyes. "Please don't say it. Don't say it."

Now his face crumpled, but when she pulled her hand away, he didn't speak.

"The last thing I want to do is bring you pain," she whispered, longing to touch his face, to kiss him, to somehow make this better. But that would only confuse the issue. "But I *can't* do what you want."

His jaw tightened. "And that is the final word on that subject as well?"

She nodded. He stepped back and she felt the loss of his

presence as deeply as if he had torn away some part of her.

"Then I suppose I should appreciate your honesty, Serafina. I will make arrangements for you to speak to the agent about the homes tomorrow. As you said, I should not be involved in your future since I shall not be a part of it beyond the pre-discussed guidelines."

She swallowed at the hardness in him now. The dark quality in his eyes spoke of volumes of pain, but pain he would never again share with her.

And even though that was what she told him, and herself, that she wanted…it felt like a stab to the core of her soul.

"I want to go back," she whispered. "Go back home…to your home."

He arched a brow and was silent for a moment.

"Of course," he finally said in that utterly impersonal tone that seemed to cut her to the bone. "I think I'll stay a while longer. There are a few people I would still like to speak to. Feel free to sleep in your separate chamber tonight so that I won't wake you upon my return."

He met her stare, waiting for her to say something. Perhaps challenging her to do so. But all she could do was nod.

"Of course. That makes perfect sense."

His lips thinned again. "I will go inside and have the carriage brought around. I'll find you when it is ready."

He didn't wait for her response. He simply turned on his heel and walked back into the ballroom, leaving her alone on the terrace, watching him through the windows.

Alone as she had claimed to desire.

Alone as she had never felt before.

CHAPTER TWENTY

Rafe could hardly see the jostling crowd around him or hear the sounds of their chatter as he staggered back into the ballroom. He had called for his carriage for Serafina, but he could scarcely recall doing so. His mind was too cluttered with her dismissive words out on the terrace.

She hadn't even wanted to hear him. He'd never even had a chance.

Suddenly there was a great clap of a hand on his shoulder, and he turned to find Crispin standing there. His brother had a grin on his face, but Rafe could see the concern in Crispin's eyes. He had obviously seen what Rafe couldn't. Crispin had known that loving Serafina could not end well.

"You were outside for a while," Crispin said, his tone deceptively neutral.

Rafe struggled to find words. "Yes. My wife had a great deal to say."

Crispin leaned in closer. "Such as?"

"Do you need to hear it?" Rafe asked.

"Do you need to say it to someone who cares only for your happiness?" his brother countered quietly.

"She does not want me," Rafe whispered, the words stinging as they left his lips. "She doesn't want my love."

Crispin stiffened. "Was your love something she had earned?"

"Yes."

Crispin nodded gave Rafe's shoulder a gentle squeeze. "I'm truly sorry, Raphael."

"As am I."

"But perhaps that makes what I came over here to discuss with you even more pertinent."

Rafe blinked. "What you came to discuss?"

Crispin nodded. "Yes. After you and Serafina left me, I was wandering through the crush to get a drink, and who did I stumble upon but our dear friend, Viscountess Braehold?"

Rafe froze at the name that fell so effortlessly from his lips. Before his marriage, he indulged in a brief night of passion with the widowed Lady Braehold. And his brother damn well knew that.

"Crispin," he growled. "What the hell are you doing?"

"Helping you, I hope," Crispin said and began to motion over Rafe's shoulder, as if to beckon someone to join their party.

Rafe stiffened as he turned and watched Lady Braehold cross the room in a few long strides. Her dark hair was bound back, her equally dark eyes focused on Rafe as she made her approach. She was very pretty, yes, and he knew exactly why he had been attracted to her.

But she did nothing for him now.

He glared at his brother for putting him in this position.

"Dear Rafe," Lady Braehold said as she reached him and took both his hands. "Or I suppose I should say Your Grace now, shouldn't I?"

He extracted himself gently and forced a smile for the woman. It certainly was not her fault that Crispin was trying to sooth a wound in this utterly inappropriate fashion.

"Yes, the past few weeks have been quite a shock," Rafe said.

"I can imagine. One moment you are a carefree gentleman, the next a duke. And married." Lady Braehold shook her dark head and the curls around her face danced prettily. "You have certainly had a very interesting month."

"Excuse me," Crispin said with a smile for them both. "I shall leave you to reacquaint yourselves."

Rafe glowered after Crispin as he walked away, but his expression didn't seem to move his brother whatsoever. With reluctance, he focused back on his female companion.

"How do you find married life?" the lady asked.

He could see the true question in the glitter of her eyes. She wanted to know if he intended to take a lover. If that lover might be her. In truth, a month ago, when he had first made his arrangement with Serafina, he might have answered those questions with a resounding yes. The lady before him was both talented and discreet.

And now his answer was very different.

"I'm afraid my brother might have sought you out under false pretenses," he said apologetically.

"And those are?" she pressed.

He looked around to make certain no one would overhear. Then he leaned in and spoke softly, "You and I shared a remarkable night, my lady."

"We did," she agreed. "And I feel a *but* coming on."

"But I am in love with someone else now," he admitted. "And until I can either convince her to allow herself the faith to feel the same or somehow shake my heart free of her, I couldn't have a mistress."

Lady Braehold stared at him. "I assume you are saying you are in love with your wife."

He nodded. "I am."

She was silent for a long moment, but then she smiled. "Then the lady is very lucky indeed."

Rafe sighed. Serafina didn't exactly feel that way, it seemed.

"Lucky and...leaving," Lady Braehold said, motioning to the ballroom door.

Rafe spun to find Serafina hurrying her way through the crowd. At the door, she stopped, and Rafe watched as his brother approached her. They spoke for a moment and she cast one quick glance over her shoulder toward Rafe and Lady Braehold, standing together.

Then she took the arm Crispin offered and allowed him to lead her from the room.

"I should follow her," Rafe said. "I'm sorry."

"Go," his companion said. "No apologies are necessary."

He wanted so desperately to hurry after his wife and brother, but the crowd was too tight. He had to all but physically fight his way through, ignoring calls of his name from those who already knew or wanted to meet him and trying his best not to elbow ladies in the face in his hurry.

By the time he got into the hall and raced to the foyer, he was breathless and anxious. Despite Serafina's rejection of him, he didn't like the idea that she would sneak from the ballroom. That act felt very final to him.

She wasn't in the foyer with the milling servants, but the door to the outside was open to allow in air and make exits and entries easier. He moved to look outside, but at that moment, his brother stepped into the house from the drive. They both stopped and the two men locked eyes.

"What are you doing in the foyer?" Crispin asked, brow wrinkling with apparently genuine confusion.

Rafe moved on him. "I'm looking for my wife, you idiot. Where is she?"

Crispin stared at him. "She went home."

Rafe pushed past him and watched as his carriage rumbled from the drive and turned onto the street back in the direction of his home. His stomach turned with the knowledge that Serafina was within that vehicle. Alone. Leaving him.

He pivoted back to his brother. "Why did you interfere?"

Crispin looked around them at the servants who were all subtly leaning in now, obviously interested in this showdown between infamous brothers. No doubt they would report back to their various masters.

Without a word, Crispin grabbed Rafe's arm, dragged him

into the closest parlor and slammed the door.

"You don't need a scandal, *Your Grace*," his brother said.

Rafe shook off his hand and glared at him. "Answer my fucking question."

Crispin took a step back. "What is *that* tone about?"

"You heard what I said. Why did you interfere?"

Crispin pressed his lips together. "How did I do that? When I bumped into Serafina, she told me that you two had already arranged that she would leave early and you would stay behind. Since you were otherwise engaged, I offered to escort her to the carriage myself."

"Otherwise engaged," Rafe repeated on a burst of laughter that was anything but amused. He paced away from Crispin, if only so that he wouldn't take a swing at his best friend. "Another moment arranged by *you*."

Crispin shook his head. "I assure you, it was not. I truly did run into the viscountess in the crush and we chatted for a moment. Did I think you should see her? Of course I did."

"Because you think I should take the woman as my lover and forget about Serafina," Rafe said.

His brother tilted his head, and there was an ugly flash of pity in his stare. "Isn't that what your wife *told* you to do?"

Rafe's shoulders rolled forward as defeat rushed through him. "Well, you can tell me, she can tell me, anyone can tell me. I cannot change my heart and I have no place in my life for a lover at present."

Crispin's frown deepened. "Is that what you told Lady Braehold?"

Rafe scrubbed a hand over his face. "Something along those lines."

He moved to the closest chair and sank down into it, placing a hand over his eyes as he tried not to think about Serafina walking away from him and the life he knew they could have together.

"Rafe," his brother said softly. "What do you want to do?"

"I don't know," he admitted. "I don't know what I can

do." He thought of how Serafina had looked at him over her shoulder before she slipped from the ballroom. "Did she say anything about me before she left?"

He looked up in time to see Crispin shift with discomfort, his face tightening. Rafe straightened up in the chair.

"What? Why do you look guilty?"

Crispin shrugged. "I do hate that my best friend is my brother. It's very disconcerting to be read from top to bottom."

"What did you do?" Rafe whispered.

Crispin sighed and moved to sit across from him. "Your wife said she wanted to leave and that she didn't know if the carriage had been called for. I offered to escort her to the foyer. While we were walking, she asked me who was standing with you."

Rafe squeezed his eyes shut. "Please tell me you didn't say an old lover with whom you hoped I would reconnect."

Crispin shook his head. "Of course not. I'm a rogue, not a cad. But…"

"But?"

"I did say she was an old friend to you. And I'm certain intelligent Serafina knew that *friendship* meant more than mere conversation."

Rafe stared up at the ceiling with a groan.

"This is a good thing, Rafe," his brother tried to convince him.

"How? I all but declared my love for her and then she's left to believe I'm meeting with an old lover not ten minutes later?"

Crispin leaned in. "You all but declared your love and she *refused* you. If she thinks you are willing to move on, at the worst, it reclaims some of your dignity."

Rafe glared at him. "And at best?"

"Perhaps Her Grace will feel a sting of jealousy and determine that losing you isn't in her best interest after all."

Rafe slowly looked at his brother again. Crispin had folded his arms and was staring at him evenly. "Are you trying to tell me that you are hoping to make my wife *jealous* in an attempt to force her to see my worth?"

Crispin shrugged but said nothing.

"But you don't want me to be married. You want me to go back to the man I was before Cyril's death."

Crispin sighed. "I want you to be happy. Only you can decide what that looks like. But if Serafina is a part of it, I would move mountains to ensure you get your heart's desire."

Rafe stared at his brother, unable to speak. Then he got to his feet. Crispin followed him in the action, wariness in his stare.

Without saying a word, Rafe wrapped his arms around Crispin and hugged him as he hadn't in years. Crispin chuckled as he returned the embrace with an awkward pat on Rafe's back.

"Don't go soft on me," his brother warned as they released each other. "Our father loved his wife and didn't become a boring sod. I expect nothing less from you."

Rafe laughed. "A lofty goal indeed. And I'll do my best, assuming, of course, that your plan does not backfire and leave my wife more determined than ever to separate her life from mine."

Crispin's brow wrinkled, and he seemed to ponder that for a moment. "Well, if she does that, then I suppose we will simply have to come up with a new plan to win her."

"You and I?" Rafe laughed.

"And Annabelle. And I'm sure Mama could come up with something devious. She pretends to be the sanest of the bunch, but she has her own wild streak. We are the Flynns—nothing can stop us."

Rafe laughed along with Crispin and he did feel joy in his heart at the thought of his family at his side as he battled for Serafina's heart.

But he wasn't certain any of this would be as easy as his brother believed. Rafe certainly wasn't sure if it was a war he could claim victory in at the end, no matter what kind of reinforcements appeared to help him win the day.

CHAPTER TWENTY-ONE

Serafina paced Emma's parlor, her eyes not really seeing her friend's room because her mind was wandering endlessly to other topics. One topic particular. One distracting and frustrating topic.

The door to the parlor opened and Emma entered, her eyes heavy with sleep and her hair simply tied back rather than styled elaborately. Serafina blushed at the sight of her drowsy friend.

"It is early, I know," she burst out.

Emma shook her head and stifled a yawn. "You are always welcome, you know that, no matter the hour."

"I'm sure your husband does not think so when you have been dragged out of bed at such an hour."

"Adrian is fine," Emma reassured her softly. "Although you will forgive him if he doesn't come down."

"How could I expect him to?" Serafina sighed. "In truth, it is you I wish to see, not him."

"Then sit down, let me ring for tea and tell me why you've traveled across town at nine in the morning to meet with me."

Serafina sank into the settee and watched as her friend called for a servant. After quiet conversation, Emma returned to take a seat in a chair beside the settee and smiled.

"They will bring refreshments for us in a few moments. Why don't you begin your tale now? I think I couldn't wait to hear it now that you've come all this way."

Serafina sighed, stiffened her spine and her resolve, and told Emma about her conversation with Rafe on the terrace the night before.

Emma stared at her, hardly interrupting her as she went over everything from Rafe's attempts to admit his feelings to her demand for a home for herself. The one thing she couldn't bring herself to say was that her husband had almost immediately found Lady Braehold, who she could only assume was a former lover, if the way they stood so close and Crispin's awkward description of them was accurate.

It was when she finished the initial tale that the door opened and a servant appeared with a tray. In truth, Serafina was happy for the interruption. As she told the story, her heart rate had begun to increase and she relived that awful night and her complicated feelings on the matter.

Emma shot her a look and then said to her servant, "Just set it on the sideboard. I'll pour for us."

The maid did as she had been told and then left the room. As Emma moved to the sideboard to pour the tea she let out a deep sigh.

"I looked for you after you approached him," Emma said. "But it was such a crush by then that I never found you again."

"I left shortly after our encounter, of course," Serafina whispered.

Emma clucked her tongue. "Rafe must have been hurt deeply by your demand that he fulfill his original bargain. If he was attempting to declare his love for you, that dismissal would have cut him to the bone."

Serafina flinched as she thought of Rafe's pained expression and his tight voice. "Yes, I thought I had hurt him and I felt badly. But—"

She cut herself off, once again hesitant to share the last part of her tale, even with her best friend. Of course it was that very last part which had kept her up all night and driven her here at this ungodly hour.

"But what?" Emma asked, her eyes widening. "What are you not telling me?"

She cleared her throat and focused her attention on her lap because she couldn't look at Emma when she spoke. "He left me to call for the carriage and I stood out on the terrace trying to catch my breath, trying to stop *feeling* anything. I could see him leave the room and then come back, and I wondered if I should go to him, try to talk to him again. I might have done except he—he found *other* company."

"Other company?"

Serafina nodded, but the motion was jerky. "He was coming back across the room when his brother approached him. And a lady. You may know her, Lady Braehold? She's a viscountess. The viscount passed a year or so ago, perhaps."

"I think I might have seen her," Emma said, her tone uncertain.

"You would know her if you saw her," Serafina whispered. "She is dark and exotic and just…just beautiful."

Emma's eyebrows lifted. "I see."

Serafina's foot began to tap beneath her gown and she clenched her hands in her lap. "You know how you can tell when two people are acquainted when you see them together? And I suppose as I gain more, er, experience I can also see when two people are more *intimately* bound."

Emma's mouth dropped open. "You think this woman and your husband have been to bed together?"

She nodded. "And Crispin all but verified it when he walked me to the carriage."

"Why did Rafe's brother walk you to the carriage?" Emma asked.

Serafina tilted her head. "Because my husband was too busy."

Emma didn't physically respond to Serafina's harsh tone. She merely shook her head before she continued, "So you saw Rafe and this woman together—and you simply *left*?"

Serafina sighed. "What was I supposed to do run up and

stake my claim?"

"That would have been one option."

"I'd only just told my husband to let me go, and I suppose it is easier for him than he pretended it would be. What more was there to say? I slipped out to maintain the last shreds of my dignity."

"And you went home," Emma said slowly.

"I went home," Serafina repeated, covering her eyes with her fingers for a moment. "I went to my chamber and locked my doors and pretended I was going to sleep."

"But you didn't."

"I *couldn't!*" she clarified. "All I could think about was Rafe's face on the terrace when he tried to tell me his heart and his face when he was talking to *her*."

"What happened when he returned home?" Emma pressed.

"I heard him at my door an hour later and I thought he might knock, but...but he didn't. He just stood outside for a while and then went to bed."

"And this morning?"

Serafina blushed. "He was still abed when I had my maid help me get ready and came here. I *couldn't* face him."

For a while, Emma was silent, seeming to ponder everything Serafina had told her. With each passing second the quiet drove her mad and finally she threw up her hands.

"Please tell me what you think!"

Emma sighed. "You may not like what I think, Serafina, and I hesitate to tell you for that reason."

Her heart sank. "No I've come here for counsel and I want it, no matter what it is. I trust you to be as honest, but as kind as you can be."

"You have spent a month with this man, claiming you want nothing to do with a future with him," Emma began. "You were reluctant about your physical bond and I understood why. And yet somehow you overcame those hesitations and I feel as though you like being in his bed now."

It was still difficult to admit that to an outsider, but she nodded. "Yes."

"When that shift happened, I hoped you would allow the same for your heart. Your qualms were reasonable at first, but I prayed that you would open yourself. And yet you didn't. You refuse to allow this man to care for you, even though he stands before you and offers you something more than you could have ever hoped for."

Serafina shifted. "I can't—"

Emma lifted a hand. "Wait." With a frown, Serafina allowed her friend to continue. "So last night he tried to tell you his heart and you turned him away, all but demanding he go back to his life as if you two had never married. And yet when he does exactly as you requested, you are so jealous that you can't sleep."

Serafina wanted to shut out the words, but she couldn't. "Everything you say is the truth," she whispered.

"Of course it is!" Emma laughed. "You wanted this! So you now have two options. You can stop being jealous and allow your husband the freedom that you claim you desire him to exercise."

"Or?"

"Or you can go and get him back," Emma said softly. "If he wanted to tell you his heart last night, I will almost guarantee that he didn't change his mind in a span of fifteen minutes. And since he returned to your home within an hour of your last seeing him, it also implies he did nothing untoward with this woman, even if they do share some kind of history before your marriage."

Serafina pursed her lips. She supposed that was true. After all, she knew from experience that Rafe was the kind of man who treated his lover with care, taking his time for her pleasure.

She flinched at the idea that he had ever done so much for Lady Braehold.

"Look at you, tied up in knots over this man." Emma smiled. "You are already lost, Serafina. You just haven't admitted it yet. And I would hate to see you throw away something beautiful in order to protect yourself. Especially since I think you've already found that pushing love away doesn't exactly make one's feelings change."

Serafina shook her head. "I don't have feelings for him. I *can't* have feelings for him."

Emma's smile fell. "If you keep telling yourself that, you'll lose everything. I hope you won't be so foolish."

Serafina got up and looked toward the door. "So what you suggest is that I go home…to his home…to—to *our* home, and I tell him what? That I'm jealous and confused and a mess of a girl?"

"I suppose that would be a start."

Serafina shook her head. "Why did he have to be *him*?"

Her friend laughed. "Because you deserve him. Now go. And tell me all about it once you're finished."

Serafina could hardly breathe as she left her friend's home and took the long carriage ride back to Rafe's. With every thundering hoof beat of the horses, her heart responded in kind, and she searched everything in her for an answer to what she would say to Rafe when she saw him.

Rafe glanced up from a ledger sheet he hadn't been focused enough to read and forced a smile for his butler. "What is it, Lathem?"

The servant glanced behind him. "It's your wife, Your Grace. She would like to speak with you."

Rafe's heart promptly lodged in his throat. He had not seen Serafina since the night before. When he looked for her, he had been told she left to see Emma. Left without so much as saying good morning. That had haunted him for hours. But now she was here.

He let out a long breath before he allowed himself to

speak. "Send her in. I'm happy to discuss anything she would like."

Lathem turned into the hallway and Serafina appeared next to him in the doorway. Her face was pale and there were hints of shadow beneath her eyes. Good. At least he hadn't been alone in his lack of sleep the night before.

"Come in," he urged, standing as he nodded Lathem away. The butler gently shut the door behind Serafina, and Rafe couldn't help but notice the way she jumped slightly when he did.

Which did not leave him feeling confident in whatever she desired to say.

"You don't ever need to be so formal as to require a servant to meet with me. Not in this house," he began, motioning toward the chairs across his desk. She ignored him and continued to stand across the room, fiddling with a loose thread on her sleeve.

"I wasn't certain how you felt after our conversation last night," she admitted. "So I thought it was better to approach with caution in case you didn't wish to see me."

He moved around the desk. "I will always wish to see you."

Those words forced her to look at him, and her expression lit a flickering light of hope inside of him. She still hesitated, yes, but there was something in her eyes that she had never shown him before. A desire that went beyond the physical, a yearning for the connection she had always distanced herself from.

"Serafina," he said, taking another step toward her. "What do you need to talk to me about?"

She drew in a breath and then shook her head as if to clear it. "Could we perhaps go for a walk in the park? The air would do me good, I think."

That request was unexpected, and Rafe leaned back to examine her face from a different angle. She was waiting, expectant, fearful, and he finally nodded.

"Of course. Will the one just around the corner do, despite it not being as popular as Hyde Park or St. James?"

She nodded. "I am not going there to be seen, Rafe. I'm going there to talk to you. As long as there is air and grass, I will be pleased."

"Very well." He reached for her and was happy when she didn't flinch as he took her arm.

They walked through the house and out the front door. She was silent as they moved through the streets, nodding hello to his neighbors and hesitating at the corner for carriages. In fact, she said nothing at all until they passed through the gates of the little park nearby.

She sighed and released his arm as she looked up in the sky. The sun reflected on her porcelain skin.

She was utter perfection.

"I have thought a great deal about our conversation last night," she said, looking at him at last.

He motioned her toward the path, and they walked together toward the center of the park. There were few others in their way, so they could talk openly.

"As have I," he admitted. "Your words weighed heavily on my mind all night."

She bit her lip, drawing his attention there. How he wanted to touch her. To kiss her. To somehow mark her as his so that even if she ran away, she couldn't fully escape the changes he had made in her.

"Did you think of me even when you were with Lady Braehold?" she asked softly, her gaze suddenly focused on the ground.

Rafe waited a moment to answer because he was stunned by that question. Here he had thought his brother a fool to try to spark Serafina's jealousy with another woman. And yet jealousy was exactly what he heard in his wife's voice, even after she had set him down on the terrace.

"Yes, actually," he admitted. "But it is obvious you have questions about the lady. Would you like to ask them?"

She froze. "It would be indecent."

He laughed. "What is a bit of indecency between spouses?"

She glanced up at him, and he could tell she wasn't certain whether to smile at his quip or glare at him for the same. She did neither in the end, but shifted uncomfortably.

"I don't—when did you—is she—" She cut herself off with a frustrated sigh. "Crispin said you and the lady were 'old friends.' What does that mean?"

Rafe cocked his head. "I suppose you want to know if she is my lover?"

She sucked in a harsh breath at his direct response to her meandering question, and her cheeks brightened to high pink. He hated himself a little for doing it, for he normally would not speak to a lady the way he was speaking to her. But these were not normal circumstances. Everything was on the line now and he couldn't be so foolish as to pretend otherwise.

"Yes," she whispered when he continued to wait for her answer. "That *is* what I want to know."

He hesitated. Telling her the truth was a risk, but he owed her his honesty. That was the only way forward, as difficult as it was. He straightened up.

"She was."

Serafina's face jerked toward his, and there was a brief moment where betrayal slashed across her features. Then she covered her emotions with long-practiced grace he truly admired. That ability had helped her survive his cousin.

But he didn't want her using it with him.

"I see," she whispered.

"No, you don't," he said with a shrug that dismissed anything he'd shared with the viscountess because it meant nothing to him. "Lady Braehold *was* my lover. Once. Before you and I met, let alone were married."

Her eyes narrowed. "Once?"

He laughed. "It is possible, you know."

"Then why were you talking to her last night?" she asked.

"Because Crispin reintroduced us. Because it would be rude to refuse to speak to a lady in the middle of a ballroom where others might see and judge us both harshly."

"It wasn't out of interest in rekindling whatever you once shared?" she whispered.

He stopped on the path and leaned into her, crowding her space on purpose, forcing her to react by leaning back a fraction. "Are you saying you care, my lady? Because I seem to recall you telling me last night that you did not. That you *would* not. And that you wanted to fulfill that bargain we once struck to live separate lives."

She clenched her hands at her sides, her cheeks darker than they had been even before and her eyes unfocused. "Will you make me say it?" she finally said, her voice broken.

He caught her hand and lifted it slowly to his heart. "You must, Sera. You *must* say it now."

"I hated seeing you with that woman, knowing that it had been implied that you were lovers," she huffed out in one breath. "She was so beautiful, Rafe, and when I looked at you two together I just—"

He grinned and tugged her against him before he dropped his mouth to hers right there in the middle of the park. She gasped against his lips, but then her arms came around his neck and she melted against him, returning his kiss with as much passion and heat and desperation as he felt.

And as much as he would have loved to lay her down and make love to her with the sun kissing her skin, not only was that very imprudent, but they were far from finished discussing the matter.

He set her aside gently and smiled down at her. "Hear me, Serafina. Are you listening, truly listening?"

She nodded.

"I will never lie to you. There were women before you, Lady Braehold being one of them. But they meant very little to me and I likely meant very little to them."

Serafina swallowed hard. "It is unfair of me to feel these

things, I know. I was the one who told you that you should carry on your life, and I know that carrying on will ultimately mean some other woman warming your bed."

He shook his head. "Don't you understand? I have no intention of taking any other lover, so your jealousy is misplaced. But I think you and I need to discuss *why* you were jealous."

Her lips parted. "You're right," she admitted, and her shoulders rolled forward. "You're right, Rafe."

"Then tell me," he urged her, motioning her to a bench that sat surrounded by rosebushes that were in full bloom.

She sat and he took the place beside her. As much as he wished to do so, he didn't touch her. From her hesitation, he knew she needed her space, her own way to come to the conclusion he so desperately needed her to reach.

"You know my past," she began softly. "You are probably the only one who knows the depth of it."

"Even more than Emma?" he asked, truly surprised at that admission.

She nodded. "I spared her from some of the worst details, but not you."

He drew back. What she said meant a great deal. It meant *everything*. "If I earned that kind of trust, I am deeply happy for that," he said softly.

She smiled at him, her hand fluttering in her lap as if she wanted to touch him, but she didn't. "You did, Rafe. But you must see how that past has mangled me, not physically, but in every other way. Do you know why I wanted us to live separate lives?"

"Because at the time we made the bargain, we hardly knew each other," he said. "Why would you want to pledge a life with someone you were marrying three days after meeting?"

She shook her head. "Of course that was part of it, and that I wanted some freedom after a life of prison was also a portion of my reasoning. But it was also that I did not want to risk a life with someone else. When a woman feels things, it makes her vulnerable. I saw that, I felt that, I learned that. It defines me more than any other thing about me."

He shook his head. "It does not have to."

She pursed her lips. "I wish that were true, but these things, these fears, they already guide my actions with you."

He stared at her. "Are you saying you care for me?"

He held his breath as she struggled for the answer, struggled to say things that he knew terrified her to the very core. Struggled to overcome her past and give them both a future he so desperately desired.

"Rafe," she whispered, turning slightly so that she faced him full-on. "I—"

She didn't get to finish the words. Suddenly there was the loud bang of a rifle from somewhere in the distance. Everything seemed to slow to half time as Serafina screamed.

Rafe caught her hand and dragged her off the bench and around behind it, hoping the stone surface would protect them from whatever was happening in the park.

"Are you hurt?" he whispered as he held her against him in the dust behind the bench.

She shook her head. "No. But Rafe, you're bleeding."

CHAPTER TWENTY-TWO

Serafina could hardly breathe as she watched a small circle of blood begin to rapidly spread across Rafe's right shoulder.

"Let me help you," she said as she moved to lean over him.

He jerked her back down. "No," he whispered. "The bench is all that's giving us shelter. If you get up, you could very well be a target."

Her eyes went wide. "You don't think that shot was an accident?"

He shook his head. "If we were in the wooded area, perhaps it might have been someone hunting for his supper where he ought not be. But out in the middle of the park? I would wager that is *not* an accident."

Their eyes met, and she could see they were both thinking about their conversation not so very long ago about all the accidents that had befallen them. Now they were being shot at...and suddenly her fears were much more founded in truth.

Her lips parted. "If we are the targets, whoever did this is likely coming for more."

He nodded. "I would guess that is true. Reach into my boot, if you will. I carry a pistol there."

She stared at him, but didn't hesitate to do as he had suggested. Indeed, there was a slender, single barreled pocket pistol hidden next to his muscular calf. She removed it and held it out to him, but he lifted a hand in refusal.

"You hold it for your protection. I assume you have shot a pistol before."

She shook her head. "My father told me that if Cyril wanted to take me on hunts, he could teach me to shoot himself. And he didn't."

"Well, you are clever, so you can do it," he said.

Her heart swelled, but she wasn't so certain. "Tell me how."

"The gun is loaded. Now fully pull back the hammer."

She nodded and did as she was told.

"It's ready now, but you will only get one shot, so don't waste it," he said as he eased up. She saw him flinch in pain with the movement, and her heart caught.

"Rafe."

"Shhh. Let me look." He peeked up over the bench and immediately ducked back down. "I don't see anything, but whoever shot at us is likely reloading their weapon. They'll have only one shot, just as you do."

"You should take the gun," she whispered, her hands and voice trembling at the importance of what he was asking her to do. "You're more likely to hit whoever is stalking us."

He shook his head. "I'm hit on my right." He made an attempt to rotate his arm and grunted with pain. "No, I shoot with my right, Sera. I don't know that I could do it. I must depend on you."

Her lips parted at that statement. Depend on *her*.

"Then I won't let you down," she murmured.

He cupped her face with his left hand and smiled at her. "You never could."

"Rafe—" she began.

"Not that I don't want to hear whatever it is you have to say, but I want you to tell me once we're safe." He flashed a grin at her despite the anxiety in his gaze. He was trying to be strong for her. "So we have to move."

"Where?" She looked around the park. "We'll be exposed

until we get off the path and into that copse of trees."

She motioned toward the trees in the distance, and Rafe shook his head.

"That is going to be a problem. I'm fairly certain our little friend is hiding there. And we are running out of time if he is reloading, so we're going to stand up and we're going to run." He rose up slightly to look toward the exit of the park. "Run toward the gate. Toward the street."

"But—"

He got up and dragged her to her feet. "Run!"

She did as he asked, lifting the edge of her skirt and running as fast and as hard as her legs would allow. The pistol was heavy in her hands and she could hardly catch her breath to do as he had asked.

"Help! Someone help us!" she screamed.

As she said those words, she peeked over her shoulder as they left the center of the park. Rafe was behind her a few paces, his hand inside his coat to staunch his wound. He was pale and sweaty.

She slowed her stride. "Rafe," she panted.

He pulled his hand free. It was covered in dark blood and she gasped in horror. He didn't allow her to say anything. He just pressed his hand to her back and pushed her.

"Go!"

The gate was just ahead of them, and she scuttled through it onto the quiet street. She spun around and recoiled. There, standing behind the entryway pillar, was Cyril's mother. She was dressed in full mourning black, with a formal veil draped over her as if she were a death bride. In her hand was a hunting rifle, which she was holding by the barrel.

As Rafe passed through the gate, she swung the gun like a cricket mallet and connected the butt of the weapon squarely with his head. His flesh on his forehead split with the force of the blow, and blood from the gash began to trickle down his face, his neck and merge with the blood from the gunshot wound to his shoulder.

He staggered, his eyes wide as he looked first at his aunt and then at Serafina.

"I'm sorry, Serafina. Run," he groaned, and then collapsed in a heap in the entryway to the park, sickeningly still and quiet.

"Rafe!" Serafina screamed and took a step forward.

"Stop," Hesper said, spinning her rifle around in order to aim it at Rafe properly.

Serafina froze in her spot. What choice did she have? Hesper could fire her rifle, and with the barrel almost pressed to Rafe's skull, he would be dead before Serafina could catch a breath to scream.

The weight of her pistol was heavy in her hand, down amongst the folds of her gown, and she glanced at Hesper. Had Cyril's mother seen the weapon? It was possible she hadn't, for she was clearly more focused on murdering Rafe than Serafina at present. And when she ran past, the gun had been at her left side, away from the woman now standing over her husband.

If she could distract Hesper from pointing her weapon at Rafe, she might have a chance to save him.

"Your Grace," she began, easing the gun deeper into her skirt to hide it. "Please, stop this madness."

"Madness?" Hesper sent her a glare from the corner of her eye. "This is not madness, little girl."

She hadn't budged her gun from Rafe's prone form, despite Serafina's distraction. And until Hesper did, she had no leverage that her own gun would grant her.

So how would she get her to stop aiming at Rafe?

The only way was to make Cyril's mother point the gun at *her* instead. Serafina swallowed and eased not forward but to the side, so that she was within Hesper's line of sight. She glanced around as she did so. No one was on the street at present, no one around to help her.

So she would have to do what Rafe had said earlier and depend on herself. It was the only way to save them both.

"This will gain you nothing, Hesper," Serafina said softly.

"Nothing will change what has already come to pass."

"No, but this boy, this awful stain on my family name, will not hold *my* son's title."

Serafina caught her breath, trying to maintain the façade of calm she had to present to counteract Hesper's insanity.

"That is true," she said. "If you kill Rafe today, then he will not be the duke anymore. But he will be buried as a duke, likely in the Hartholm plot, with full respects due to that station."

Hesper's face twisted. Clearly this plan of hers might be well planned, but not well thought through. Which gave Serafina hope that she could inject enough reason into the situation that it would end without murder and further destruction.

"I don't care where they bury him," Hesper said, shaking her head. "Just as long as he is dead and gone."

Serafina flinched as she glanced at Rafe briefly. He was still enough that she feared Hesper already had her wish. He was losing so much blood and she had no idea how bad his injuries were.

She wanted to throw herself against him, to render aid and bring him back to life. But that would not help either one of them now.

All she could do was be strong. Strong like she had been during the years of torment with Cyril. Strong as Rafe said she was, said that he admired.

She owed him that.

"Very well, so my husband will be dead. But his brother will inherit the title from him, so the Flynn line will continue to carry Cyril's dukedom into the future."

Hesper's lips pursed. "Yes, a troubling thought. The younger brother is as bad as the older. Perhaps I will have to see him dead as well."

"But they are the last to inherit." Serafina shook her head. "If they are gone without heirs between them, then the title will revert to the crown. It will die with them."

"Thank God," Hesper said with a smile.

It was an almost angelic expression, as if the thought gave her enormous pleasure that could not be fully expressed with words. It was a terrifying look, for it revealed how far gone Cyril's mother was. How she could not be brought back from this plan she had formulated possibly from the moment her son had died and it was clear Rafe would inherit.

"You did those things," she whispered.

Hesper tilted her head. "Things? I assume you mean all the 'accidents' you've experienced since you met your husband?"

Serafina nodded. The dowager's smile broadened, and Serafina knew the answer.

Hesper had insured Rafe's horses went wild on their first ride together. She had arranged for the carriage that had nearly mowed him down. She had planned the fire in his kitchen. This madwoman's need to destroy what she couldn't have, like a petulant child, had nearly killed them both.

It now left Rafe in a heap on the sidewalk.

Serafina had always been good at controlling her emotions. It was something she had forced herself to do over the years. And yet now a set of feelings washed over her that she could not control. She was *enraged* as she stared at Hesper.

And if she could get that damned woman to put the gun on her instead of Rafe, then she would have a chance to end this. And also a chance to say everything she'd ever wanted to say to Hesper, to Cyril, to her father...

"Thank God?" She forced a smile. "Perhaps so. Except that if Rafe dies with an heir on the way, then your plan is far more complicated. After all, you would have to kill Rafe, kill Crispin, kill me and my child."

Hesper's eyes bugged out. "Are you with child? *His* child?"

Serafina swallowed. Although she and Rafe had made love so many times that she couldn't count them, she'd had no indication that she had a child growing within her. But the idea of that child, formed in the passion and the love she felt for

Rafe, had a power that was staggering.

Love. In this moment, she knew that was true. She loved the man slumped by the gate. She loved him with everything in her.

And she would do *anything* to save him and build the life with him that he had offered—and she had foolishly tried to push away.

She slid the hand that didn't contain her hidden pistol over her belly and smiled at Hesper. "You'll have to wait and see, if you strike down Rafe. How long will it take you reload that gun? Long enough for me to escape."

Hesper's hands shook, and Serafina could hardly breathe. If her finger twitched on the trigger, Rafe would be gone in an instant and none of this would have been for anything at all.

"I'll find you. Find his brother," Hesper said, almost with a feral growl.

Serafina shook her head. "But I know the truth. I know you're after us all. The precautions our family will take to protect my husband's son will be limitless. And *you* will likely be arrested and put in Bedlam after this."

"Then I'll hire someone," Cyril's mother said, but her tone was becoming less certain.

Serafina shook her head. "Certainly you wouldn't be able to afford that. After all, the reason Cyril was marrying me was to get at my inheritance. Could you *pay* for the murders of us all?"

Hesper shook her head. "You are trying to distract me, but it doesn't matter. This one will be dead and you will be destroyed. The rest will follow."

She settled the gun harder into her shoulder and Serafina took a step forward.

"Your son was a bastard!" she screamed. "An abusive idiot, and I celebrated his death. He was not half the man as Raphael Flynn."

The result of her accusation was exactly as she had hoped. Hesper let out a primal, guttural sound and swung her gun up and away from Rafe.

"I'll kill you!" she screamed.

The next moment seemed to move in half time. As Hesper began to press the trigger of her rifle, Serafina pulled her pistol from the folds of her skirt and aimed it at the other woman's chest.

She heard the massive explosion of both guns firing in time and squeezed her eyes shut. She braced herself to be hit by the heat and pain of the round lead ball that would tear through her flesh and render her hoped-for future mercilessly short.

But there was nothing. She heard the zing of a ricochet off the wall behind her. Slowly, she opened her eyes.

Hesper lay on her back, eyes open and glazed. Serafina's bullet had hit her straight in the chest. The rifle was at her side, smoking from being fired. But the reason the projectile hadn't hit her was that Rafe's hand was wrapped firmly around the other woman's ankle. He had yanked her off balance as she shot and made her fire wildly.

He lifted his head. His face was a mess of blood, pale and drawn as he looked at her.

"Are you hurt?" he asked, his tone strained.

"No," she panted. "Rafe…"

"Good," he groaned, and then collapsed back against the paved walkway.

"Rafe!" she repeated, this time on a scream. She dropped to her knees and fought to turn him over on his back. She cradled his bleeding head in her lap and tore at his shirt to make something to staunch the seeping shoulder wound.

Behind her, across the street, she heard doors open, people rushing out now that the gunfire was over.

"Someone ran for the Guard after the first shot," one man said as he moved to look over Hesper and then to Rafe. "What were they fighting over?"

Serafina ignored him as she smoothed her hand over Rafe's cheek. "Rafe, I love you. I love you. Please hear me.

Please don't leave me. I love you. I can't lose you. Please."

But he said nothing, he did nothing, and he didn't move even an inch.

CHAPTER TWENTY-THREE

The parlor at the bottom of the stairs was crowded to say the least, but it wasn't noisy. In fact, the silence seemed eerie and unnatural to Serafina. She paced across the floor and felt five pairs of eyes upon her with every step.

Annabelle and her mother sat on the settee, ignoring the tea and mounds of biscuits the servants had placed there as some kind of offering of solace and solidarity. Serafina's father was at the fireplace, alternating between staring into the flames and watching her.

And Crispin stood at the doorway with the inspector from the guard, a thin, direct man named Simpson who had questioned Serafina about the death of the dowager duchess of Hartholm.

She could hardly recall what she had said to the man, but was grateful to her uncharacteristically pale brother-in-law for taking over the duty of dealing with the Guard and its representatives.

They spoke too quietly for her to hear for a moment, and then the inspector crossed the room to her.

"Your Grace, I will leave you now. There may be a few questions I'll have later and I will be sure to call on you if they arise."

She stared at him, for it took too long for his words to sink in past the fog of her worry. "Will you arrest me, then?"

At that moment, she didn't care if she was to be taken into custody, but she wanted it to be done after she knew that Rafe, upstairs with the doctor, would survive his injuries.

The young man shook his head and actually looked surprised at her question. "No, my lady. The statements from those across from the park who saw the altercation from their windows, along with your explanation makes it clear what happened was unavoidable self-defense. The matter will be closed once I file my report."

She might have felt relief in that statement, but there was no relief at present. There would be none until the doctor returned.

"I hope your husband will make a recovery, Your Grace." The officer tipped his hat to her. "Good day."

She nodded, though she hardly noticed when he walked away. She turned back to her window and stared out at the garden without seeing it, either.

"Serafina?"

She jolted at the sudden touch of a hand on her elbow and turned to find her father at her side. She sucked in a breath. "I'm sorry, Father, but I cannot hear haranguing at present."

His eyes flashed down, as if with guilt. "No. No, that isn't my intention. I wanted to say—to say that I am sorry."

She blinked. "Sorry?"

"I am the one who pushed you toward Cyril and into the path of his mother. I only wanted to give you a better life."

"You wanted to give yourself a better life."

He hesitated, but did not snap at her as he might have a day before. He only sighed. "Yes. I wanted to further my own desires. But I am truly sorry that it has ended this way."

She jerked her gaze to him. "Ended. It is not ended."

He caught her hand, and she stared down at their intertwined fingers. It was the first time she realized her gown was still covered in blood. Rafe's blood.

She could hardly breathe as she extracted her hand. "He *will* live," she said firmly.

Her father nodded. "I'm certain you are correct."

He moved away from her, and now it was Crispin who walked up to take his place.

"You should go up to change," he said softly. "Your maid is ready to help you wash and—"

"I can't be in a state of undress," she whispered, "where I can't go to him in a moment's notice."

Crispin tilted his head as he looked at her. "You love my brother."

She nodded, but now the tears sprung to her eyes. "Do you think he knows? Do you think he heard me tell him?"

Crispin swallowed, and she saw his tears sparkle in his eyes too. "I hope so. It would give him a reason to fight."

They stared at each other, silent in their grief and support, until they were interrupted by the sound of a clearing throat at the door. When Serafina saw it was the doctor, she rushed forward with a cry.

"What is it?" she asked, trying to read his expression but unable.

"I have stitched his head wound. As for his shoulder, we are lucky that the bullet went straight through and did not damage his bones," the man said.

"But will he live?" she asked, holding her breath.

He nodded. "Yes."

She heard nothing more, leaving the rest of the family behind as she bolted up the stairs and down the hall to the bedroom they had shared for over a month. The door was open and she all but bowled over Rafe's valet as she skidded inside. The servant smiled weakly and then left, closing the door behind him.

Rafe was propped up on his pillows, eyes shut. He was no longer in his bloody clothes, but was bare-chested with the sheet pulled up to cover his stomach. His shoulder was bandaged and his arm pressed against his chest in a sling.

"Are you going to stand there all day or come and sit with me?" he asked.

She jolted at his voice, for she had thought him still unconscious. But the sound of it was like music to her ears, and she rushed to him as he opened his blue eyes and smiled at her.

The smile fell when he saw her gown. "Were you injured?" he asked, sitting up and then wincing.

She touched his hand and urged him back. "No, no, the blood is yours. I didn't want to clean up for fear the doctor would have news before I had changed and I would not get to—to—"

She broke off as the tears she had been holding back began to stream down her face.

He pulled her to the bed beside him and wrapped his good arm around her. "Shhh, shhh, love. I'm fine. I will be fine. Though maybe a little scarred."

She looked at the stitches on his head with a frown. "I've heard some ladies find a scar rakish," she managed to quip.

He smiled. "Do you?"

"On you? Most definitely." She couldn't believe she was laughing with him when they had both nearly been murdered just a few hours before.

"Then I will wear it with pride," he said. After a moment, his laughter faded. "You saved my life. By telling my aunt how much you truly hated her son."

She nodded. "At least I got to share that fact before she left this earth. And it made her turn the gun away from you. But you saved me too. Grabbing her ankle made her misfire."

He stroked her cheek. "You said something else to her too, Serafina. Even through my fog, I heard it. You said you were with child. Is that true?"

She looked up at him and once again was hit with a pang of longing to make what had been a lie into an utter truth.

"No," she whispered. "At least, not that I know of. I only wanted her to turn her hate away from you. I would have said or done *anything* to save you."

"Including sacrifice yourself," he said, his face falling. "Even though I told you to run away."

"Would you have run and left me if our roles were reversed?"

He smiled. "No. But we are different, you see. I love you, Serafina, and for you, I would die."

"You very nearly did," she said with a shudder. "But we are not so very different."

She felt him tense against her, though the smooth stroke of his hand over her cheek did not change. "Aren't we?" he said, his voice strained with hope and fear.

She sat up and looked at him straight on. "Are you saying you didn't hear what I said to you after you collapsed the second time?"

He shook his head. "It was only blackness once I knew you were safe."

She leaned in, nearly kissing him but not quite. She held his gaze solidly as she said, "I begged you not to leave me, Rafe. I told you I loved you."

He tilted his head, edging even closer than she was. She felt his breath on her skin, felt his warmth and his life. Having been so close to losing him, she reveled in his nearness.

"Did you mean it?" he murmured.

She cupped his cheeks gently and met his eyes. "I meant every word, Raphael Flynn. I love you with all my heart, and it thrills me and terrifies me. But since I almost lost you already, I cannot bear to think of losing you again. I would rather tell you my heart and hope that you will keep it safe than resist what you have already offered me and live in isolation from you."

His gaze lit up, filled with the love he had already declared and with the promise of everything she had ever desired and thought she would live without. She saw in his eyes the children they would have, the home they would make, the laughter they would share, the passion that would stoke them on for years to come, decades. She saw it all, and she could no longer resist leaning in for the kiss they had been teasing about.

His good arm came around her, holding her close as their

mouths tangled in a desperate meeting that spoke of fear and desperation and of love, always love.

When they broke apart, she smiled as she traced the lines of his face with her fingertips once more.

"Well, that is resolved," she said.

He laughed. "What is resolved?"

"We love each other and we shall be happy together—I hope in this house rather than the ducal home—for the rest of our days."

He settled back on the pillows with a great sigh. "Yes, that is resolved."

"Then we should likely allow your family in. I know they have been as terrified as I have been as we awaited the doctor. I have no doubt they are huddled about your door waiting to have their turn to see you are whole and unharmed."

He caught her elbow and pulled her down across his body. His fingers threaded into her hair and just before he kissed her again, he whispered, "Let them wait just a moment longer, Sera. Let them wait."

And he kissed her.

EPILOGUE

Six months later

Rafe strode into the parlor and grinned at the sight of Serafina reading on the settee, feet tucked beneath her. Every time he walked into this vision, it thrilled him beyond reason.

She glanced up with the smile that lit up his life on a daily basis and moved to get up, but he crossed to her and sat down to keep her in her spot.

"*You* are to be resting," he said with a playfully stern glare as he placed a hand over the slight swell of her belly.

At four months, she had just begun to show her condition, and now that he could see true evidence of the baby inside her, he wanted to dote on her in a way that would have made his old, rakish self roll his eyes.

She smiled as he brushed a brief kiss over her lips. "I'm fine. You fret like a mother hen."

He laughed. "I will show you I'm nothing like a mother hen."

"Cock of the walk is more like it," she said through her own laughter.

He arched a brow. "Saucy wench."

"So what did your sister want to see you about?"

He leaned forward and poured himself some tea and grabbed a biscuit from her plate. She arched a brow at him, but said nothing as he wolfed down half in one bite. "Annabelle has announced she would like a Season."

"A Season, as in, with us as chaperone?" she asked, blinking in disbelief at him.

He laughed. "With *me* as chaperone. You will be round and ready to pop by then."

"I'm not sure she'll get much help from either of us," Serafina said. "The *ton* still buzzes about your aunt's attack and subsequent death. We are a scandal of epic proportions."

He lifted his brows. "True or not, that has not slowed the invitations made to us. Annabelle knows from experience that this family tends to live in a constant state of notoriety, so I suppose she believes the sooner, the better—before Crispin decides to publicly declare his love for a horse or Mama takes up walking the boards."

"I think your mother would be a fine actress," Serafina teased.

He smiled again. The past six months together had seemed to put all her fears at ease. And he was more in love with her than he had ever been. A fact he put into practice by settling his plate aside and slowing easing himself over her.

She wrapped her arms around him without hesitation and smiled up at him. He saw her gaze linger on the scar on his forehead, but she didn't shudder as she had for so many weeks after the attack that had nearly killed them both.

"What about you?" he whispered.

"As an actress?" she teased softly. "Oh no, I never have to act anymore, Your Grace. My feelings are perfectly true."

"And they are?" he pressed.

She drew him down, closer and closer until her lips brushed his. "That I love you more than anything. And I would like to show you just how much this very moment."

He said nothing more. He required nothing more. He merely melted into her kiss and showed her how much her love was appreciated and returned.

Other Books by Jess Michaels

THE NOTORIOUS FLYNNS
The Scoundrel's Lover (Book 2 – March 2015)
The Widow Wager (Book 3 – 2015)

THE LADIES BOOK OF PLEASURES
A Matter of Sin
A Moment of Passion
A Measure of Deceit

THE PLEASURE WARS SERIES
Taken By the Duke
Pleasuring The Lady
Beauty and the Earl
Beautiful Distraction

MISTRESS MATCHMAKER SERIES
An Introduction to Pleasure
For Desire Alone
Her Perfect Match

ALBRIGHT SISTERS SERIES
Everything Forbidden
Something Reckless
Taboo
Nothing Denied

Jess Michaels raffles a FREE Kindle or Amazon gift certificate
EVERY month to members of her newsletter, so sign up on her
website:
http://www.authorjessmichaels.com/join-the-jess-michaels-
newsletter/

Take a Sneak Peek at *The Scoundrel's Lover*

Book 2 of the Notorious Flynns:

CHAPTER ONE

April 1814

The rain slid down the windowpane like tears down a woman's face and Annabelle Flynn turned away with a shudder. She didn't want to think about weeping at present. She didn't want to think about heartbreak or failure or humiliation, either. Not on the eve of her first Season in the highest of Society. Instead, she smiled at her brother Rafe and his wife of less than a year, Serafina.

It was hard not to smile at them, standing across the room, heads close together, her once-rakish brother's hand resting protectively on the swell of his wife's pregnant belly as they waited for their son or daughter to kick again. They were the picture of domestic bliss and true, passionate love.

Things Annabelle didn't want, nor expect, as she prepared herself to wade into the deep waters of the ton.

"Serafina, do you have any advice for tomorrow's ball?" she asked.

Her sister-in-law blushed as she looked up from her belly. But it was her brother who laughed.

"You do not ask me?" he teased as he managed to remove himself from his wife's side. "The duke? Your chaperone?"

Annabelle rolled her eyes. "Your title is only good to gain entre, my dear brother. But you've not yet been a duke for a year, so what would you know?"

He staggered back, gripping his chest with both hands as if he had been shot. Annabelle saw Serafina flinch a little at his playful act. Her brother had been shot not long ago and his wife still thought of that day, as she had told Annabelle time and again.

"You wound me," he teased. Then he shrugged and walked to the sideboard to fetch a glass of port. "But you are correct. My wife is certainly the better guide for you."

Serafina moved toward Annabelle, taking her hands gently. Annabelle smiled. She had grown deeply fond of Rafe's wife over the months. They had become friends and sisters of the heart, as well as marriage. It was a lucky thing, no doubt, as Annabelle had many friends who despised the mates of their siblings.

"You and I have gone over the rules and expectations so many times since you announced your interest in a Season, you know them like your own hand," Serafina reassured her. "Be your lovely self beyond those rules and no one could dare do anything but adore you."

Annabelle kept a smile plastered to her face, but inside her heart sank. Be herself. Oh no. That was the very last thing she would ever be. The last thing she would show anyone.

Herself was a very dangerous creature, indeed. One best kept hidden.

"I do wish you could be there," she sighed.

Serafina touched her belly again. "I show too much or I would." She smiled at Rafe. "But your brother has been reminded time and again to be on his best behavior. And you have become friends with Lady Georgina. She won't steer you wrong."

Annabelle nodded. She had met Georgina at one of Serafina's gatherings a few months ago. Although a few years younger than Annabelle, the daughter of the Marquis of Willowbath was well versed in everything Society. They had become friends of a sort.

So she would not be alone. Even though it sometimes felt very much that way.

Annabelle shook off her thoughts when she caught Serafina watching her closely. It would not do to worry her sister-in-law.

"Mother was very sorry she couldn't make it with me tonight," she said as a way to change the subject. "She has not been sleeping well and she is overly tired."

Rafe's smile fell at that statement. "Yes, she looked tired the last time we called. What keeps her up?"

Annabelle arched a brow. "Would you like to hazard a guess?"

Rafe let out a long breath. "Crispin?"

She nodded slowly. "Our brother's troubles seem to mount each day. I have never seen him so wild."

Serafina dipped her head. "Since we married, he does seem to struggle."

Rafe turned on his wife and shook his head. "Crispin's decisions are his own, do not take responsibility for them, my love."

"It's true," Annabelle tried to reassure her as she reached out to squeeze her hand. "Our brother has been adrift for some time, you and your marriage did not change that."

"Only magnified it," Serafina said softly.

Rafe shrugged. "He will overcome it, he always has."

Annabelle tensed. That was what Rafe had been saying for months, and yet she didn't feel that Crispin was overcoming anything.

"How can we help him? What should we do?" Annabelle asked.

Rafe arched a brow at her. "There is nothing we can do. If Crispin wants to wreck himself, all we can do is wait for him to come to his senses."

He paced away and Annabelle's shoulders rolled forward. She'd had this conversation with Rafe, Serafina and her mother enough times that she knew her brother wouldn't change his thoughts. He had always been so close to Crispin that Annabelle feared Rafe might be blind to the truth.

That their brother was spiraling out of control, to his detriment, but also potentially to her own. Their family's tenuous inroad into societal acceptance was predicated on Rafe's newfound title, inherited the year before from their rotten cousin.

But Annabelle's chance at a good match and a calm and ordinary future hinged on behavior as well as rank. Both her brothers had endangered her standing before and Crispin might do so again if his antics grew too out of control.

She didn't want to see either of them hurt by his current woes.

Serafina wrapped an arm around her and drew her back to the present.

"Will you stay with us tonight?"

Annabelle smiled. It had become a common occurrence for her to sleep at Rafe and Serafina's, chatting half the night and enjoying long mornings at Serafina's side.

"Of course," she said with a smile. "I have heard from Rafe that you are finished now with the nursery."

Serafina's face lit up and her beauty, which had always been at the highest level, was almost too much to look at. "We have."

"Well, I would love to see it," Annabelle said as she took her sister-in-law's arm and hugged her.

"Come then," Serafina said as she led her from the room with Rafe at their heels. "I would love your opinion on the colors."

But as Annabelle smiled and nodded at Serafina's joyful descriptions of her future child's future chamber, she couldn't help but have her thoughts wander again. And again they landed on deep and abiding fears that her Season's debut would be nothing but a failure and her future would be destroyed in one broad brushstroke...

Coming March 2015

ABOUT THE AUTHOR

Jess Michaels writes erotic historical romance from her home in Tucson, AZ. She has three assistants: One cat that blocks the screen, one that is very judgmental and her husband that does all the heavy lifting. She has written nearly 50 books, enjoys long walks in the desert and once wrestled a bear over a piece of pie. One of these things is a lie.

Jess loves to hear from fans! So please feel free to contact her in any of the following ways (or carrier pigeon):
www.AuthorJessMichaels.com
PO Box 814, Cortaro, AZ 85652-0814

Email: Jess@AuthorJessMichaels.com
Twitter www.twitter.com/JessMichaelsbks
Facebook: www.facebook.com/JessMichaelsBks

Jess Michaels raffles a FREE Kindle or Amazon gift certificate EVERY month to members of her newsletter, so sign up on her website:
http://www.authorjessmichaels.com/join-the-jess-michaels-newsletter/

19472603R00145

Made in the USA
San Bernardino, CA
27 February 2015